A DESERT BETWEEN TWO SEAS

WINNER OF THE *Flannery O'Connor Award for Short Fiction*

A. Muia

A DESERT BETWEEN TWO SEAS

A Novel in Stories

THE UNIVERSITY OF GEORGIA PRESS ATHENS

Published by the University of Georgia Press
Athens, Georgia 30602
www.ugapress.org

Designed by Mindy Basinger Hill
Set in Adobe Caslon Pro
Printed and bound by Sheridan Books, Inc.

The paper in this book meets the guidelines for permanence and durability of the Committee on Production Guidelines for Book Longevity of the Council on Library Resources.

Most University of Georgia Press titles are available from popular e-book vendors.

Printed in the United States of America

25 26 27 28 29 P 5 4 3 2 1

Library of Congress Control Number: 2025934429
ISBN 9780820374383 (paperback)
ISBN 9780820374390 (epub)
ISBN 9780820374406 (PDF)

For Alan

Y así fue la campana:
cantó cuando vivía
y ahora está en el polvo
su sonido.

And that's the way the bell was:
it sang while living
and now its sound lies
in the dust.

FROM "ODE TO A FALLEN BELL"
BY PABLO NERUDA

CONTENTS

ACKNOWLEDGMENTS

With great thanks to the Baja California ranching families and guides who shared the trail, stories, and songs: José María Arce Arce, José Antonio Arce, Jorge Guadalupe Fernandez Delgado, Isaac López Chavez, Cecilio Osuna Salazar, Simón Peralta, Josefina Romero Gerardo, Juan Jacobo Rousseau Moreno, and Humberto Verdugo; to Elizabeth Camacho Espinoza for her hospitality and guidance on the history of Santa Rosalía; to William Burley and Debra Valov for sharing their love for Baja California flora and opening my eyes to all that grows in that wondrous landscape; to Arnulfo Estrada and Dr. Mario A. Magaña for their scholarship of Baja California history and native peoples; to Francisco Meza, Nayely Murrillo, Jesús Ortega Lizardi, and Mario Rocha for imparting their knowledge of the territorial prison of Mulegé; to José Ernesto Yee Aguilar in recognition of his prolific study and generous help with the history of Mulegé; to Jane Beard Ames for her decades of work with San Ignacio oral histories and the use of her wonderful Baja California library; to Rogan Shannon for graciously reflecting on the experience of a character without ears; to David Kier for his passion for all things Baja California; and to Shameen Rathnayaka for his beautiful map. A special thanks to Trudi Angell and the mules—who guided me to ancient places that captured my imagination—and Rodolfo Palacios Castro for his reading, suggestions, and enthusiasm. I am also deeply grateful for my Seattle writing colleagues for immersing themselves in Baja California stories for so many years; to Greg Wolfe, Scott Cairns, Robert Clark, Gina Ochsner, and Chigozie Obioma; to the team at University of Georgia Press; and to Lori Ostlund for her editing and encouragement.

"The Vermilion Saint" was published in *Image Journal* in 2014.
"La Santera" was published in *Zymbol Magazine* in 2015.
"Las Salinas" was published in *The Baltimore Review* in 2017.
"Las Flechas" was published in *West Branch* in 2018.
"The Good Confession" was published in *Raleigh Review* in 2018, and reprinted in the 2019 *Orison Anthology.*
"La Mula Milagrosa" was published in *Beloit Fiction Journal* in 2020.
"Dolores-Born-without-Ears" was published in *Water~Stone Review* in 2022.

The poem "Ode to a Fallen Bell" was originally published in *Fifty Odes* by Pablo Neruda, translated by George D. Schade, Host Publications, January 28, 2001. Used with permission.

ALTA CALIFORNIA
N
W
E
S
Santo Tomás
Santo Domingo
San Quintín
Pabellón
El Rosario
Velicatá
Agua Dulce
Santa María
Country of Stones
SONORA
Calmallí
Santa Gertrudis
Malarrimo
Sierra de San Francisco
San Ignacio
Santa Rosalía
Guadalupe
Mulegé
VERMILION SEA
San Bruno
Comondú
Loreto
San Xavier
PACIFIC OCEAN
BAJA CALIFORNIA

Espín

The Vermilion Saint

SANTA ROSALÍA DE MULEGÉ

— 1820 —

Some say the Virgin guards her pearls, and for that reason, the church is never locked. The stone mission of Mulegé, set among rugged hills above the river that flows to the bloodred waters of the Vermilion Sea, had no doors to lock. The entrance stood open like a great dark maw, and the people passed in and out. Even when workers hung the carved wooden doors on leather hinges, the doorway remained open, for the saints watch out for what is theirs.

The Virgin at Mulegé had a bowl full of pearls. Ship captains brought them, and soldiers brought them when they took pearls from the Cochimí. Sailors carried them to the Virgin when their children were ill. The commerce of prayer took place every day in the church: a pearl for my child, a pearl for my husband, a pearl for my mother. We have no pearl, but we shall light a candle. We have no candle? Only a prayer then. And if no prayer, just a sigh. Tomorrow we will look for a pearl. I know a man who has one. His son is also sick? Then we shall ask someone else. Do not be afraid. There is a way.

Father Magín Matías Espín, the priest of Mulegé, kept count of the pearls. He stroked their shiny surfaces and put them to his teeth and tongue, and he knew each one by heart. The gray-green pearl that restored the life of the blacksmith's youngest boy. The pink pearl—odd in shape but beautiful in color—that brought a baby to Juana Amawayahá. The white oval-shaped pearl, though the wife died later. There were pearls for dead children and lost husbands and accidents and nightmares. A hundred tiny seed pearls, gray and small as widow's mites, for what petitions Fr. Espín did not know. He counted every pearl before he went to bed, and the next day he would find one more.

Fr. Espín kept a native boy, one of the Cochimí. The boy had no Cochimí name, but only a baptismal name—José María—for his mother died before giving birth. Fr. Espín carved the fetus from the water of the woman's womb, and as he lifted the infant for baptism, the child surprised him with a mighty breath, a giant indignant outcry. The boy cried and cried; it seemed he should never run out of air. Fr. Espín found a wet nurse from the monjerío where the native women lived, and for a time the boy was cloistered among them. But when he grew, the priest took him out and began to instruct him.

—What is the seventh commandment of the law of God?

—We must not steal, said the boy.

—What is the fifth commandment of the law of God?

—We must not kill.

José María went with Fr. Espín into the hills to persuade the Cochimí to the mission. They went to the fields where the people were toiling, and into the adobes where they lay dying. The boy spoke on behalf of the priest, who could not understand the language of the people. José María translated every word—the mundane words, the rude words, the pious words. He told the secrets of the Cochimí. And when he heard mention of some sacred thing—a cape of human hair, or a stone pipe to pull sickness from a person's body—he told that to the Father also, because no one would speak openly to Fr. Espín about sacred things, not even at the wooden box where they made their confessions. In this way, the priest collected strategies to conquer the people.

At dawn the priest knelt before the altar in his study, waiting for the boy to ring the Angelus and summon the people to prayer. The boy came every morning, calling Paili!—for when he was very young, he could not say Padre.

—Paili, what do you have in your pocket?

Fr. Espín watched the boy from the corner of his eye and delighted in the small earnest face. He produced a peach and said, A sailor brought this to me, and I will share it with you.

—Paili. I saw workers returning from the brick lots too early. They are hanging around the monjerío, calling to the women: Come out, are you lonely? And the women are calling back with a bad kind of laughter.

—And what else?

The boy rubbed one sandaled foot with the other and waited for a group of men to pass.

—Tonight there is to be a dance of the wrong kind.

—You said this yesterday. I believe you have run out of things to tell me.

José María pressed his nose to the Father's sleeve and inhaled. Fr. Espín smiled.

—My son, why do you do that?

—For the smell of you, Paili.

The priest took the boy's hand in his. You are a good boy, he said.

—Are we going to the villages today?

—Not now, Fr. Espín said. Walk about, see what the people are doing. Then go down to the sea. Come to me quickly when you are finished, come directly.

To make the boy leave, the priest gave him a cake of brown sugar in the form of a lamb, for the boy loved sweets.

Fr. Espín sent José María to the sea every day in the summer, when pearling was best. The boy would wait on the shore until the sun rose high in the sky, illuminating the water, and then he took the balsa the priest had given him and rowed this reed canoe into the waves and dove for pearls.

He brought all the pearls to Fr. Espín. The priest made a necklace for the Virgin, a black strand that stretched to the floor, and a smaller white one for Santa Rosalía, the patroness of the mission. He placed pearls in the Virgin's outstretched hand and decorated her crown and dress with them, alternating pearls of black and white. While the Father stood gazing at the Virgin, José María stood looking at the Father.

One night, Fr. Espín was ruminating and quiet. When he finished recording the pearls in his book, he turned to José María and said, Are you afraid down there, in the depths?

—No, Paili, José María answered.

—Do you enjoy going to the sea?

—Yes, Paili. I am the only boy with a balsa of my own.

—You do not think it dangerous?

—No, Paili.

—And you are never afraid, not even a little.

—No, Paili.

The priest was relieved and pleased. Someday I shall take you to Loreto with me, he said. I will show the governor what a jewel I have, the kind of gem we are hewing out of this field of stones.

José María came early to the sea. The wind was at his back, blowing down from the dark mountains of the Guadalupe, born from volcanoes of long ago. The mouth of the river was a broad wash of swirling sandbars, covered with gulls. Egrets high-stepped among the mangroves, and a solitary heron moved on fragile legs—regal as a bishop—with yellow eyes that snapped to and fro.

On the shore, an old Cochimí was fishing. The man was from the mission but did not wear the cotón. The skin of his middle gathered in narrow folds that had fallen upon his hipbones and he stood on the sand with wide, planted feet. José María watched. At intervals the man cast a line of agave fiber into the sea and pulled out a roosterfish, which he placed in a woven bag. The old man looked back at him, but neither spoke, and the man turned away toward the line.

José María sat licking sugar from his fingers, staring at the man. Then he held his breath to prepare himself. He rolled the balsa over and examined the bindings that held the rushes in their tight bundles.

Beside the canoe he kept a stone with a rope tied about its middle, and he slipped his foot into the loop. The stone would carry him to the depths and hold him there, and it must not come loose. He sat on the sand and listened to the haw-haw-haw of the pelicans as they dove in turn. The sea had cast the corpse of a dolphin upon the shore. Its face smiled with lean bony jaws, and José María could smell the reek of its dark flesh. Turkey vultures landed, and he disturbed them with pebbles and they darted away and back again.

When he felt the sun's heat atop the crown of his head, he pulled the balsa to the water. He placed the paddle on it, and the stone, and the knife with the curved blade, and a sharp-pointed stick, and the net he wore about his neck to collect the oysters. He shaded his eyes and looked over the sea. He knew the place he must go; winds of pleasure fluttered in his chest and he knew.

He rowed out. The sound of the waves against the canoe reminded him of animals when they chewed the brush. He looked back and the fisherman was watching him. José María smiled to himself, for on the beach the old man had stared meanly at him, but now wanted to see where he was going, where the good pearls were found.

He stopped rowing and looked down into the sea. He had come to a deep place. Below lay an underwater mountain, the crags and gullies thick with shells. Other men were afraid to venture inside the fissures for fear of being drowned. José María was not afraid. His back was scarred from the rocks, but he knew his own breath, and he knew the moment to ascend, and this was the place to find the best oysters, which avoid the strong currents of unprotected seas.

José María never took a man to accompany him. He used a long line tied about his waist to fasten him to the canoe above. He took the stone in one hand, and secured the net around his neck, and took the pointed stick in the other hand. He took three deep breaths, and said a prayer to Saint Peter the fisherman as the priest had taught him. Then he slipped over the side.

The water was thick and warm, growing cooler as he descended.

The pulse of his heart began to slow, and he felt dreamlike as the water cradled him down. The surface became its own clouded sky and the sun was large and glimmering, then shrinking into a ball of white. All the colors of the world surrounded him—blues richer than the Father's festival garments, white ribbons of sunlight, red from the clouds of tiny animals that in seasons of great quantity give the Vermilion Sea its name. Far below, the water grew cold and black, a grave beneath José María's feet. But he would not descend as far as that. As the stone carried him down, the water above grew heavy, and he felt the mighty explosion within, and that was his eardrums. Then he must be watchful; the blood would attract sharks.

When he came to the underwater mountain, he grasped the barnacled outcroppings to stop his descent. Small crabs went skittering and wide-eyed fish flitted away. A strange music surrounded him, clicking winds and the heavy hum of quietness, and he heard the beating of his own slow heart and the creak of held breath. He saw a dark form near the surface, following his movements. The shark had a flat plank head and eyes on either end, the kind called Cornuda cruz, the horned cross. Salt burned José María's eyes, but he looked down and saw the black aperture of a cave beneath him.

It was narrow and dark. He slipped his foot into the loop of rope and the stone kept him from rising. The sides of the fissure were covered with oysters, their mouths open as if breathing in sleep. As he passed his hand over them, the oysters snapped into tight little stone castles. He took his pointed stick and pried one loose, and then another, putting them into the net. He did not work quickly and fearfully as other men, but carefully and dreamily, and the sea was cool and undulating. He felt he had been absent from the world above for many days.

Now he felt the spasm in his chest and the burning of his throat, but he looked once more, and how had he not seen it? A great oyster, fancy and ugly with tiny waving weeds around its mouth, an ancient and rubbled grandfather who must conceal a pearl. He reached out. The lips closed with a puff of cloudy water. He brandished the stick and forced it to the root where the oyster clung to the rocks, but it would not let go. He pushed harder, and pried with his hand, and finally it gave. He slipped the oyster into the net and turned from the darkness toward the dim blue crack of the entrance, and his abdomen burned and his mind pressed him to inhale and he did not listen.

Slipping into the open water, he kicked his foot free from the loop and the stone fell down and rested among the coraled hummocks. He began to rise. He looked toward the surface of the sea which had become the sky, and the sun grew larger and rippled outward as he ascended. He knew he must take care, for the eyes could deceive and cause a person to panic. The surface could be very near, or still far, and he must go slowly upward without even a thought that might use what little breath he has saved for the last.

Fr. Espín sat in the dark stone church, counting pearls and waiting for José María. He kept a silk cloth tucked into his sleeve, and he lifted the bowl of pearls from the niche at the Virgin's feet and poured the pearls onto the cloth. He kept an ivory blade of the kind heavyset men use to slip into their shoes, an odd gift to a priest who for poverty's sake could wear no such shoes. He used the blade to separate and count the pearls, and he herded them like sheep about the silken cloth.

Two days before, the boy had brought a new pearl, blackest of miracles and perfectly round. Fr. Espín held it up. The skin was smooth, unblemished, and darker than iron or night. Candleflames shone on its surface like stars in a tiny universe. He put the pearl to his teeth, and his tongue tasted the salt.

Once, a visiting dignitary, sweating and taking refuge in the cool church, remarked upon the collection of pearls.

—The boy dives not for me, but for the Church, Fr. Espín explained.

The visitor nodded and wiped his brow and said the mission was very fine.

—I want there to be no misunderstanding, Fr. Espín pressed. You will find no secret mines here or Indians working them for silver. No, the Cochimí bring these pearls voluntarily.

The visitor waved a bored and acquiescent hand and rose to leave, and Fr. Espín pursued him and said, I myself live quite simply. But we treat our saints as well as we can.

Now the priest waited alone in the church. Candles fluttered like small feathers of fire in the darkness, placed before the altar by soldiers and sailors and wives. He looked up. The Virgin, standing in her niche, was watching him. He leaned to the right and the left; the smile and the eyes followed him. Across her forehead and around her wrists lay shining strands of black pearls. She looked like a mermaid, and the dark church with its walls of waving candlelight was the depths of her sea. He went back to counting.

Suddenly he was aware of a presence behind him. He rose to greet the boy, but an old Cochimí man and woman were coming instead. Fr. Espín covered the pearls with his hand.

The man wore the simple cotón of the neophytes, and his wife wore the rough woolen skirt. They came on their knees, and the woman lifted her skirt and the priest looked away. He could hear them scraping toward the statue of the Virgin. They paused and whispered to one another. Fr. Espín looked over. The man's tone was instructive, and the woman nodded. Then they blessed themselves and went out.

He went at once to the statue. One never knew what offering one might find—a cactus heart, or a bone, or some feathers. Once he found a bat, wounded but still struggling, which he crushed and threw away. He peered into the bowl at the Virgin's feet. In the bottom lay one tiny pearl.

He held it to the candle to examine it. Tiny, ugly, neither gray nor brown, and pitted with cavities. He rolled the pearl in his hand, appraising it for something he might have missed. No, the pearl was as it appeared. He chuckled, such had been the couple's formality. He returned to the corner and sat on the wooden bench to resume his business, and the Virgin watched.

The hour grew late and the boy did not return. He replaced the pearls and opened the shuttered window and peered out. His heart leapt at the sight of a boy coming along the path, but the boy was not José María. He donned his palm hat and climbed the knoll behind the church, looking down toward the river. The hilltops were red in the late day sun and the arroyo below had already fallen into shadow. The palms shivered and scratched one another in the evening breeze. Brood hens bobbed about, looking for a speck of something. A few men were coming from the brick pits. They saw the priest and one called the customary Amar a Dios on behalf of the group. They stood watching him. It was past the hour that the bell should ring.

Fr. Espín went to the belltower himself and pulled the rope. The bell tolled and men entered the church, speaking in low tones. Women carried their mats for kneeling on the flagstones, and the soldier arrived and took his place along the wall.

The priest stood before the Cochimí and he shivered. There are so very few, he thought. Sickness has taken them all. Soon shall there be none?

Yet he must begin. He intoned the prayers, and the people recited the Doctrina and sang the Alabado. Still the boy did not return. Dust blew into the church from the open door and swirled around the bodies of those seated on the ground. The soldier watched from the wall to make certain that none slept.

How I will scold him when he comes, the priest thought. As he raised his hand for the final blessing, the hand faltered and he steadied it with the other. The people rose and exhaled as they left the church, as if all had been holding their breath within. They went to their homes and their suppers, and Fr. Espín called the soldier to him.

—What is it, Father? the soldier said. Are you ill?

—It is my boy, my son José María.

His voice failed and he turned to the altar as if to pray but turned again to the soldier, unsure of whether the prayers had finished or were just to begin. His fingers trembled upon his throat and he said,

My son José María went to the sea . . . he loves to fish for pearls, you know. He has not returned. Will you go with me, will you come.

—Of course, Father.

The soldier followed him down the hill and along the river. When they reached the mouth of the estuary, Fr. Espín began to run.

A group of Cochimí fishermen were gathered on the beach. They were haggling over José María's canoe, and the boy lay at their feet still tethered to the boat. Fr. Espín knelt before him and with shaking fingers untied the knots that held the body fast, and when the boy was free, the Father fell upon him and wept.

The fishermen sat down and cut the net and pried open the oysters, and when they came to the last and largest they had difficulty opening it. One of the men took a knife, slipped the blade into the crevice, and severed the muscle. The halves fell impotently apart, and into the hand of the knifeman rolled a shining pearl of pink.

—Here, Father, he said.

The priest would not take it. He gathered the boy into his arms and pressed the small gray face into his robes and held him there, cradling him beside the sea.

In the morning Fr. Espín carried José María to the church and stayed with him. The soldier told the people that the Father must not be disturbed. At evening the priest left the boy. He went to his study and lay down, and did not know who rang the Poor Souls' Bell or if anyone did. He turned toward the wall and covered his face.

At some hour in the night, he rose. He wrote no letter to the superior and blessed no one nor prayed. Abandoning all the sacred things, he slipped into the wilderness, a poor and exiled Cain with only the hand of God to recommend him.

When the soldier discovered the priest gone, he went to the sea and found the Cochimí fisherman and pocketed the pearl. There was a girl down at Loreto he was thinking of.

La Niña

SAN FERNANDO REY DE ESPAÑA DE VELICATÁ

—1843—

For years he had hidden himself at San Bruno on the coast. Among the creosote and the mesquite, he found a crumbling foundation of coquina stone and walls of worked rock, the ruins of the tiny fortress of Atondo's men now two centuries gone. He lived on fish and hares and pitahaya fruit and spent his days alone, looking out toward the sea.

One day some fishermen happened upon his camp, surprised to find a man living there. The priest denied who he was, but they knew, they recognized a telling gravity in his manner. They carried news of him to Loreto. Pilgrims followed; they pressed him unmercifully. Just a prayer, Father. You will hear our confessions? We've been so long without anyone.

They brought their children. He wept when he saw them, and turned away as the people said: See how much he loves them. With burning soul, he flew from them in the night.

He went north, crossing the territory of the Monqui and the Didiu, veering away from the sea, coming to the barren country of the Cochimí. He slept in the desolate missions, the only catechumens the vulture and the dove and the quail who called cuidado as they scurried away. At night he heard the mournful songs of long-dead Indians he had known. Sometimes he wept for them, and sometimes he wept for the drowned boy he had forced to fish for pearls, and he hurried away like a ghost before it was light.

When he came to Velicatá he found the old mission fields, overgrown with bursage and willow, beside the low stream of reeds. The adobe church rested on a platform of hard packed earth cut into the hillside, planted to the ground like an old man in siesta who had passed away sitting up. The chapel was long and narrow, without cross or bell or ornament. One small wing jutted from the side—a room for a priest, perhaps.

He climbed the few steps and pushed the door open. Cholla and burro weed were growing through the floor. Light crept between the fronds of rotting roof thatch, scattering dots of brightness on the mud walls. The church had an altar of piled-up stones; that was all. Not a sign of any pilgrim, not so much as a single votive. Yet it held a familiar peace. He set his palm hat and cow-horn canteen in the empty niche at the rear wall, and unrolled his bundle and slept.

He made his home there. From time to time the boy came to him in dreams, bedecked with pearls about his throat. On those nights Fr. Espín would take to the road, wandering south or as far north as he dared, shying away from the territory of the lone priest at Santo Tomás, in the frontera. Only once, tortured with thirst, did he stop at the solitary ranch of Pabellón to inquire at the house for a drink, and a good woman attended him, and he took the road home again.

One afternoon he returned to the chapel from such a journey, coming just ahead of the rain. He could see it on the road, a dark sheet following him, and he heard the thunder. He unfastened the strap that held the chapel door, ducking inside, and hung his hat on the peg. The rain swept over the earth, puffing the dust, drumming the new roof of palm branches. A crude table of cardón wood stood in the center of the room, and he lit the candle.

A child was sitting on the floor. He stepped back. At first he feared the boy José María had surfaced from his dreams, had come incarnate into the chapel. But when he looked again, he saw that the child before him was a girl. Older than one year, but not yet two. She wore a dress of cotton sacking and sat among some gray woolen wrappings that did not belong to him.

She neither cried nor smiled when she saw him. Her face was dirty, her eyes red. They looked at one another in the dim lamplight and his hand went to his throat. She could not have been there long. He went to the door and stepped out. The rain had faded to a drizzle and the darkness was moving away toward the east. He hurried to the road, but the land was cloaked in fog and he could see no one. He went back, his face lightly misted as though sweating. The girl was sitting in the same place as before.

He had not held a child since he was a priest, all those years ago. He baptized the infants of the Cochimí, and soon they died of disease, most of them. Even then, he held them only for a moment—to quickly perform the rite—and the mothers carried them away to their huts, or into the circle of women who slept in the stone-walled monjerío where he forced them to live, in those close dark quarters where they coughed and succumbed to fevers. He could not remember individual children. In his mind he could see only the rough form of them, one like another. But he remembered José María's infant face, tucked into the circle of his arm like a small round bread.

He looked at the girl and shook his head.

—Who brought you here?

The red line of a scratch lay across her cheek. When he knelt and brushed the matted hair aside, he saw she had no ears at all, but only pinpricks of holes where the ears should have been. He clicked his fingers but she did not turn. She kept watching his mouth.

He paced the room, going again to the door. Water dripped from the thatch. The low hills were steaming and the brush was bright; within the hour there would be flowers.

He was no one to care for a child. But he could not leave her on the floor. He lifted her up, and now he remembered how a child felt in his arms. The clinging hands, the chin upon his shoulder. The boy used to sniff the sleeve of his robe. His throat caught and he set the girl down. He busied himself getting a cup of water from the olla and he gave it to the girl and sat at the table watching her drink.

She had soiled herself. He got up and carried her down to the stream. He kept scanning the road. Someone would come. Someone. He could take the girl north, quietly, to Santo Tomás. But he could not face the priest.

He sat her down in the watercourse among the rushes and she did not kick or slap. She seemed accustomed to a world which moves languidly past, bringing what it will, and there is nothing one might do. He pulled her up by the arm and washed her quickly and set her on the bank while he scrubbed her dress and laid it out to dry, and then he took her inside away from the sun.

He clothed her in the old woolen wrappings and they sat at the table, she in one chair and he in the other. She scarcely glanced around. With reddened eyes she looked right through him to some other place that held a greater fascination. He had seen that look before, in the very old and the dying. Her lips moved without sound, like a small fish, and he thought of the boy in his dreams, mouthing some message of condemnation or pardon, he did not know. He got up and brought some agave mash and fed her with his own wooden spoon.

In the evening, he carried her to the bank of the stream. The moon was out, ringed and ghostly white against the fading sky. Dragonflies hovered over the water. The cacti on the high hills were alight in the setting sun, like crosses of green flame, and then all went into shadow. She was watching him. He knew she could hear nothing, but he said: You would be wise not to grow accustomed to me.

When the last of the softening light faded behind the hill, he brought her back to the church.

As a boy he had slept poorly, had never recovered from the habit of sitting in the black friendless hours through the long watches of the night. He had continued in the same way as a priest, waking himself hour by hour, keeping vigil. Now he watched the girl. When she lay too still, he felt her nostrils for breath, and she would wake up crying and he permitted her to sleep on his chest.

He began carrying her in a blanket on his back, like the old abuelitas did, and she rode everywhere with him, quiet and observing as he gathered firewood and checked his snares for ground squirrels. There was a small ell to the side of the mission with a few graves, and in the evenings he carried her among them, reading what names could be found there, and he talked to her of such things. Of heaven and the Christ.

One morning he found some pitahaya fruit in the hills and brought it home, but she turned her head away and would not eat. She was hot from play, and he set her on the floor with the wooden spoon. Her cheeks were red, her eyes bright. He felt her brow and got up quickly and carried her to the stream. He soaked a cloth in the water and wiped her face. She cried a low and listless sound.

For three nights he did not sleep. He sat beside the cot, holding the small hand that was like a fire unto itself. He poured droplets of tea into her open mouth, and she coughed and swallowed. Her shining eyes were fixed on the roof thatch. On the fourth night, he dragged the cot before the old altar of piled-up stones and lay down beside her, and it seemed the two of them shared a single sepulcher of wood, lacking only the sides. He lifted her to his chest and sang until his voice gave way to groaning, and then to silence.

In the morning, she woke him. She clutched his beard and he pulled her hand free and sat up. He touched her face. Her brow was cool, her eyes clear and no longer shining. He kissed the small fingers, and for the first time, she laughed.

In the late day, he heard someone walking along the road. He looked out and saw a young woman, alone and on foot, thin and resolute with a torn rebozo about her head and shoulders. She was out of breath and paused for a moment, then kept coming. He ducked inside. He looked at the girl—sitting on the floor with the wooden spoon—and he could hear the woman's footfalls drawing near, first on the hard packed road, then on the loose pebbles of the lane.

He went out and stood in the path. The woman smiled, her face mottled from the sun, her nervous hands clutching the old rebozo beneath her chin as she sheltered inside it. He could hear the girl in the house, the pounding of the spoon, the hesitation and the silence. Now she was crying for him.

—She can't hear but she can make quite a noise, the woman said.

—Who are you, he said.

—I just left her a little while.

—Who are you, he said again.

—Her mamá.

The girl's voice grew insistent and he told the woman to wait but she was already going around him, this grinning mother of sorrows bedecked in black, pocked with pieces of straw from wherever she had slept. The girl looked up when they came in. Her mouth hung open. She reached for Fr. Espín, but the woman picked her up and kissed her, and now he could see the echo of the same face: the miniature visage that the world had not yet vanquished, round and smooth, and the other drawn from the toll of men and the road and time.

—Oh my girl, the woman said. Littlest little girl.

The woman kept smiling, and he saw from the lines on her face that she held this expression all the time. She sat at the table and petted the girl's hair, arranging it over the place where the ears should have been. The girl was very still, watching Fr. Espín.

—I knew you would care for her until I came back, the woman said.

—You did not intend to come back.

—Oh yes, I did mean to.

The girl sucked her hand and he brought a cup of water and the woman took it from him and drank. He brought another for the girl. The woman laughed a little, seeing the child hold the cup. He stood above them, addressing the woman in a tone that had gone weak from disuse.

—Where have you come from? he said.

She started to speak and caught herself. She looked away, still smiling, and picked at her fingers like a woman at the confessional, half ashamed but not fully free from the delight of whatever she had done. She was scarcely more than a child. He felt a small compassion rising.

—I shall tell you what to do . . .

—Are you the priest of here? she asked.

He looked sharply away. No, he said. There is no priest anymore.

—You're not the priest of here but you are a priest. I know by the way you talk. And a priest can't have a child.

The girl wanted to get down; she struggled and kicked. The woman set her on the floor and Fr. Espín picked her up.

—And what have you to care for a child?

The woman stopped smiling, the lines on her face severe. She got up and stood at his elbow.

—I'll tell people, she said.

The girl clung to Fr. Espín and he held tight and turned away.

—Come now, you are frightening her.

But he was the one frightened. He returned to the table and sat with the girl on his lap and lit the candle. The woman looked from his face to the child and back again. She smiled.

—Do you think she is a good girl?

He sensed a trap; he was afraid to answer. The woman's eyes took in the shelves, the cot, the olla of water and the stacks of provisions: some dried meat, pitahaya, and the severed pads of cacti, stripped of thorns.

—We could stay here awhile.

—Where is her father, he said. Where is your home.

His voice faltered. Now she came boldly and lifted the child from him.

—If you don't want us, we'll go.

—It is late, he said quickly. You cannot take the road now.

—I believe we will go.

—She is tired. Sleep here tonight.

Her eyes flicked to the cot.

—I give you the house, he said.

The girl reached for him but he dared not kiss her hand; he dared not look at her.

—I knew a priest would help, the woman said.

—I am just a man, he said. An ordinary man.

She was already going to the shelves, taking some fruit and eating it quickly and giving some to the girl. His hands were shaking, but the woman did not see him anymore.

He took a blanket and went out, hesitating beside the door. He heard the girl fussing and the woman moving about. The clink of the cup against the olla of water, the woman laughing softly. The girl padding toward the door and the woman gathering her up. The girl was crying for him. The woman crooned a tuneless song. He heard the creak of the cot, the woman whispering, and the quiet.

She would go with any man. She had done. He recalled her smiling face, grinning as she spoke of the girl she had abandoned. Even he—as profane as he was—had not done such a thing. He had not smiled once since the boy died.

He walked down to the stream, standing at the water's edge among the reeds. The woman was dirty. She carried nothing with her, as though the only resource she possessed was herself. No, she had the girl. He felt an anger rising.

The sun was low in the sky and he looked to the barren fields where a bevy of doves darted down and away. The stream was clear and fast from the rain. He knelt and cupped his hand to drink. The last light shone on the skin of the water, and the pebbles in their depths were round and small and gleaming, each one a shining pearl. He withdrew his hand and sat back, trembling, and wiped his face.

The sun went down and only a red line remained along the ridge of the far hill. The cacti were like dark men with their arms raised, a host of them. He turned back toward the church. He heard the echo of the woman's voice: a priest cannot have a child. But he was no longer a priest.

He waited until the late watches of the night, slipping off his sandals and stepping across the threshold, moving silently in the darkness. From the shelves he took dried meat and pitahaya, putting them into a sack. With shaking hands he set the bundle outside. Once more he went in.

The moon shone through the door, and in the dim light he could see the still forms of the woman and the girl. He stood over them, listening to their breath. The woman did not smile in sleep. Her brow was drawn, her heavy hair encircling her. She looked smaller, as though she were sibling and not mother to the even smaller form beside her. One hand rested on the girl, the nails gnawed to the quick. He should have blessed her. He hovered there, just for a moment, his shadow covering them both. He almost turned away. But he lifted the girl, putting her to his shoulder, hesitating as the woman shifted in sleep, and he went out.

He walked north through the night, wearing the girl on his back, and she slept. In the morning a wagon was passing, and the driver invited them up.

The girl's name was Dolores, Fr. Espín said. She was his sister's child and he was returning her to Pabellón. The man looked puzzled and replied that he knew the ranch at Pabellón and he believed the good couple there were childless, God preserve them. Fr. Espín ducked his head and the man asked no more questions. On the final league, Espín took the girl from the blanket on his back and held her, blessing her under his breath, over and over, and he smiled as she held tightly to his beard. He asked if the driver would let him off and deliver the child himself, since he was already passing that way.

The Good Confession

SANTA GERTRUDIS DE CADACAMÁN

— 1843 —

In the uneasy morning light, Barros the gravedigger of Santa Gertrudis pushed his hand-hearse from the abandoned mission to the campo santo. He walked slowly, stopping to wipe his brow, and put a hand upon his heart to feel it stutter. A vulture wheeled above. He sat down for a moment before going on.

The cemetery was overfilled, bursting with the remains of the Cochimí—the aged and worn, the robust and brokenhearted and accidented and diseased and wasted. The born—legítimo, natural, adulterino, bastardo; and the baptized—standard and provisional, privadamente, in articulo mortis, in periculo mortis. A few markers of stone leaned into one another. Men of stature lay in repose under flat table tombs. Mounds of bones congregated beneath. The forsaken campo santo was soundless in the wind.

Barros smoothed the half-hearted furrows where coyotes had been digging. He went to the corner and worked into the earth with his spade, loosening the soil and sifting the ground. He pulled up bones to make more room, for everyone must have a consecrated burial at least once.

The bones disarticulated in his hands. He blew dust from their fissures and placed them in the hand-hearse. A mist lay across his brow, and he sat back on trembling shanks. The vulture alighted on the half wall, watching with a red-rimmed eye. Barros did not know whether it favored the bones, or him.

When the cart was full, he hoisted it by the handles and rolled toward the charnel house. The hand-hearse groaned on wooden wheels and he eased it around cholla and creosote and old man cactus and giant cardón, the profane creaking trolley jumping over the rutted desert like a merchant at sale. In the cart he carried the remains of three infants, or perhaps four. When he began sorting them, he would know.

Bones clicked and settled as he pulled up to the door. In days of old, a soldier had taken a skull from the charnel house and mortared it above the lintel, without a jaw but somehow grinning at those who passed underneath.

The sun came over the hill. Across the arroyo he saw the whitewashed stone of the deserted mission where he still tended the luminary—that tiny burning light—though the holy presence had long departed. There was no one to call to Misa, no priest or soldier or people. The Angelus hung silent. Barros removed his hat and began to sing:

Ya viene el alba
rompiendo el día
digamos todos
Ave María.

The solitary voice drifted along the arroyo and across the empty corrals and into the church and out again. The scrabbling of birds in the brush fell silent. He pressed a palm to his chest. He felt the faltering rhythm, and rasping he pushed the hand-hearse into the charnel house.

The ossuary was low and narrow, leaning sidelong upon its foundation and covered with an arched roof, like a wine cellar. It was windowless and lit by two tallow tapers, glowing on either side of an iron cross with a figure of Jesucristo dying upon it. The floor was cured in blood.

On the ground, stacked in neat bundles like cordwood, lay the long bones—femurs and tibias and ulnas. On the lowest shelf, Barros placed the curved bones that would not stack easily, like those from rib cages. Smaller bones, such as carpal bones and talus bones, he put on the second shelf. He fit the bones tightly, as a mason might do. On the top shelf he arranged the skulls in rows like catechumens, front-facing and staring toward the door with empty eye sockets darkened into round wells by the candle glow behind them. Uncle, aunt, grandfather of grandfather. Desiccated acolytes. Soldier tucked with indigene.

As a young man, Barros feared the bones. He snapped the spines of the dead when no one was looking, so they would not return to bother him. But in time, he kept company with them. Brittle parishioners in the dark sacrosanct chapel, and he the lone unkempt elder at Lauds.

A few bones remained in the cart. He reached for them, but his heart floundered and he sat down on his cot. The ossuary disappeared and his feet could not feel the ground. He found himself within a cloud. Fearing that he might float away, he clung to the wall of bones. No one was about. Only Jesucristo hanging upon his cross with the weight of iniquity tearing his hands.

When the cloud passed, he was sitting again upon his bunk. He kept a flagon of wine beneath the cot and he brought the wine to his lips, good wine from the mission vines. The cloud desired him. He did not know when it would draw him inside for good. Today, or tomorrow perhaps. His days were spent, and no priest had come or would come.

He got to his feet and removed his hat. He explained to the bones that he had something to tell them. He must finish before the cloud enfolded him. Perhaps he had no right to disturb them in such a way, but he hoped they might listen.

Years ago at the mission, there lived a young plowman who carried many grudges. He slashed the earth with his tools and thought of his enemies and made his terrible plans. Everyone feared falling beneath his vengeful eye. It was widely known that the plowman had poisoned his own father by grinding a black widow into his food.

The old white-haired priest of Santa Gertrudis was always working on him. Forgive, forgive, the priest admonished. Unforgiveness is a millstone no man can carry.

One morning, the plowman discovered the priest was right. Trapped under the weight of many grudges, with his own guilt added besides, the plowman could not rise from his bed. He had never confessed his many murders, for he was afraid the soldiers would carry him away to hang. But as he lay there, crushed beneath the load of wrongs and scarcely able to breathe, he vowed he would live a different way. He would learn to forgive.

The plowman never spoke of this vow. But with forgiveness the weight lifted, and he was able to rise again, and one day while out walking, he came upon a man named Peti Juan.

Peti Juan was a leader among the Cochimí. He guarded the sacred things the priests worked to destroy: bull-roarers and tablets and capes of human hair. There were many dead and dying in those days, and Peti Juan roamed the hills and found the sick and sore-covered and suffering. Though the priest always tried to arrive first, everyone called for Peti Juan, and at the risk of his life he attended them.

Peti Juan was a great protector of the people. When he saw the plowman, he threw a stone and hit him in the face.

—Hey you killer, Peti Juan said. Why don't you leave before something worse happens to you?

The stone put out the plowman's eye. The priest punished Peti Juan by putting him in stocks, but the people rejoiced in the plowman's misfortune. For years, everyone had feared him. They didn't know of his vow; they didn't know he was trying to live a different way.

That night, the plowman went to see Peti Juan in the stocks. The people hurried to surround Peti Juan, afraid the plowman would try to avenge himself. But the plowman said only, The matter is settled. I forgive you for putting out my eye.

No one believed him. Everyone thought he was trying to make Peti Juan relax so he could kill him.

Peti Juan was sentenced to the stocks for three nights. On the third night while everyone slept, a rabid skunk reeled by and attacked him. Everyone woke to Peti Juan's screams. By the time the priest arrived, Peti Juan's arms and legs were flayed open with bites.

The priest beat the skunk to death with a hammer from the forge. Peti Juan trembled with fear. Let me out, Father, he begged. But it was too late; he was already afflicted. The priest ordered that no one come near, and tried to give what comfort he could.

In a week's time, Peti Juan burned with fever. He jerked about and tried to free himself. The mission rang with his wails. The priest came to perform the offices for a dying man, but Peti Juan lunged at him, biting and straining. The Father had to bless him from a distance. Horrified, the people watched Peti Juan's misery—his contorted animal face—and the Cochimí wept for their good leader, who had comforted so many but would receive no comfort himself.

In the night, the plowman came in secret to Peti Juan. The poor man lay raw and bleeding, twisted in the stocks. Spume dripped from his mouth.

—Kill me, Peti Juan whispered. Free me from my suffering.

The plowman looked around. The hammer that killed the skunk lay nearby. He picked it up and hefted it in his hand. Then he put it down.

—I have killed too many people, he said.

—Please, Peti Juan begged.

—I cannot harm another man, the plowman said. I have vowed to forgive.

He went away as Peti Juan thrashed and bit himself. The anguished cries kept the plowman awake for three days until Peti Juan lay dead, and still he heard the cries. The Father told him to take the body and bury it in the campo santo.

The plowman thought continually of the way Peti Juan had suffered. He saw the twisted face and the rolling eyes. The screams followed him everywhere he went. He carried the weight of that forgiveness for many years.

Barros slept for a time and woke trembling. One of the tapers had gone out. He put a hand to his neck, and his heart beat feebly on, and he got up and relit the wick. The flame sprang up and settled back. A shadow passed the door and he turned to see if the priest had come, but it was only a bird dipping in flight and soaring away.

Slowly he straightened the bones, tucking them into place until weakness ranged over him again. He lay back, puffing shallowly like a fish, and took another swig of wine. A dark hand lay upon him, and he brushed it away and found it was his own. When he could speak, he turned and addressed the bones again.

In those days a woman named Manuela de casa served as the key matron of the mission. Everyone called her de casa because she lived in the monjerío, where the single girls were kept. Though she was old, she was also unmarried. After the death of two husbands, she had given up.

Manuela de casa watched everything the girls did. She went to bathe with them; she accompanied them to meals and to the Misa and back to their beds. No one could speak to the girls without the permission of the priest, who trusted their oversight to Manuela de casa.

One day she caught a man looking at her during Mass. It was the stonemason, a man shunned by the people because he built boxes for the dead. He had not chosen this profession, but the priest forbade the Cochimí to burn the deceased according to their custom, and someone must handle the bodies. The people decided upon the stonemason, who was already something of an outcast.

The stonemason was younger than Manuela de casa by many years. His face was scarred from an accident in his youth, but his nose was straight and his teeth fine. Despite his reputation, Manuela de casa found herself looking at him during the prayers. She wondered what he intended. One morning when the priest turned around, the stonemason made a gesture with his fingers that no one could misinterpret. Manuela de casa flushed and led the girls back to the monjerío.

That night she heard him outside the window. Let me in, he called. Manuela de casa stole to the door and unlocked it. She stood there flaming like a young maid in the moonlight. The girls were asleep. She could not believe her good fortune. She had been beautiful once.

But the stonemason said, I have come for the girl called Tomasa. I am burning for her, I can't stop thinking of her.

Manuela de casa saw that all his overtures had been a pretext to gain entrance to the monjerío. But she had been alone a long time.

—Lie with me, she said, and then you can go to the girl.

—I'm not going to use myself all up on you, he said.

—You don't have to use yourself up. Just hold me in your arms.

She would not let him come into the monjerío if he did not agree. She had her own little room, and he lay on her cot and held her, and she pressed his hand between her thighs. After a while she brought the girl to him.

Manuela de casa stood outside the door. She could hear Tomasa protesting, but soon the girl quieted, and the stonemason left before daylight.

He came again the next night, and lay with Manuela de casa, and then the girl. Manuela de casa could not believe the glow she felt. She thought the flame had died away long ago, but it hadn't. She dreamed of the stonemason and his rough hands all day long—while teaching the girls to mend the Father's robes, when bringing meals to the sick, and even during prayers.

As for Tomasa, she stopped laughing with the other girls. She sat in the Misa and neither spoke nor sang. The priest asked if she were ill. He told Manuela de casa to watch Tomasa carefully, for many had died of sickness and he was worried for her.

It went on like that for a few weeks. The stonemason came to the monjerío every night. Soon the girl began to wait for him. When the others were sleeping, she came to the door and listened for his footsteps. She stayed outside Manuela de casa's room until they were finished, and then she hurried in to lie with him.

Soon he stopped visiting every night. It fell to twice a week or sometimes once. Manuela de casa and Tomasa waited for him together, but when he arrived, he looked unhappy. Manuela de casa listened outside the door. She could hear Tomasa crying. The stonemason came out and Tomasa clung to him and he brushed her aside and left.

—Why have you driven him away? Manuela de casa scolded. She struck Tomasa atop the head and sent the girl crying to her pallet.

A week later, the priest called for Manuela de casa and the girl. When they came to his study, the stonemason was there. Manuela de casa looked nervously at the priest, but he turned to the stonemason and said, This girl likes you very much and wants you to be her husband. What do you say?

Manuela de casa could see the girl's eyelids fluttering like hummingbirds. The stonemason looked at the girl. I do not like you, he said. He bowed to the priest and went back to his stonemasonry. The priest told Tomasa to choose someone else for a husband and come back and see him again.

Tomasa didn't go back to the priest. She died the next month from shitting sickness and never had the chance to marry anyone.

Later the stonemason told Manuela de casa that he did like Tomasa, but he did not love her. He felt it was best to set Tomasa free to marry someone who did. In truth, he said, it was Manuela de casa that he had come to love.

Manuela de casa was filled with joy. She had been carrying a terrible burden for what she had done, ruining a girl just so she might feel that old glow again. But the love of the stonemason would lift her spirits. He would come to comfort her.

The stonemason said he would not. Because of the suffering he had caused the girl, he vowed that he would seek love no more. Manuela de casa wept and tore at him, but he would not relent. To make such a vow seemed a foolishness to Manuela de casa. Now everyone was alone.

Barros sat before the bones. A bat shuffled along the ceiling and disappeared into a shadowed corner. He took another sip of wine. A fog was descending and he gripped the cot. But it was only the wine.

The meter of his heart swelled and waned. The skulls gazed at him, unrelenting. The cloud hovered around. He held up his hand to stave it away, and turned to the bones and spoke again.

By this time another priest had come. The people called him Father Blacksnake because of his dark robe and his fondness for the whip. The priest did not understand why the people should take offense at this, for he flogged even himself.

Father Blacksnake had but one follower, the man who served as sacristan. The sacristan had no wife or children, and the people looked upon him as the source of every evil and trouble. Twice they had driven him out, but he always returned, for he had nowhere to go.

The sacristan felt grieved that his only companion was a blacksnake who caused the suffering of others, but he stood beside the Father as he made the mysteries. The priest would gently beat his breast and say, Mea culpa, mea culpa. The sacristan alone understood this.

One night, Father Blacksnake came to the sacristan's room. In the darkness, the priest knelt and confessed that he was afraid of the people. He had whipped them mercilessly, and now he feared the punishments they might think of, like hanging and dragging and cutting. He spoke about the priest of Mulegé, who had fled his mission and lived as an ordinary man somewhere in the wilderness. No one knew where he had gone. Father Blacksnake said he wished he could do the same. He was ashamed of his fear, and begged the sacristan never to speak of it.

—There is forgiveness for you, Father, the sacristan told him.

The priest wept and whispered, Perhaps on the day of judgment, God will have mercy.

But he continued his days in fear. Vow that you will stand with me if trouble comes, he pleaded. And the sacristan made that vow, for he knew what it was to be a man despised.

Not long after, Father Blacksnake died unexpectedly in the night. The Cochimí crowded into the chapel to see the dead priest. A late fog drifted in, moving like smoke around their feet, into the church and out again. Candles flicked shadows onto the Father's face. He seemed at first to smile, and then to frown, and children watched from the door with interest.

The sacristan arranged the Father's black cloak over the white tunic, and made the stiff hands to clasp a small wooden cross. He placed the priest with his head toward the altar as the Father had once instructed him, should anything happen. But without the priest, the mission lost its fearsomeness. All the mystery had departed with the man. The people grew restless. They came to the corpse and pushed the table because they knew the Father wanted to be arranged in the other direction. They began pulling the robes from him. For years the Father had forced them to cover themselves with abrasive cotton garments. Stripping the priest seemed a fitting thing to do.

The sacristan remembered the vow he had made. He tried to put himself between the priest and the people, but they fetched the blacksnake. They whipped the sacristan into the corner, and they whipped Father Blacksnake. They pulled out some of the priest's hair. Father Blacksnake himself had taught them this, the power that resided in the corpses of religious men. Soon the Father was half-bald on one side, naked and hanging sidelong off the table. The sacristan crawled over and hoisted him up.

Some of the people began to leave; they had no interest in staying at the mission to await another priest. But others held a cold justice in their eyes. From that moment, they decided their labor would end. No one would make bricks, tend the gardens, weave, or look after animals. They talked of how many cattle each person could eat. They spoke of all who died of sickness. The priests repaid us badly, the people said. For all the work we did. Who built the godhouse? We did, with our sweat and blood. We paid with our lives.

They looked at the corpse, and the sacristan saw a dark notion forming. He lifted Father Blacksnake's naked body. Drops of blood fell from the sacristan's face onto the priest.

—The Father is dead, the sacristan said. There is nothing more to be done to him.

Trembling, he took a step. He moved like a bier through the sea of people. They murmured against him and he hurried on, struggling with the cadaver across the arroyo to the cemetery, looking back the whole while. He had no time to wrap Father Blacksnake in so much as a cowhide. He began digging. The grave was very shallow, but now the priest was safe in the ground.

The sacristan returned to the church to gather his things and leave, but the people were inside. He hid beneath the eaves and listened to their complaints. Some felt that justice had been satisfied, for the priest was dead and they themselves were living. Others cried that all should remember the many who perished because of the fathers.

Then the sacristan heard a man boasting to the others, saying, Let's go to the campo santo and get that priest.

The sacristan stole away from the wall and ran to the storehouse and filled a jar with lamp oil, as much as he could carry. He took it to the cemetery and knelt at the shallow grave and began digging. He dug until he felt the priest's hand. He pulled the Father from the earth. The priest's mouth and eyes were filled with dirt.

—I am sorry, Father, he said.

Near the campo santo were stone pits for curing hides. The sacristan put the priest into one of them and covered him with lamp oil and set him alight.

The smell was terrible. Black smoke and ash rose like grainy incense into the dark red sky. Cruelty and love and fear drifted upward—the sum of all the priest contained. The sacristan added wood to the blaze: the skeleton ribs of dead cacti and what kindling he could gather. The fire burned hotter.

He tended the flames throughout the night. At dawn he heard men tramping along the arroyo and cracking through the brush. They looked into the pit and shielded their faces from the smoke and covered their noses from the stench. The priest was black, already breaking up.

—This is the wasp's stinger, the sacristan declared. The end of it.

The men laughed. You've saved us a lot of trouble, they said. Who could think of a better justice? Now there is nothing left of the priest to ascend to his god.

Then the sacristan remembered how the Father had told them of the great rising of bodies on the final day of the world. In vowing to protect the priest, the sacristan had barred him forever from the day of mercy.

With a cry he pulled brush from the flames and threw handfuls of dirt upon the priest until the fire lay extinguished. But it was too late. The Father was all earth, sand, and ash. The sacristan stood with smoldering hands, and one by one the men went away satisfied.

After that, the Cochimí abandoned the mission. They went to their relatives in the hills, free to live in the accustomed way. The sacristan was the only one left. Because of what he had done, he made a vow never to leave the Father. He would stay and keep him company. And if the great rising of bodies should ever occur, he promised not to rise with them.

Barros sat in the charnel house until the sun hung low over the land. Carefully, with moments of resting, he placed the remaining bones among their brethren. He sat before them, hat in hand. The candles drew into themselves, and in the darkness he watched the bones. The skulls regarded him, but no pardon was offered.

He waited through the watches of the night, but the spirits were gone to the place they had gone and no forgiveness would come. He extinguished the tapers and went out. Under the young white moon he walked slowly toward the garden of the dead. Twice he sat down before going on. In his pocket he carried a handful of shells.

He tottered through the gate and placed three shells upon the grave of Peti Juan, and three upon the place where Manuela de casa lay. He placed three shells on the grave of the girl Tomasa, and again over the mound of Father Blacksnake's ashes. Three shells he guarded in his hand.

A night wind had come. He sat on a stone and watched the moon. A bat flitted down and away, and he saw its gray shadow sweep the ground, a ghost bat following. He looked up. Another shadow was rising from the brush—the figure of a man, wearing a hat of woven palm and an old blanket about his shoulders. The figure was no priest that Barros knew, and he did not know if the man was even a priest. Still he said, Father.

Barros tried to rise. His heart stammered and he struggled up, reaching out.

—Father, he said again.

The man shook his head and held up a hand—as a man might protest—and Barros was surprised to feel one vow lift from his chest. Then another, and finally a third. He put a hand to his heart, and a lightness lay upon him. When he looked again, the man was going off. Barros could see the palm hat moving away, and the shadow receded, and finally the sound of his steps echoed and failed through the brush.

In every campo santo there is a separate space for the very young. Bells are rung not mournfully, but joyously, for an infant has died in purity. A cross is carried, but without its staff, for a life incomplete.

Barros, now having made a good confession of his heaviest sins, went to the grave he had prepared for himself. It was a fine grave, empty of other individuals, a spacious place in the corner of the innocents. He spoke over himself as he remembered: Quia apud te propitiátio est. Requiéscat in pace. He placed the remaining shells beside the grave. Sitting on its edge, he watched the moon yield its place to the sun, and he looked forward to the sight of another sky.

Las Salinas

THE BAY OF FIVE HILLS

— 1852 —

Fr. Espín walked north along the Camino Real, a wizened man in peón clothes bearing only a walking stick and bundle, slow of gait in the light of the moon. He passed the ruins of Santa María in the country of stones, the old Cabujakaamung of the Cochimí. Of the adobe church only two walls remained, their high gables facing one another, with a weathered altar of earthen brick and a floor of soil bleeding down from the walls.

He skirted the towns, hiding in the brush when he spied a rider. Even in a poor man's clothes I have the look of a priest, he thought. They will want prayer, and blessing, and counsel. To kneel before me. To adore me without knowing anything of the one they are loving.

Near the waterhole of Agua Dulce, a scrabbling in the brush startled him—the frantic struggle of something bound. He moved closer. The mesquite trembled and ticked. He used his walking stick to part the sea of chaparral, and the brush emitted a hoarse whisper that ended in a single plaintive note.

A donkey was trapped in the thicket. It was the gray variety called Jerusalem—a fog-colored coat with a dark cross upon the shoulders. It was oddly shaped, gangly with overlong legs, and it saw the priest and skittered, looking sidelong at him. The donkey wore a jáquima and the rope was caught in the brush.

Fr. Espín pressed through the scrub. The donkey leapt sideways and pulled at the rope, eyes rolling. Drops of blood bloomed on the priest's hands as he worked. He yanked the jáquima loose and the donkey turned and bit him. He clung to the lead, the animal's hindquarters crashing through the brush, until they stood free of the chaparral, shivering and sweating.

—I am also alone, Fr. Espín said. Perhaps we can go alone together.

He gave the rope a gentle pull. The donkey resisted.

—Do not worry about a thing, the priest said. You are in good hands.

The donkey clopped its jaws and huffed in the morning chill. It watched Fr. Espín's hands, and the dark eyes brimmed with judgment. It seemed to know what he was.

The priest released the rope and the donkey kicked away, leaving him alone in the vastness and the wind. The donkey stood at the horizon, very small under the sky.

—I promise I won't strike you, the priest called out.

The donkey stretched its neck and bellowed.

—And I will not ask you to carry anything.

The donkey pawed the ground.

—Don't go, Fr. Espín pleaded.

The animal stood regarding him. At last Fr. Espín turned and began walking. He followed a coyote trail toward the coast, and the trail led to a spring. He filled the cow horn he carried and went on. The donkey shadowed at a distance, stopping when the priest stopped. Fr. Espín began talking to it as he went. The donkey shook its head.

Late in the day, from atop a low hill, he spied an abandoned corral of stone. His feet ached and he went gingerly down and passed through the gate. He did not dare make a fire, for fear of setting the floor of hard packed manure into flames. There were two spines embedded in his hand and he dug them free and cleaned the wounds with saliva. Then he peered over the wall. The donkey lingered at a distance, watching him.

I wish I had an orange, the priest thought. I could lure you with an orange. Ay, Dios. I have been alone for so long.

Night was coming on. He lay against the stones, sheltered from the wind, and heard the dolorous call of a coyote and sat up again. He kept thinking of his children. José María had not appeared to him in some years. Perhaps the boy had grown weary; he did not know. He could never determine what the boy wanted. And he missed the girl.

He lay down and curled his legs to his chest, legs all skin and sinew that must carry him to Pabellón. He would go as a passerby or a beggar, and he knew the girl would not remember him. He wished only to glimpse her once before leaving this bitter country forever, for word had come to him that the priest of Santo Tomás—the one he feared to meet so long ago—had closed the churches and not a single priest remained in the frontera save himself, and he was no longer one of them.

At last he fell asleep. He dreamed of his vows. He saw the bishop sitting upon the faldstool, the oil of righteousness warm on his palm. The stone mission of Mulegé and the faces of the Cochimí. Pearls surrounding him, the sole salvation from a grim and beautyless call. He opened his eyes and lay panting in the chill. Behind the dark drapery of the sky, the glow of heaven poured through tiny pinholes with a light weak and cold.

Sometime in the night he heard a clop and another clop. The donkey was standing in the corral. Fr. Espín got up carefully and closed the wooden gate. He counted eight long hairless furrows across the donkey's back, beginning at the withers.

—Pitiable puma who tried to eat you, he said. I imagine you kicked the very guts out of him.

He pulled back his sleeve and examined the bite that was going from red to black.

—I believe I will call you León.

Some hours later he woke in darkness, stiff and shivering. There was no promise of light to the east and he did not know what hour it was. He heard León snoring. He thought of the donkey's warm flesh, and he crept over and lay against him. The donkey startled. It whipped around and bit him on the shoulder, and all became a tangle of reedy legs and striking hooves and flailing hands. The donkey landed three good kicks before Fr. Espín could trundle away to the opposite wall. He felt one tooth go sideways and come out in his hand when he tried to put it right. He spat blood, and León stood huffing and unrepentant.

—You would kick a priest as you would any other man, Fr. Espín said, fingering his cheek. The thought gave him a strange satisfaction.

They spent the next day at rest, and in the evening he saw figures riding from the south along the coast. He looked about. This was open country, the vegetation small and spare. The riders would see the corral as he had seen it. With León he could not go quickly away. The donkey watched with ears alert. A man and woman were drawing near.

—Buenas tardes, the man called.

The priest lifted his hand in blessing and quickly dropped it. Buenas tardes, he said.

The woman was pallid and drawn, and she stared over the long horizon as if there were anything to see. The man asked if they might stay. They had food to offer, even limes for León.

I should tell them to go, Fr. Espín thought. But he was hungry.

—You may, he said.

The man helped the woman slip from the saddle and led her to the cold circle of the fire. He put the horses in the corral and relieved them of the weight of their gear. He carried a pan and some wrappings to the fire, and a bundle which he placed beside himself but did not untie. León stood at the gate of the corral and watched the priest.

The man worked at making a fire. We are going to Santo Tomás, he said.

The priest was afraid to say anything. He knew only how to speak as an ecclesiastic; there was a certain lilt to the voice. The woman observed him with clouded eyes and looked away.

—What happened to your face? the man inquired. Have you come upon rough men? Take care. There are many in this country.

Fr. Espín was afraid. The man could see that he was not rough, and he wondered what else the man could learn of him so easily. He looked into the fire and put a hand to his jaw.

—The roughest of men, he said. My donkey.

The man covered his smile.

—I have not seen a donkey like that before, the man said. With such long legs.

The man stoked the fire and dished the food and set a plate before the woman. She looked beyond him and would not eat.

—Belén, the man said to her. Belén.

He touched her hair and whispered to her. Fr. Espín busied himself with his meal and offered the rinds to León. The donkey snuffed them from his hands and the priest returned to the fire.

—You travel alone? the man asked.

—Yes, Fr. Espín said. With the donkey.

—Where do you come from?

The priest did not want to speak of Velicatá, or San Borja, or Santa María, or any place with a mission.

—From the south, he said.

—You have no family?

At this, the woman reached for the bundle, and the man blocked her hand. She fell across his lap with a strangled cry, her palms toward the heavens. Fr. Espín turned away. He imagined what the bundle carried, what lay in the dark folds of coarse cloth wrapped with string. His heart seized.

—We go to Santo Tomás to find a priest, the man said. There was none to speak a blessing when our son was lost.

—Are you certain there is a priest there, Fr. Espín said.

—We believe so, he said. It must be so.

Fr. Espín lowered his head. The donkey looked at him and bellowed like a grate of iron swinging shut. The woman pulled at the man's clothes and begged him to bury her with the boy, to put her in the ground.

—Forgive us, the man said. We did not mean to bring sadness to your fire. But we have suffered alone.

Fr. Espín stoked the coals and kept his head low. The bundle lay on the ground, vermilion in the firelight. The man soothed the woman's brow and began to sing:

Nana, nanita
El chiquito dormirá
en un ratito ya.

Nana, nanita
El niñito está
a punto de dormirse,
en un ratito ya.[1]

The moon came up and the coals burned low. Smoke passed before the man's face.

—Have you a wife? he said.

—No.

—Have you never? the man asked.

He was fearful again that the man should guess, but the man did not await an answer. He looked down at the woman, and Fr. Espín saw that she slept.

—I fear for her, the man said. If we should find no priest to help us.

In the night he could hear them. The man's low murmur, the woman's protest. Their movements composed a sad refrain: the discord of limb and garment, the coda of a sigh. He heard the woman weeping and the man spoke a failed comfort and the priest went to the corral among the animals so he would hear no more. The horses dozed with low-slung heads and León came to stand with him.

---

1. Lullaby, lullaby, the little one will sleep in just a little while. Lullaby, lullaby, the boy is at the edge of sleep, but not just yet.

He could relieve their suffering. A simple prayer, a gesture or a word. But he was a minister of death and there was no absolution, even should he seek it. He was no one to bless a child or anyone, and he could not abide the blind, miserable adoration that would come.

In the morning he helped them prepare the horses. The man secured the bundle behind his saddle, and Fr. Espín would not look at it. The woman mounted and stared ahead with unseeing eyes. The man shook the priest's hand and said, Que Dios le acompañe. The hand was very cold. Fr. Espín did not know what to say, what a common man would have offered or in what manner.

—The same to you, he said at last.

He watched as they rode away. He pulled the jáquima over the donkey's ears and looked at his hands, as dirty as the next man's. Still, he thought, they would have kissed them if they had known.

He continued north with León beside him. The donkey clopped his teeth, and when he kicked sideways the priest did not prevent him.

The country was ironing out. Toward the coast the mountains melted into foothills, and the hills flattened to low dunes. Scant vegetation grew by the sea, and the land was empty of game. In hunger his body seemed to consume itself. The sand was fine and kicking up in the wind, and he wiped his eyes and wished for the donkey's long lashes. Toward afternoon a haze covered the sky, and they passed through a country of gray sand and sea and heavens.

At Socorro he spied the inlet called the Bay of Five Hills. His heart quickened; he was near Pabellón. Salt pans lay along the coast like shining white mirrors among soft gray dunes. He led León through the salt brush, stopping by lagoons thick with brine. The beach was long and curving and empty, the sand sculpted by the breeze into winding furrows. The sea was restless, and he saw black volcanoes rising from the earth like the rounded tops of men's hats.

He could see figures ahead in the salt pools. The figures bent, gathering crystals with their hands, and their backs made dark islands in a strange white sea.

León's ears pricked up at the sounds of men. He stopped. Fr. Espín saw their camp with the low fire, and his mouth watered at the thought of salted meat.

—Come, León. They may be willing to share with us.

The donkey would not go. Fr. Espín gave the jáquima a gentle pull. León anchored his hooves in the sand.

—All right, Fr. Espín said, you have won. But if you miss a meal, it will not be my fault.

He turned the burro's back to the wind and secured him with hobbles. He took the cow horn canteen and poured water into his hand. León gulped through velvet lips and bristles, sighed, and put his head down to nibble at the sea grass.

Fr. Espín took a kerchief from his pocket and tied it low over his eyes; the blowing sand and the brightness of the salt pans could blind a man. By now the figures had seen him coming. One waded out of the brine to watch him approach, and turned to the others, and they all straightened up.

There was one white man in a short-brimmed hat, and one Indian in a long leather coat such as soldiers wore. There were two Mejicanos in soiled short pants and tunics. Their pitted faces were the same; he thought they might be brothers. They had a small cart, filled with salt baskets, but no animal.

The man wearing the short-brimmed hat said, Have you come for salt.

—No, he said.

—What are you looking for?

—I am going north. But I saw your camp.

The man's trousers were caked with salt. His face was ashen, the color of one who drinks too much liquor. His ears protruded from under the hat, and one of the ears was notched in the manner of former prisoners. He stepped close.

—And you thought it would be good to share our fire.

Fr. Espín felt very small among them. He did not like the look of the brothers, gaunt and loco-eyed and mean. He tried to speak as he had heard other men speak: And what of it, cabrón.

The brothers laughed. The white man looked at the priest's worn clothes, the matted hair, the beard and staff.

—Gather salt for us, he said. And you may share our fire.

Fr. Espín looked back at León, small and gray in the distance. The donkey's head was up, watching him. The men were looking down the coast at León. I should take him and go, Fr. Espín thought. But hunger held him.

The sand, blown by persistent winds, made low walls of earth that set off the marsh from the sea. He removed his sandals and rolled up the legs of his trousers, and took a basket and waded into the pool. The salt heaped itself into islands and isthmuses, pushed by the wind and tides, and where the pools were deep the color was green. In one pool the crystals looked like rice, white and clinging to one another. In another pool, where the salt had collected over time, the crystals were large and resembled ice and burned like ice. The brine was so thick that on the tongue even the smallest taste would make a man shudder, even a confident man who tries to test himself.

He worked silently and the men kept looking at him, all but the Indian. The water was oily with salt, and the wind needled his face. His palms began to burn as he filled the basket, and cuts opened in his feet. He hopped around like he had been stung.

In the evening he rinsed his legs in the sea and went to the fire with the other men. He did not know their names. He thought of the white man as Short Brim, and the pitted men as Brother One and Two, and the Indian as Soldier Coat.

Soldier Coat went to the sea to fish. He stood on the sand and cast his line into the waves. The men sat in silence. They did not seem to like one another. The red sun broke through the gray at the last moment, rested on the sea, and went down. The sky began to clear. The moon was coming up, a bright, full moon of white. The priest watched pelicans descend into the surf, rising with glittering fishes in their beaks, and the waves were wild and pounded like drums. Short Brim walked off to urinate in the grass. He carried his satchel close. Brother One lay back in the sand, and Brother Two smoked and looked out over the sea.

—Are you traders? Fr. Espín asked.

Brother Two turned. Why, do you have something to trade?

—No, he said.

—And you, what do you do?

—Nothing. I am just walking, going north.

Brother Two looked at him with vicious eyes. Fr. Espín was afraid. He thought again of taking León, but the fear was like wine to him. The men and their talk slowed, and his thoughts eddied. He took the cow horn and poured water over his stinging feet. Brother One came and sat beside him.

—Do you work for yourself or for other men?

—Just myself.

—Have you a ranch, then?

—No.

—A ship?

—No, only the legs I walk upon.

—What equipment do you have.

—Nothing, a little water, that is all.

Soldier Coat was coming back, carrying fish. He squatted and began arranging them over the fire. Brother Two blew smoke and scrutinized the priest. Fr. Espín was glad Soldier Coat was there. He moved closer to him. Soldier Coat said nothing, preparing the fish and whistling to himself. In his nervousness Fr. Espín whistled too, the song of the boy at the edge of sleep.

Short Brim came to the fire and said, Hurry up. I am hungry.

—Oye, I am sick of fish, Brother One said. He had a deep cut on his forearm and cradled the arm between his legs. The edges of flesh were turning black. Short Brim held a bottle and he stood behind Brother One and splashed drink into the wound. Fr. Espín watched the man cry out and dance. Brother Two kicked at the dancing feet. Soldier Coat poked the fish and turned them.

Fr. Espín felt Brother Two's dark eyes upon him.

—What kind of man are you, Brother Two said.

—Just a man. Like you.

Brother Two spat into the sand. You are a liar.

Fr. Espín looked up. What do you mean?

—You are not a man like me. You are afraid.

—I am just an ordinary one, he said, looking away. The wind carried the smell of brine, salted like blood. He swallowed and stood slowly and slipped into his sandals.

—What is your hurry, Short Brim said.

—I must water my animal.

Brother Two handed his half-smoked cigarillo to his brother. We saw your donkey there, he said.

Fr. Espín shivered.

—Are you going to La Esperanza? Short Brim said.

Fr. Espín knew of La Esperanza, a place for gold-diggers.

—No, I am going north.

Brother One came close. Going north, you say?

He stood in the dark breeze. Sand peppered his legs, raising goose-flesh.

—Let him go, Soldier Coat said. He has nothing you want.

—I am not so sure, Brother Two said. Here we have a cart, and no animal to pull it.

In the moonlight, Fr. Espín could see the gray fleck that was León, hobbled in the sea grass. The donkey lifted his head and looked at him.

—He is my only companion, Fr. Espín said. He rubbed his chilled arms. The men were silent, hovering. They could force me if they wanted to, he thought. They will kill me, and take León.

He could bless the food. Or offer a phrase from the Mass. He had no idea of the white man or the Indian, but the brothers could never harm a priest.

The sky had gone dark. He was floating above, seeing himself as the men must see him, a small and dirty thing with strange voice and odd gesturing hand. A man who seemed at once greater and less than what he was. He closed his eyes. He felt that León, watching him, must know his thoughts. And he turned away to the fire.

Short Brim set out along the beach toward the donkey. The brothers crouched and began eating. They pushed pieces of fish into their mouths and ate like those who have not eaten in a long time.

The wind chilled him. He saw Short Brim coming back and leading León. The brothers turned to each other. Fr. Espín saw them nod, saw them signal with their eyes. The wind trilled in his ears, a high warning like a whistle through the fingers.

He walked away from the camp. When he had gone a short distance, he looked back to the low coals of their fire. What if they strike him, he thought. Or starve him. He felt a tottering resolve but sat down. I will stay nearby and see what happens. León may shake them off and God return him to me. Or perhaps tomorrow I will stay with León and go with them.

Sometime in the late hour he fell asleep and woke with cold. Clouds covered the dark sky, and he looked at the red dot of the fire on the dunes. He closed his eyes and the red dot remained. He listened to the waves and suddenly he heard a loud bray of alarm. The note rose and rose and broke into short bursts of panicked cries and the final cry was chopped short and the note died away on the wind.

He flushed with dread. He squinted, wishing the moon might appear from the clouds so he could see. He got up, stumbling, and the bunchgrass raked his legs as he ran. The men were crouching in a circle with their knives, and he saw the low gray form among them.

León had died kneeling, with his nose touching the earth. The priest shivered with cold and sorrow, and the men did not acknowledge him. They continued cutting. León lay in pieces, and the men were putting strips of meat across the fire.

Soldier Coat got up. He held a foreleg and offered it to the priest. Fr. Espín trembled, his arms across the cold cavity of his chest, and Soldier Coat set the leg on the ground and took off his leather coat, holding it out. The priest slipped it on. The man's warmth was still inside it, the warmth of his exertion.

Blood trails wound serpentine through the sand. When the dark tendrils trickled to the priest's feet, he turned and walked back to his fireless camp. He could see the bright red star of fire in the distance and he closed his eyes. He woke only when a coyote came to sniff him, and the animal startled and trotted down the beach.

At dawn, the new sky was a soft blue and blushed with red clouds. He looked toward the camp and saw a host of gulls and heard the sharp cries. He got to his feet and brushed the sand from himself and walked toward the place, and at last he ran and sent the cloud of birds into the air. The men had gone. The sand was black with blood, the fire cold. The ground was covered with the tracks of coyotes.

Not even a hoof remained. He walked around the fire and saw the deliberate footfalls of men and the skittering round prints of hooves and the two long impressions of the dying, kneeling forelegs. He saw the trail of men going east. Their tracks lay deep in the sand from the load they carried.

The ground was scattered with clumps of hair. He knelt and hugged the coat around him. Gulls swarmed and darted down and watched with red-rimmed eyes. He gathered the gray hairs with rushing fingers, as an ordinary man might slip beads of prayer through earnest, work-worn fingers, and he rose and continued north, holding the salvation of no one in his hands.

La Mezcalera

SANTO DOMINGO DE LA FRONTERA

— 1852 —

When Inés was a girl, her father acquired land at Santo Domingo, two hundred leagues to the north of Mulegé along the western sea. He built a ranch at the foot of Red Rock, a humped-up hill of stone with a dark cleft in the middle, as if a giant had split it with an axe. To one side of the house he added a generous ramada that sheltered vats and mauls and clay pot stills, and a circular mill that crushed the hearts of agaves to make mezcal. Her father was a man much occupied with the mezcal works, and Inés cared for him instead of marrying. In time, she performed the requisite burial at the small adobe church which had not survived long enough to be built into a mission of stone, and as if from some unspoken indenture, she took up her father's trade.

It happened once, driving an old Kiliwa man before them. They were in no hurry but walked the man ahead of their mules, with a dog following, and they stopped to purchase mezcal. They had the man bound by the wrists. Inés asked what crime he had committed. They said he claimed to own land in the north, at the frontera, but the land was not his and they were moving him along to El Rosario.

So far the old man had said nothing. She asked if the land was mission land, meant for the indios. They said the governor had given land grants and the man's name was not among the listed.

—You can read the documents yourself if you're concerned, one man said.

—I am.

You can address the governor. See what he will say.

—Take as much mezcal as you can carry, she said. And leave the man.

They refused at first, but she filled their cups and on the fifth round they went back north along the road, loaded with bottles and little memory of why they had come. Inés untied the old man and he sat rubbing his wrists and looking around. The dog sat beside him.

—Are you harmed, she said.

—I thought that was the end of me, he said. I was ready to go off wearing my crest of stars.

—Not today, she said.

—No, not today.

—Do you have land at the frontera?

He said he was born not far from Red Rock and his people used to walk these hills. He said this had been their custom until some years ago when the priests arrived and caused considerable trouble, and his people quit the land and settled in the east.

He got up to examine the clay pot stills.

—Do you intend to harvest every agave on the land?

—No, she said. Some are left to flower so more might grow.

She told him this was what her father had done. She expected him to inquire of her father, but he did not, and she remembered that among certain tribes one does not speak the names of the dead.

His name was Manolo. They sat passing the time, and he did not appear to want to leave. She offered him a cup and he declined. But after that day, he took to staying at Red Rock. He addressed her as sister and sometimes he worked as the jimador of the agaves, prying them from the ground, or tending the firepit where the hearts lay buried and roasting, or leading the black donkey Frijolito in circles around the mill, mashing the roast into a slurry bound for clay pot stills and bottles and to El Rosario to be sold. Sometimes Inés would not see Manolo for days or weeks, and the house became desolate beyond endurance, and she imagined he went to Arroyo de León where the Kiliwa people had settled, for he had a true sister still living among them.

Inés had been a child at the mission of Mulegé in the year 1820 when there were many Cochimí in that place. Her father was a soldier, and she still lived with the memory of what had occurred there. She seldom slept, because in those hours of stillness the boy's voice would rise, calling to her from beneath the faraway Vermilion Sea. She could never understand him, and did not know whether he spoke her tongue or the tongue of the Cochimí, or whether in the next life everyone spoke the same.

On one such night, she got up and sat in the caneback chair she reserved for the long hours before dawn. She rubbed her temples.

—I can't know what you want, she said.

Somewhere over the hills, the coyotes were calling. Outside the window, she heard a dove flush from the mesquite. She lit the lamp. The trunk with her father's effects lay under the bed where he died, the bed she now occupied herself.

The boy whispered and she walked the room. For a distraction, she slid out her father's trunk and opened it. Within lay the saber and the pistol, a sheaf of papers in spidery formal hand, a letter addressed to her which contained the particulars of the mezcal works but carried no sentiment at all. His old breeches lay next to his retired boots. The cuera he had worn as a soldier at Mulegé. Copper coins, green with verdigris, that she placed upon his eyes when he passed.

She lifted out the cuera. The leather was soft and smelled of animals and her father in particular. She recalled his scent more than anything he had ever spoken. As she refolded the garment, she felt a tiny weight within the folds. A stone or a nut or perhaps a seed. She shook the garment, but nothing fell out. She turned it inside out and discovered a pocket sewn shut. She fingered the leather, wondering if a bullet lay within. A memento of her father's life spared, or another's. The lamp guttered and flared up again.

She got a knife and slit the pocket. Inside, she found a kerchief bordered in lace, tied in a series of knots. She began untying them. The last was tied with a man's strength and she thought of cutting the fabric but finally retrieved an awl and forced it through the center of the tangle. She worked it loose, and the folds fell away. Into her hand dropped a shining pearl of pink. The boy spoke in an urgent whisper. The hair on her arms stood up, and she closed the cloth around the pearl and sat listening.

The next day she was surprised to see the three men from the frontera returning down the road, one fat man and two slight men behind him. She invited them to drink but they would not dismount. They asked after Manolo.

—He is not here, she said.

—Where has he gone?

—Who inquires?

—Some say he was seen at the frontera.

—That is unlikely.

—So you do not know where he went.

—It is a free world to wander.

They said they would stay and drink after all. They got down and went to the shade of the ramada. She did not bring chairs, but they drank standing. The fat man complimented her on the quality of the mezcal and passed her some coins. She saw the men watching her eyes and she was careful not to look to the road.

They were a long time in finishing. Finally she said she had other matters to attend to and she collected the cups. The fat man saluted her and signaled the others, and they tarried a moment before mounting up and going north along the trail.

In the morning she saw Manolo returning across the arroyo, thin of body but square in face, gray-haired and bowlegged, though he rarely rode, wearing sandals of agave fiber and picking his way along the rocks. The dog followed. She left the clay pot stills and came out from the ramada and called. He stopped as though she might be warning him of something and he looked around, but then raised a hand. Together they walked to the house and sat under the eaves.

He asked who had come in recent days, and she named the names but did not mention the men from the frontera. She asked if anyone had bothered him on the road, and he said no. He presented to her a small sack of datilillo dates and she asked if he cared for a cup of mezcal but he declined. She rubbed her eyes.

—Have you not slept?

—No. I heard a boy speaking.

—A coyote pup can sound like a boy.

—It was not a coyote.

He sat thinking. Even a goat, he said.

—It wasn't any goat.

—Well, he said.

—I want to show you something.

She went to retrieve the pearl. She carried it in the folds of the kerchief. Manolo peered at the pearl with interest but did not touch it.

—This is not from the western sea, Manolo said.

—How did you know that?

—I didn't, he said. I was only beginning a conversation.

—It is from the Vermilion Sea, she said. At Mulegé.

—How did you come by it?

—It lay among my father's things.

She looked out to the road and folded the cloth over the pearl and beckoned him inside. They sat at the table, and the dog lay underneath. She released the pearl from the cloth and it spun in a shining orbit and came to rest. It flared in the light of the lamp and might have been a small lamp unto itself. Manolo picked it up.

—This is a good pearl, he said. These you cannot find anymore.

—My father intended this for a woman, but she refused him. I did not know he still possessed it. Did you know my father was a soldier at Mulegé?

—No, he said.

—I was reluctant to tell you.

Manolo put the pearl to his teeth.

—When I was a girl, she said, there was a priest at Mulegé. Thorn or Needle was his name. Espín or Espada. He had a son. Not his own son. A boy he had taken from the Cochimí.

Manolo waved a hand.

—Sister, this is the worst kind of story.

—The priest did not like me. I ran wild, I had no mother to teach me. I would go down to the place where the river met the sea . . .

—I believe you have not slept. It causes one to think of sad things.

—The priest made the boy fish for pearls, just a small boy.

—Don't tell me. Don't say another thing.

—One day some men came towing the boy's canoe with the boy floating after it.

Manolo returned the pearl to the table and did not touch it again or look at it.

—There are methods to drive a ghost away, he said. If a ghost is bothering you.

—I do not want to drive him away. His blood calls to me from the ground.

—From the sea.

—Yes, I mean from the sea.

—Get rid of the pearl and the ghost will follow. That is the best way.

—Have you been listening? I am trying to know what the boy wants.

She got up and refilled Manolo's water cup. She took a drink herself and handed it to him.

—Someone is coming, she said.

Manolo looked around.

—No, not now, Inés said. I believe that is what the boy is telling me. Someone is going to come.

—This talk unsettles me, Manolo said. I am going to bed. Good night.

She woke him early because she still had not slept. They loaded the donkey Frijolito with the crates and mallets and the coa for harvesting agaves. Manolo told the dog to stay behind and keep watch, and the dog thumped its tail once and they set out.

A morning dew lay heavy on the old fences of prickly pear, on the old mission huertas of fig and pomegranate. At the widest point of the arroyo, on a terrace of earth, sat the abandoned chapel of Santo Domingo and its quadrangle of crumbling walls. As they passed the church, a bevy of swallows flitted out and away. They approached the cemetery, and she set aside the fallen gate and passed behind the half wall and paused for a moment among the cairns and wooden crosses at the grave of her father. She thought of speaking to him, but he had never been one to answer.

Manolo waited at a distance until she had finished. They took the side canyon in the shade of grassy mesas, passing the broken acequias that once carried water to the mission. When they came to the small stone fort where soldiers had once surveyed the people, Manolo looked away.

They ascended the slope. The hills looked soft and brown from a distance until one stood under them, and then they were rough with chaparral. In years of rain, the hills gave birth to flowers—colonies of bright brittlebush that made wide bands of gold in the crevices where they came spilling down. But the years had been dry, and the brown grasses hissed and bent in the wind.

Agaves covered the hills. Some were tiny pups growing pulga by pulga flea by flea and others were in midmaturity. Inés stopped at the crest of the hill beside a plant she had castrated the previous year. The agave was swollen with sugar intended for the severed flower stalk that now lay on the ground.

Manolo moved Frijolito off. Inés took the coa, and with its flat blade she severed each leaf. She chopped at the root until the core sprang free and she rolled it over with her foot. The heart of the agave resembled a great pineapple with wounds of white flesh. Manolo took the coa and split the core in two. He struck again and now it lay in four, and then eight. Inés sat down and fanned herself with her hat.

—I was curious what else he was saying, Manolo said.

—Who?

—The boy, Manolo said.

—I thought you did not wish to speak of the boy.

—I wasn't speaking of him. I was inquiring of him.

Manolo led the donkey over and hoisted the agave fragments into the crates. Frijolito's head hung low, dispirited under the weight. Manolo bundled the lead rope and secured it and patted the donkey's rump. Frijolito started down the trail with Manolo and Inés following.

—Perhaps he wishes me to return the pearl to the sea, Inés said.

—Good. We have a sea here, ready to receive it.

—I mean the Vermilion Sea. At Mulegé. Or perhaps to his grave.

The trail led through the golden earth. When they came out above the mission, Inés held up a hand and Manolo stopped. A man stood below in the cemetery. He wore a palm hat but his face was nearly black, as though he lived all his hours under the sun. Wearing a soldier coat such as her father possessed. It gave her a chill, this apparition in a cuera standing beside her father's grave. He was picking among the stones with a staff, stumbling as an older man on uneven soil where the bursage was pushing up the ground around the markers. He stooped to read the names and straightened up again.

—You better go on alone, Manolo said.

—If ever he was a soldier, he is not one now. He is just an old man.

Frijolito was already going down. Inés turned once to look at Manolo. He waved her on but kept watch. The donkey blustered and the man looked up as Inés came into the dusty yard and stopped at the cemetery gate.

—Perdón, he said. I was looking for someone.

He told Inés he was traveling north with the intention of abandoning the country, but he wished to visit the resting place of a priest he had known some years ago, one who had been a friend to him in his younger days.

She led him to the corner of the campo santo where a tilted and weathered headstone without ribbon or candle or flower leaned against the half wall. She asked if this was the person he sought. He knelt and brushed the stone and said yes.

—The name is all but obscured, he said.

—I am sorry, she said.

—It does not matter, he said. Whether a priest or an ordinary man, all are buried alone.

—I shall leave you, she said.

He looked up. Would you stay, he said. It is a lonely thing after so many years.

She knelt beside him and asked where he had traveled from. He said he had come from Pabellón, where he had gone to find a child he had once known. To see about her welfare.

—And was she well?

He said he had only seen her from the road. That she looked well. He shook his head and did not say any more. She turned discreetly away and beckoned Manolo. When she turned again to the kneeling man, the boy began whispering. She looked to see if the man could hear, but he kept clearing the gravestone.

The man blessed himself and thanked her for staying with him, and at once his voice recalled something to her. She looked more closely. The man was not a soldier. He was the priest of Mulegé, the one she remembered from girlhood, the very man who caused the death of the boy. She sat back on her heels. She had not known the priest was still living, but now he appeared in the campo santo as if she had summoned him.

There was little priestly about him now. He was no longer the fragile and refined person who scolded her with his slight gesture while the Cochimí boy rested in the circle of his arm. Now his face was coarse with sun sores and a patchy beard that in times past he never would have allowed. She went to the yard where Manolo waited.

—You are trembling, Manolo said. Did the man threaten you?

—No.

—Did he?

—No. He is the priest I told you about.

—Of the pearl and the boy.

—Yes.

For once Manolo made no comment. The two watched the priest struggle up and wipe his face with a sleeve and come to the gate.

—Sister, do not invite him, Manolo whispered.

—I do not wish to.

—But you will.

—Yes.

—Is the boy speaking?

—He was.

—This is a bad business.

She helped the priest secure the gate. She told him of her ranch at Red Rock and invited him to come and eat.

—It is a quiet place, she said. Just myself, and Manolo.

—Thank you, he said. In truth I am worn out. Thank you.

They went slowly along the arroyo, talking of mezcal. The priest laid a hand on Frijolito, walking alongside. He asked about her house at Red Rock. She said nothing of her girlhood at Mulegé or how much she knew of him. Manolo followed at a distance, and when they came to the house she showed the priest to the room where she slept before her father died. She told him to rest. She said she would call him to supper and he lay gratefully down and she let the curtain fall across the door.

In the kitchen Manolo waited.

—Come outside, he said.

She followed him to the ramada. In the dirt beside the clay pot stills lay the dog, matted and sticky with its own blood. In the dust she saw the footprints of men. Manolo showed her where the three mules had come into the yard.

—Perhaps you should go away for a time, she said. To Arroyo de León.

—I am reluctant to leave you.

—Because of the boy.

—And the priest. These events.

—The boy wishes no harm to me.

—How can anyone know what the dead desire?

—The issue is not the boy. It is these men. Tell me, do you truly have land at the frontera?

—No, he said.

—Then I will tell them so.

—You will tell them.

—Yes.

—And will you also tell the priest to leave?

—I do not know. I believe the boy has directed him to come.

—I will sleep out here tonight. I cannot stay under the same roof with a priest.

—He is not a priest now.

—A priest in the coat of a soldier. What could be worse.

They buried the dog, and in the night she thought she heard the boy again but it was only the wind. She went to check Manolo. He slept in the corner of the ramada, away from where the dog had lain. He breathed heavily, his arm over his eyes. The moon was hidden and she went down to the arroyo to listen but heard nothing.

When she returned to the kitchen she found the priest asleep at the table, an overtired man who could not rest until he had given up the night. She lit a candle and took the chair across from him. She watched as he slept.

She had perceived no malice in what the boy said. Merely an urgency, some task that must be performed. She found herself arguing with the boy. The priest is going north, leaving the country. Who am I to prevent him? As a child I held no favor with him.

She got up and began to build a fire beneath the grate of the stove. The priest sat up and rubbed his eyes.

—It is some time since I slept in a proper bed, he said. It was strange to me.

—How long have you traveled?

—Perhaps the better part of my life.

—Sometimes it can seem so.

He said his name was Magín Matías. She did not know if this was true, for she had never learned his given names or even that he possessed any. He said his surname was Espín. She said her name was Inés, and her friend was called Manolo, and there had been some trouble. She told him of the dog. He shook his head and said that men were cruel, that he had seen much ruthlessness in men.

—Are you not a man yourself?

He did not answer. She turned to the fire and prepared the coffee and he cradled the cup but did not drink.

—Have you been long alone? he asked.

—I am not alone.

—I am sorry, he said. Do not listen to me. I am tired.

—I told Manolo to leave for a time, but he does not seem inclined, she said.

—Because of you.

—Yes. He is a good man.

She told him of the death of her father some years before. How she managed the mezcal works, and at times had thought of giving it up but continued in her father's name. The priest said she had done well, that her father would be pleased. She said she did not know.

—From girlhood I have been one to do for myself, she said.

—That quality is an admirable one.

—For a boy perhaps, she said. But no one praises such a girl.

He rubbed his eyes and she felt sorry for testing him.

—I will not stay long, he said.

—You can stay for a time, she said. If you wish.

A rooster crowed and the square of the window was growing light. Manolo stood in the doorway. The priest greeted him, and Manolo took coffee and went out.

—He is a quiet one, the priest said.

—No, she said. He is not.

In the afternoon the priest offered to assist her with the mezcal. They went behind the house, where Manolo had already built a fire in the pit. They lowered stones into the embers and waited for the stones to heat. She watched the priest. She had not recalled that he was a man for work. He now seemed not a priest at all, but an ordinary man, except for something in the high voice, perhaps learned long ago. And a gentle manner. Magín Matías. She found him looking at her and she wiped her brow and saw the soil on her hand and glanced away.

The agave heart lay in eight pieces on a cowhide, and the priest set to chopping. He and Manolo lowered the fragments to the hot stones and covered them with damp grass, and the three took shovels and buried the severed heart in the earth. They sat around the newly created mound as if to observe the fragments under the ground, in roast. The priest kept looking over, as though he wished to say something, and once he started but checked himself.

Finally Manolo said, You appear well and rested.

The priest blushed and said, Yes. I will soon be on my way.

—There is no need to hurry, Inés said.

Manolo rose to leave and stopped. Inés saw a man riding up the road, one of the three from the frontera. He came into the yard, a fat man under a broad hat, well established in his short jacket and vest with pocket chain. A jovial face that belied his intention. Frijolito blustered at the approaching mule.

—Buenas tardes, the fat man said, gesturing to Manolo. Here is the very man we seek. One might think he resided here.

—He resides where he chooses, Inés said.

Manolo moved to stand between Inés and the man.

—You would like to come with me? the man said. Would you like that?

Manolo did not reply. The man turned his attention to the priest.

—And who is this other?

—A traveler, Fr. Espín said.

The man rubbed his chin in thought. He looked at Inés.

—What would your father say about these men living here?

—I wonder more about what you yourself are saying.

—I only wish to take this old indio to El Rosario.

—You and which others?

—Respectable persons. Names you do not know. Is it right for this man to cause anxiety to good families living on land rightfully given them?

—He seems to cause anxiety only to you, she said. I wonder that a man such as yourself would worry so.

The man lifted his hat to her. You are the true daughter of your father, he said. Only lacking the saber.

—There is nothing untoward here, Espín said. A kind woman offering shelter. And the jimador of agaves. That is all.

—Out of respect for your good father, the man said to Inés, I will do nothing before your eyes.

—My father is gone, she said.

The man looked at Manolo and touched the brim of his hat. He nodded to Inés.

—Nothing before your eyes, he said again.

He turned the mule, walking at first, and spurred toward the arroyo in a kick of dust.

—Manolo, she said. Will you go to Arroyo de León.

—And bring this trouble upon them?

—Come. Let us take supper.

Manolo went to retrieve the tools, and he knelt to touch the warming earth where the pieces of agave lay buried. The priest spoke to Inés in a low voice.

—Is there any danger to yourself? Perhaps you should make him go.

She turned on him. Would you abandon a companion so readily?

The priest glanced away. I do not know what is wrong with me, he said.

—Nor do I.

When she looked again for Manolo, the tip of Red Rock was aflame with the setting sun and he was but a small form growing smaller in shadow as he made his way along the arroyo to the east.

The boy came to her in the night, whispering incessantly until she got up and lit the lamp. She went quietly to the kitchen, but the priest had now accustomed himself to the house and slept in his room. She sat at the table. Once she thought she heard him up and moving. She went to the hall and paused outside the curtain that covered the door. Now the boy began to speak in urgent utterances. She retrieved a candle and came again to the priest's door and carefully lifted the curtain. He lay sleeping, and the shadows cast by the flame upon his face made him appear as a corpse she had once seen in the church of Mulegé, reposing in the candlelight. He opened his eyes and she nearly dropped the flame. The priest groped at the blanket and held up a hand against the light.

—What is it? he said.

—Nothing.

He was sitting up now.

—Are you all right?

—Did you hear whispering, she asked.

—What?

—Whispering. Speaking.

—Come here, come here.

She stood at the foot of the bed. She clasped her shawl to her throat with one hand, and the candleflame shuddered in the other. The priest held still, listening.

—Have the men returned? he asked.

—No, not the men.

—What then?

—Never mind. It was a dream.

—Tell me of your dream.

—I am going. I am sorry to disturb you.

He took hold of the edge of her shawl and released it. Please stay, he said. You need not speak of the dream. Just stay and speak to me.

She turned to the door, but the gentle voice held her.

—Here, he said. Let us go to the kitchen. To the table. Yes, that is more seemly.

She went to sit with him. The boy's voice had fallen silent and she stayed with Espín at the table, passing the night by speaking of commonplace things which were a comfort. It was nearly sunrise when they bid each other goodnight and went to their rooms. She stood at the window and looked out upon a country of unceasing wind and gray sky. Fog and dodder hung upon every wizened branch in a manner that made even living trees appear dead. She turned. Her father's things were piled about her in a room that had never been her own.

When she lay down, she heard the boy whispering again. She said if he would only show some patience, she would do the thing he asked.

On the fourth day they unearthed the heart of agave from its burial place. The fragments were charred and steaming and full of sugar.

Frijolito lifted his head and snuffed the scent and tried to move away, but Inés pulled him to the round mill. She fitted him with the collar and hitched him to the traces while the priest forked the fragments into the ring of stone. The donkey walked the circle, scarcely lifting his feet, as the wheel crushed the agave into mash. Inés sat with Espín beneath the spare shade of the tamarisks her father had planted long years before, and they watched Frijolito going around.

—A la mujer y a la mula, she said, por el pico les entra la hermosura.

He laughed and asked if this were true, that a round woman and a round mule were equal in beauty. For the first time she smiled and told him it was only a saying, and she did not know why she repeated it.

He ate a small piece of roasted agave and gestured that she should hold out her palm and he placed some in her hand. The breeze was warm. He removed his hat and fanned himself. She offered him a cup of mezcal and he apologized but said that some years ago he had given up drink because he had seen its effect upon men, and he had enough difficulty with himself alone. He said he meant no disrespect toward what she had built.

—My father built it, she said.

He gestured toward the house. It is a fine concern, he said.

She said that concern was the correct term. That in truth she cared little for the mill that had belonged to her father, or the drink that made men sullen or unbridled.

—Why then do you continue?

—For my father's sake.

—For your love of him.

—For his sake.

Frijolito was slowing. Inés got up and flicked his flank with a palm branch and he trotted two steps and returned to his heavy pace. She went to the house and returned with vinegar water. She gave it to Espín and he drank and sighed. She sighed too, watching Frijolito. She sat hugging her knees and looking up at Red Rock. Espín said it was a singular landform, and she said she wondered what made it red. He told her that in the earliest days, priests had made their rituals in the cave by the light of tallow candles. And before them, the shamans. He asked if she had ever climbed it.

She said her father had taken her once. She recalled many rough shelves and knobs for handholds and she almost lost her footing. From the top, one could see the high hills rising from the canyon that led to the mountains. She told him she felt the canyon promised something. She wondered where it terminated. Even Manolo did not know.

She looked to Red Rock again. To the west, she said, one could see the broad mouth of the arroyo that led to the sea and the shining salt pans of white.

He coughed and replaced his hat and removed it again.

—Would you allow me to speak to you, he said.

She smiled. Have you not been speaking to me? she said.

—Something of import.

She was a long time in answering. She could feel her heartbeat in her throat and she took a handful of dust and sifted it in her fingers as she had often done as a girl. Then she put her hands in her lap and looked at him. His face was earnest, one hand at his temple.

—You are free to speak as you wish, she said.

A little wind came up and he wiped a speck of dust from his eye. Inés held very still.

—When I was a younger man, he said, I lived at Mulegé.

She had expected another kind of proclamation. It took a moment to comprehend what he had said, what she knew he was going to say. She looked away. She had thought he could become a companion or perhaps more than a companion, but he could be nothing other than what he was: a priest or sorcerer who had lulled her, who had made her forget herself. And now he wished to unburden himself to her.

When he began to speak again, she half-rose to leave but she wished to know how he would contrive the story. He seemed to be having difficulty. He said again that he was from Mulegé. She kept silent and he finished his drink and set the cup on the ground and wiped his hands though they were not wet. He replaced his hat and picked up the cup, staring into it as a man might read leaves of tea.

—I know the mission there, she said. Above the river that flows to the Vermilion Sea.

He looked at her with surprise.

—I know what you wish to say, she said.

—You cannot know, he said.

He pushed back his hat and looked at her face and she did not shy away.

—My father was Don Mata the soldier, she said. Of Mulegé.

He kept studying her but without recognition. She felt a cruelty rising within herself.

—I know you are that priest of Mulegé, she said.

The donkey stopped in his traces, stamping and swishing his tail at the flies.

—Who told you.

—Myself alone.

He looked toward the sky. I was once a priest, he said. I am no longer.

—You do not remember me. I am the girl who played beside the river. And the sea.

—The daughter of Don Mata, he said. I remember now.

—I do not believe you. But I remember. You and your Cochimí son.

The priest gestured idly with a hand as if persuading his congregants of some truth that was not to be relied upon.

—He was not truly my son.

—He was the son of your heart. What other kind of son is there?

His hand went to the back of his neck. He wiped his eyes, and without another word he got up and went to Frijolito. He took hold of the jáquima and pulled the animal forward. He walked behind, pushing the wooden beam and his share of the giant stone wheel.

She left him and went to the house and took the trunk from beneath the bed. She crouched there, listening, but the boy was silent and she took this as approval of the right course. She lifted out the cuera, and the boots, and for a moment she held the funerary coins in her hand. She took the kerchief and came outside. The priest continued in his course with Frijolito circling ahead of him.

—Padre Espín.

He stopped. She imagined it might have been years since anyone used the title. Without ceremony, she unwrapped the handkerchief and held it out. He leaned in for a moment to see what she had brought, examining the pearl without knowing what he beheld, leaning in again. Then his face creased with recognition.

—He wishes you to take it, she said.

The priest nodded without understanding.

—The boy, she said. The boy wishes it. He has been speaking to me.

—That is not possible.

—Yet it is so.

The priest studied his hands and said, He used to come to me with pearls about his throat. I thought it was a dream. Or perhaps a vision of my own self, accusing myself.

She held out the handkerchief but he would not take it.

—You know this is the very same one, she said.

—Yes. I know it.

—I do not believe you, for on that day you had eyes only for your dead son. But believe me when I tell you this is the pearl that purchased his very life.

The priest went to sit under the tamarisks. He put a hand over his face. She sat beside him.

—I will tell you what must be done, she said. What the boy desires. And you must do it.

—I can do nothing, he said.

—Return this to Mulegé.

She took his hand and placed the handkerchief in his palm.

—He desires the pearl?

—Take it to Mulegé. That is all I know.

He looked to the hills. For a long time he did not speak. She could scarcely hear him.

—Does he. Does he pardon me.

She got up. She took Frijolito by the collar and pulled him forward. The priest walked alongside and they went circling. He did not utter a word until they had forked the slurry into bags to ferment and returned to the house. He stood at the window until the sun fell behind a line of clouds, and finally he said, Manolo is coming.

They sat in the kitchen, and for the first time Manolo asked for a cup of mezcal and she gave it to him. He ate and drank, and Inés ate after him. The priest would not take supper, but he also took a cup of mezcal and she said nothing about it. They all sat quietly, she and Manolo at the table and the priest in a chair beside the cookstove, watching the dying flame.

Inés did not ask Manolo what had occurred on the road, but after his meal she brought him a cake of brown sugar and waited. He sat looking at the priest, but the priest did not get up. Finally Manolo said he had met two of his kinsmen on the road to Arroyo de León and they turned him back.

—Because the men from the frontera were waiting for you, Inés said.

—Yes. Putting questions to my sister and others.

—Tomorrow I leave this territory, the priest said. You are welcome to accompany me.

—You suggest taking him to the frontera, Inés said. Where men are waiting to seize him.

—I believe he is safe in my company, the priest said.

—Yes, because you have cared so well for others, Inés said.

The priest did not look up.

—Never mind, Inés said to Manolo. He is not going to the border, he has somewhere else to go.

Manolo took a bite of the brown sugar.

—Where are you going? he asked the priest.

—The boy gave him the pearl to take to Mulegé, Inés said.

—The boy gave it to him?

—The boy told me to give it to him. And now it is out of my hands.

—Good, Manolo said.

—The boy himself has not asked me, the priest said.

—She is asking you, Manolo said.

—You disregard your own child, Inés said. After everything, you disregard him.

—And you a priest besides, Manolo said.

—I am not a priest.

He fished into his pocket and took out the handkerchief. He spread it on the table, and the pearl swirled in a circle and came to rest in a seam. He took a cup and filled it from the flask and went from the kitchen. Inés watched him go. She collected the plates and cups and put them into the bucket of wash water. The pearl lay still. Frijolito was calling from his pen and she went out.

The night was quiet and she scratched the donkey's ears, looking toward the house. The light went out in the room of the priest and she shook her head. She heard the door open and saw the figure of Manolo going out to the ramada, walking slowly in his contemplative way. She called goodnight to him and went to her own room. She lay down fully clothed, got up and lit a candle, and then extinguished it.

The three-quarter moon made a bright ribbon on the floor, and a moth came and went. The boy began speaking. He kept whispering and she objected but he would not relent. She pulled the trunk from beneath the bed. She took out the leather coat and the saber. The handle of the pistol was worn smooth, as though for her father's hand alone. She folded the breeches and set aside the leather boots, and finally she took out the coins that had covered his eyes in death.

She went to the window. In the moonlight, the mesquite resembled fishbones standing on end. The coins were cool in her hand, chilled as though they still lay upon his frigid body. He had left her long ago. Had left long before he died. The boy began to speak again and she held up a hand.

—If you have anything else to say, she said, tell it to the priest.

In the dark watches of the night, she went out to Manolo. He was awake and tending the stills under the light of a single candleflame, observing the steady drip into the pots. He inserted a finger and put the finger to his tongue. When he saw Inés, he got up.

—I am going to Mulegé, she said.

—For what? The boy wants the priest. Not you. Not even the pearl.

—But the priest will not go.

—Sister, what has this to do with us?

—I also have something to cast into the sea.

She opened her palm and showed him the sepulchral coins, dark and desiccated from handling, worn beyond recognition or value. She told Manolo of their use and he looked away. He asked why the coins were not buried along with the man.

—I kept them, she said.

He asked if this denied the man passage to the world of the dead, and she said she did not know. But she wished to be rid of them. She put the coins into her pocket.

—Will you go with me, she said.

For a long time he stood without answering. Then he said, You will not return to Red Rock.

—No.

—The boy wants the priest, Manolo said again.

—But not for vengeance.

—What then?

—For the same reason he calls to me.

Manolo shook his head. He went out toward the ramada and she followed. In the darkness she heard him arrange his pallet and lie down.

—Please go with me, she said.

She stood listening. No reply came but a single sigh, and she went back to the house.

In the morning before first light, she placed the pearl and the coins in a tiny purse of leather and hid them beneath the folds of her skirt. She made ready for Mulegé, saddling her mule and loading Frijolito with provisions which the priest helped her to secure.

—If you will not do what the boy asks, she said, will you at least stay here. Manolo will tell you what to do.

Manolo turned to the priest. I will indeed tell you what to do, he said. Take the pearl and go to Mulegé yourself. Go on your knees as your kind are inclined to do. Or go walking. But go.

—I will stay, the priest said.

When the sun rose above the hill, Inés mounted up and started from the yard with Frijolito following. Manolo called to her. She stopped and turned. He went to the corral and saddled the other mule and got up. They set out and the priest waved, though no one waved in return. When the two had gone into the arroyo and were some distance away, the priest blessed them and returned to the house.

Some days later, he went into the hills. He pulled the cart himself and chopped a heart of agave in rough fashion but sufficient to get it free. He brought it down to the house, and with some effort he buried it, and after three days he exhumed the fragments and forked them into the mill. He took up the wooden shaft and pushed. The wheel would not move. He rocked it back and forth until it gave, and began circling. He kept circling long after the fragments had gone to mash.

In the morning, men from the frontera came to the house at Red

Rock but found the fires cold. Mash hung fermenting in sacks, and the stills had overrun their catchments. The men helped themselves to what bottles they found, and they waited. When Inés did not return, they examined the tracks around the house and rode to the coast and kept going south until they spied the old traveler walking along the trail.

They drew alongside and stopped him. He stood shakily in the sun, mopping his brow with an aged handkerchief of lace, and they kept badgering him, asking if he had stolen the cloth from the doña. He insisted that she had given it to him. He said he was going south with the intent to look for her, if they would only yield the road.

Sombrerito

SANTA ROSALÍA DE MULEGÉ

— 1852 —

When Inés arrived at Mulegé, she did not go to the old mission or down to the sea. She went to the adobe where she had lived as a girl. The house stood on a hill overlooking the river with its palms crowding the banks below, and she could see the single belltower of the church, rising from the brush on the opposite side.

She stood at a distance from the little adobe, a one-room block of earthen brick beneath a roof of aging gray thatch. At first she thought the house was vacant, but a girl emerged and lingered in the doorway. A voice called the child to come inside. The girl didn't go, but looked down toward the river, giving Inés the unsettling sensation that she was watching herself, and she half-expected the next voice to be that of her father. But when she looked again, she saw the girl had a tidy braid wound around her head with a ribbon, so the girl could not be an apparition of herself. There had never been a woman to care for her as a child, not even a cook or a nursemaid, for her father was a hard man and no woman would live with him.

The girl saw Inés and smiled shyly as though caught, and the voice called again and the girl turned and went inside. The mission bell began to ring, calling the midday hour, and Inés felt an unexpected chill and wished she had not come. She walked the road down the hill again.

The town and even the river seemed smaller than she recalled, though there were more houses, with orchards of olive and date and fig, and even a tienda by the parque. Someone had put a bench of mesquite beneath some date palms, and she sat down and wished

Manolo had stayed with her. When the two of them had neared the village, he was reluctant to enter, for he did not know the attitude of those who lived there. She asked if he would tarry a single night to rest, and said she would pay for lodging and something to eat. He said he had witnessed her safe arrival and would go on.

—Where will you go, she asked.

—Sister, I am far from home, he said.

—It is dangerous for you there.

—Nevertheless I am going.

He did not speak of the pearl she carried in its leather packet, or the funerary coins that had covered the eyes of her father before he was buried. He did not ask what she would do. He did not inquire of the boy, or whether he still spoke to her, or what the boy wished or wanted. He only patted her arm and looked as though he did not want to go. She said it was all right. He smiled a little and said he had seen a farrier at the edge of town, and he would board the mules if she wished. She said he must take the donkey and his mule and not think anything of it, but she would be obliged if he would board her own. She gave him money and asked if it would be enough for the journey, and he said it was, and she gave him some more.

When he was gone, she walked along the river toward the sea. There were houses now where none had been before, set back from the bank, jacales and adobes with roofs of tightly woven palm. The path had grown wide through use. Where the river narrowed, she removed her shoes and lifted her skirt and waded across. Gulls flocked on the sandbars and a solitary crane minced away, watching the current. She knelt and put her hand into the water, and when the ripples stilled, she was surprised to see a grown woman there. She washed her face and went on.

At the sea, fishermen stood on the shore with full buckets. She could see the gaping heads of snappers and triggerfish, and dogs were slinking about. One of the fishermen said good day and she returned the greeting. She walked along, listening, but the boy did not speak.

She kept going until she came to the place near the tombolo and the tiny island of rock where so long ago the men had gathered about the boy's canoe while he lay face down on the sand. She recalled how the priest had come running, how she had never seen him run before. Until that day he had not seemed to her like other men; he wore a robe and handled sacred things, lifting them in front of the people and reciting his litanies. But the day the boy died, she saw the priest run, and weep, and she turned away because she was ashamed to see him like an ordinary person.

Then he surprised her by arriving at her ranch and staying with her. He said he was no longer a priest, and she thought he had come to love her. But he never confessed it, and said he would not go to Mulegé with the pearl as the boy wanted him to. Now she held the very pearl in her hand, along with the funerary coins of her father.

She walked back to the fisherman who had greeted her and asked if he had a canoe. He pointed to a boat resting on a hillock in the sea grass. She asked if he would ferry her out. She said she would pay him.

—Not far, she said. Just a ways from the shore.

He asked if she wanted to fish and she said no. She said again that she would pay him, and he went to retrieve the boat. She knelt in the prow and he waded into the water, dragging the boat free from the sand, and he climbed in and began to row.

She could see Punta Concepción to the south, and to the north lay the Bay of Santa Inés for which her father had named her. She held tight to the coins, which were hot from the heat of her hand and from her nervousness. In the other hand, she held the pearl. When the boat had gone some distance from shore, she asked the man to stop rowing.

The canoe rocked on the waves. Somewhere behind the brushy hills lay the small mission of stone above the river, and the house of her girlhood on the opposite hill, and the high ragged mountains of nothingness beyond. Her throat tightened and she held the coins out, over the waves. She hesitated for a moment. The man made no comment but held the paddle dripping across his lap, watching without expression. She wondered if he had ferried others, what other burdens he had seen cast into the sea.

She offered no word of farewell. Such a time had come and gone. She dropped the coins into the swell, watching them turn and wink in the sunrays until they tumbled from sight. She sat back, and a sudden lightness came upon her. She put a hand on the gunwale to steady herself and she almost laughed. The man asked if she were all right and she said she was.

They had drifted farther out, and the town was laid before her. She saw it now for the oasis it was: the thick stand of palms along the freshwater river, the clusters of homes, the groves of lime and pomegranate, and the plots of corn and wheat and beans. Cerro Colorado, bright orange in the sun, and the hill of Sombrerito—though as a child it was lost upon her that the mound resembled a hat, resting in the sea.

She held the pearl. For a moment she sat listening. She leaned against the side of the canoe with her closed hand extended, and suddenly the boy spoke. She looked up. The man sat holding the oar, quiet and looking out over the waves. She could not understand the boy's words and she held her hand experimentally over the water and this time he spoke in a torrent. The hair on her arms was standing, though she was not cold. She withdrew the hand and now she was angered.

—If it is the priest you wait for, she said, you will wait a very long time.

The boatman asked her pardon, for he did not hear what she said. She extended her fist again and a chill ran across her neck and she was afraid to look into the water, afraid the boy might raise a hand from the sea and clasp her arm. She shivered and thought she would ask the man to throw the pearl for her, but a stream of words swirled about her and she said again: The priest will not come, not for your sake or mine.

The lightness was gone and she held the pearl in her lap. The man asked if he might row back to shore. He spoke carefully, as though he feared she might step from the boat.

—Yes, she said. Let us go back.

He rowed slowly, and when he had pulled the canoe ashore and helped her down, she gave him some coins. She asked if anyone could go into the church, if a priest was in residence. He said there was no priest anymore, but she might go if she wished. He said he thought she should go.

She thanked him and started away. She carried the pearl in her pocket, and the boy was silent and she told him she would not throw the pearl into the sea but would dispose of it in her own way. That she did not wish to keep it, nor did she want the boy following her.

She kept to the river until she came to the rising road that led to the mission. At the top of the hill, she stopped. The church was not as she recalled. An unadorned square front of fitted brown stones, and the eastern wall painted white with cal. The church appeared to her now as a garrison, with a single window above the door where a sentry might keep watch. She remembered a half wall that once guarded a pomegranate tree from which no one was allowed to eat. But as a child she had eaten. The boy had told, and the priest scolded her, but her father did not care to say anything of the matter.

Now the wall was gone and the trees had been uprooted or burned for wood. The yard had succumbed to rock and dirt and dust, and some of the roof stones had fallen and broken on the ground. The western wing was weathered, the windows shuttered. Though the great wooden doors of the entrance stood open, she could not see inside for the darkness. She went forward.

The church was cool inside, too small to inspire awe. When her eyes adjusted to the dim light, she saw that everything had been taken—the tabernacle of Solomonic columns that once guarded the host, the oil paintings of saints, and the saints themselves. Santa Rosalía, for whom the mission was named. Even La Santa Virgen, who the priest had once adorned with pearls, and the bowl that rested at her feet. Only the altar of stone remained, and someone had placed a candle there.

Inés stood in the half-light, holding the pearl in her hand. She tried to imagine Fr. Espín in this vault of a room, speaking to the Cochimí and performing his works. She wished to be angry with him but could not recall what he looked like as a young man. She could only see the man she came to know at Red Rock, the ordinary man who reclined beneath the tamarisks and placed a bit of agave in her hand. She could not envision that man at the altar, the man who persuaded the boy to the sea and counted pearls while the boy was in the very act of drowning.

The room was growing darker in the waning day, and a heaviness settled over her again. She felt as though the boy stood behind her, and she was afraid to turn around. It was not only the boy; the room was filled with the Cochimí, women and men and little ones, crying softly to whoever might hear. She listened to their laments, silently bearing witness, and when the cries subsided, she went out. The boy whispered a final word, and she was still holding the pearl. She heard the boy sigh, the solitary utterance of a satisfied child before sleep, and then he was gone.

She put the pearl in her pocket. She followed the road to the house of the farrier and she spied her mule in the yard. It trotted to the fence. The farrier's wife bid Inés a good evening and said she was welcome to stay, that she would charge only for the mule. Inés thanked her and said that tomorrow she would look for an adobe in the village to purchase, for she was waiting for someone to come. The woman smiled and said that from the mouth of the river—atop the hill shaped like a man's hat—one could see the road, and from that place, many women had watched and waited. If one wished, the woman said, one could be the first to see a new person arriving.

La Santera

NUESTRA SEÑORA DE GUADALUPE DE HUASINAPÍ

—1852—

The ruined mission of Guadalupe de Huasinapí sits below the black heights of the Sierra San Pedro, an odd presence of right angles among rugged dark hills. The church's rude crown is a mere covering of reeds; the stones have tumbled and the adobe walls are melting. Doves pick at strands of straw that poke whisker-like from the crumbling mud and they make their nests in the rushroof above. To one side of the church sits the small sacristy, cool and quiet and vacant of sacred things.

There are stone corrals that hold no cattle, and huertas where the trees for want of pruning have cast their fruit to the ground: orange, plum, fig. But the fences of prickly pear remain, and pilas to hold water, and aqueducts that once baptized the soil. A hot empty wind blows through the palms in the arroyo, and the emboldened quail have multiplied and run through the brush as quickly as those who pass this desolate place.

Some leagues distant from Guadalupe, in a village near the sea, lived a saint-maker named Juana Antonia. She had inherited one resolute line of an eyebrow from her mother, a broken and sideways nose from her first husband, a lonely ache in her heart from the second, and a son who could not speak from the third. From her grandfather, she learned the secret of making santos.

La Santera Juana Antonia was well known in the village. The neighbors were accustomed to seeing her with Pablo her son, who had grown into a young man but followed Juana Antonia like a boy or a pup. When the neighbors saw them go into the hills, they felt a small rush of holy pleasure, for saints were about to be made. Juana Antonia knew a secret stand of güéribo trees, and she harvested wood to carve the santos with her grandfather's good adz.

When a saint, beginning as a güéribo, had been adzed into human form, coated with yeso and painted, Juana Antonia finished it with resin of creosote to seal the colors. A saint finished with creosote resin smells like the brushy hills from which it came, so it might always remember its humble beginnings. Juana Antonia and Pablo smelled strongly of the resin themselves, for the sala of her house was also her workshop.

The people of the town bought the santos. They placed the saints upon their home altars, and some of the statues even traveled across the gulf to important churches on the mainland. But there were some santos Juana Antonia would not sell. These were her own private saints, crowded upon a table in the corner of the sala, and she dressed them with clothes of silk and linen. She knelt before them three times a day, and she had but one prayer. Santa Rita, she would say, or Santa Clara or San Borromeo or San Gregorio. San Whoever, let my son speak.

Juana Antonia had prayed this from the time Pablo was a little child, from the very day when Nacha the neighbor said, There is something wrong with your son. Why doesn't he talk?

Pablo could make noise. He could cry, and he could groan, and he could grunt. He could chirp when he was happy. Juana Antonia tried not to worry, but as the years passed and Pablo grew to the height of a man and did not speak, she began to lose hope.

—He is a good boy, a gentle boy, she said to Nacha. What more could a mother ask for?

—A lot more, Nacha said.

Juana Antonia increased her prayers to five times a day and began to fast twice a week. She sewed new clothes for all the saints and hung silver medals upon them. She brought her son to the altar, and he held his mother's hand and chirped with contentment. Little birds, hearing him, flitted to the window and ticked their heads to one side to listen.

—This is a good sign, she told Pablo. Who knows but that these birds are messengers, who hear our prayers and carry them to heaven?

But Pablo still could form no words. The town watched the increased devotion of Juana Antonia, and when Pablo did not improve, the people stopped buying her santos. A saint-maker with a mute son, they whispered. If the one who creates the saints has fallen under such a terrible curse, what hope is there for any of our own prayers to be answered?

Juana Antonia began to punish the santos. She stripped them of their clothes and buried them in the ground to their necks. She would not relent when ants marched across their heads, or even when dogs passed by and watered them. She left the saints outside in a storm, letting the raging waters take them. When the sky cleared, she went to find them. Santa Rita she found cast into some mesquite. San Miguel she found half-buried in sand. San Antonio de Padua she did not find at all.

Each night she lay next to Pablo and spoke to him softly, coaxing him. When Pablo did not utter a word, she turned the saints upside down in the earth.

The people of the town wondered about this holy experiment, for they too had santos that could be punished if their long-dead hopes could turn into miracles. They watched Pablo. They goaded him and tried to make him speak. He ducked, he dodged, he laughed at the attention and did not see their anger rising.

Juana Antonia was working in the back courtyard when she heard the cry. She ran through the house and into the street. Pablo was folded upon the ground, bleating and covering his face with his arms. Ashamed, the townspeople dropped their stones behind their backs. Juana Antonia helped Pablo to his feet. He looked at her with confused and pained eyes, and the bridge of his nose was torn. She led him back to the house.

—Enough, she said. I will make no more santos. The saints you see here? On the shelves, on the table, on the floor, under the bed. These saints deserve me no more.

One by one the neighbors began to visit again, and the town pulled back from its madness and resumed praying in the customary way. But Juana Antonia the former santera gave all the saints away, even her private collection and all their clothes.

For a while she felt satisfied, but soon she became troubled. She thought of her grandfather, the famous santero, who had trusted her with secrets that would be practiced no more. Every night her hands were restless for their tools. Then she imagined the saints were trying to trick her.

—Ho, I see what you are doing, she said. And it will not work.

She kept her hands occupied. She swept the floor, pounded soil from the clothes, patted tortillas and tied up strings of garlic. She brushed her hair and Pablo's hair too, and her hands were restless still. Finally she sat unhappily in front of the house, watching the children of the village playing in the street. They had twigs for men and pebbles for animals, and Pablo sat with them. When the children scolded him, he lumbered away and Juana Antonia watched him look for his own small stones. An idea came to her.

She went inside and took the carving tools and a good piece of güéribo that she had not yet burned for kindling. Her hands began to work.

—I will make toys instead, she said.

From that moment, Juana Antonia La Santera became Juana Antonia La Jugetera, the toy-maker. Her hands worked deftly and confidently. Pablo, sensing importance in the air, came and watched. Sometimes he dared to gently blow the wood curlings away when too many had gathered.

The first thing Juana Antonia created was a horse. She put pins in each joint so the legs could move freely, and she bored a place on the hindquarters to insert a tail of real horsehair. She made a hole in the jaw for the bit and left a generous impression upon the back for a rider. Then she set about fashioning a man.

The man's legs must be bow-legged to seat correctly, and when the rough little form stood on the table she chuckled, remembering her third husband who spent all his days on muleback. Pablo laughed too. Then she held the figure at arm's length and drummed her fingers on her brow.

—What do you think, Pablo?

The adz slid along the surface of the wood. She carved a helmet and breastplate and pushed a hole through the hand for a sword. Halfway along she stopped.

—Dios mío, what have I done.

She set the figure down and shook her finger at it.

—Santiago the Conqueror, she said. You sly thing, you thought I would not recognize you. What do you mean by showing up here? I said I would make no more saints and I meant it.

She took the horse apart, and Pablo wrung his hands.

—Do not worry, she said. I have something else in mind.

She shortened the legs of the horse. She flattened the back and blunted the nose. She removed the ears and fashioned new ones, long ears but thick so they could not be easily broken off. Pablo, seeing a donkey appear before him, clapped his hands.

Then she turned to the man. She shaved the armor flush and began again. Now she carved the simple garments of a peasant—ragged pants, a long shirt, a serape for covering. Into the fist she inserted a staff. The body was smaller for her mistake, and the head a little greater, but the disproportion gave the figure a whimsical quality. She snapped the man into his seat upon the burro and walked it across the table toward Pablo.

He hummed with pleasure and walked the figures back and forth and picked them up and looked into the man's face.

—Hand them here, Juana Antonia said. I will coat them and we will sleep while they dry. Tomorrow I will paint them for you.

Pablo hugged the figures to his chest and would not meet Juana Antonia's eye, for he had never disobeyed her and did not know how to bear it. He turned toward the hearth and rocked the wooden man.

Juana Antonia knelt down.

—Keep it then, she said, if that is how you want it. They are yours, my love.

Pablo lay down on his pallet. Juana Antonia took the broom and swept the wood shavings into the hearth. Pablo played with the figures until the hour grew late, and she snuffed the candle and went to her own bed. In the darkness she could hear the low unknowable utterances and the clop of wooden hooves upon the floor and she smiled and turned to sleep.

In the morning, Nacha appeared at the door. She looked at Juana Antonia and her tools.

—What is this? she asked. I heard you were finished as a santera.

—Yes, Juana Antonia said. I am making toys.

Nacha came inside. On the table sat a house with a roof that could be removed, and one chair to put inside. Nacha picked up the little chair. Then she noticed Pablo and the figures he held. She whisked the rider and donkey from his hands and turned them over.

—Those are not for sale, Juana Antonia said. They belong to my son.

Pablo moaned and reached for the toys, and Nacha turned aside.

—But could you make others? she said. A horse instead of a donkey. My son, he is crazy for horses already, and barely walking.

Pablo circled around and raked his hands through his hair.

—Give them back to Pablo, Juana Antonia said. Then we will talk about something for your son.

—Just a moment, Nacha said.

She used her elbow to keep Pablo away. He lunged for the toys. Juana Antonia tried to stop him, but he had become a man with all of a man's strength and she had not known he could use it. Nacha fell back and the bench clattered and she tumbled over it. Her fingers curled under Pablo's foot, and Juana Antonia heard the crack. Pablo swept up the fallen toys and scrambled to the corner.

Nacha cradled the twisted fingers.

—You demon! she cried.

—He is sorry, he is very sorry, Juana Antonia pleaded.

Nacha struggled to stand. She dipped in a near faint and Juana Antonia tried to steady her but the woman pulled from her grasp.

—Let go of me, madre del diablo!

She spat at Pablo and spat at him again while he cowered. She went out.

Juana Antonia paced and thought of the twisted fingers and the anger of a town who tried to stone her son.

—All this because you cannot speak!

Pablo covered his eyes and knelt with his head to the ground.

—Do you understand? Now you are a man who has attacked a woman and I am afraid for us both. I am afraid, Pablo!

She closed the shutters and pulled the leather doorlatch to the inside. She did not allow Pablo to go out, and they lit no candles when the sun went down. Each time a man or animal passed in the street, she held out her hand to quiet her son. Anxious, he watched her face. When the village fell quiet, she lay down with him, and when he was sleeping, she got up and gathered some clothes, dried goat meat and tortillas, a container of water, and her grandfather's good adz. Then she lay down and listened.

In the late watches of the night, she awakened him.

—Pablo, she whispered. Walk with me and bring your blankets and your toys and do not make a sound.

She took his hand and they went out by the light of the moon. When they had passed the last house and were well beyond any hearing, she turned to Pablo and said, There is a man I have heard of. I do not know if he still lives. But if he is there, I will make him help you, for he was once a priest and a priest cannot turn us away.

They traveled the road toward Guadalupe, crossing arroyo upon arroyo and winding through the dark canyon where the cottonwoods grew, passing wild strangler figs with their ghostly white roots stretching over the rocks. On the fourth day she found the overgrown trail to the mission itself. As they came into the clearing, the birds disappeared into the trees and she warned Pablo to be still. They stood before the old church with its crumbling walls and the bleached carcasses of the reeds that covered them. A turkey vulture sat on the roof, spreading its wings to dry. The windows were shuttered and she wondered what eyes might gaze from the dark seams. All around was silent and she said to Pablo, The very trees in this place are unaccustomed to callers.

The door was ajar. They came to it quietly and it creaked upon leather hinges. She looked inside. The nave was quiet. Tiny motes of thatch dust rose and fell in strands of sunlight. Leaves lay on the floor, palm upward, dry and withered supplicant hands. Doves flapped and chirred, and bats had found their high dark corners and hung upside down as San Pedro crucified. Rude niches in the stead of transepts stood empty save ribbons of guano. The reredos was gone, and the church was without imagery except for one underrated wooden saint with missing feet. Someone had built a stand, but the statue had tipped over and lay on the altar as a man fallen from his crutches.

—Come, there is no one, she said to Pablo. But they entered carefully and Pablo clung to her hand.

The floor was dotted with dung. They paused in the crossing, and Juana Antonia looked back to the open door and wondered what goat or cow came at night to stable. The wind sighed through the windows, and she asked, Are you afraid, Pablo? because she herself was a little afraid.

She walked to the crude altar of wood, gilded only by the dotted light from above. Her hand, remembering, crossed her breast. She dipped down on one knee and Pablo did the same. A small rasping sound came from behind the altar and she jumped and wondered what had come in through the door and hidden itself. She moved forward and dared to peer behind.

A man scarcely garmented lay against the wall. His eyes were half-open and unseeing. His feet were unshod, the nails yellowed and curled. The once-tonsured hair—the beloved crown of thorns—had grown into an untended thicket, and though his hands were rough from labor, she imagined they had not always been so.

—The man who was once a priest, she whispered. Pablo, bring me the water.

Pablo hurried for it and she lifted the olla to the man's lips. He showed no sign of understanding, but the Adam's apple remembered and moved up and down as he swallowed.

—Do not be afraid, she said.

His cough was ragged, his breathing labored. She wet the corner of Pablo's blanket and bathed the priest's face, his neck, his hands. She refilled the olla at the stone reservoir and returned to kneel beside him. She removed the outer shirt, and within the pocket she found an old handkerchief of lace.

—There must have been a woman once, she said, because you have kept this near your heart.

She slit his undergarment. She told Pablo to turn away, and she washed the priest where he had soiled himself. When he was clean, she removed the stained clothing and covered him with the blanket and made a cushion of her shawl for his head.

Pablo, sweep the animal refuse from the church. And close the door. No bestias in here tonight.

For three days and nights she cared for him, and Pablo went out and threw stones until he killed two quail. She boiled them into broth, which she fed to the priest a few drops at a time. On the fourth day she told Pablo, Sit with him while I clean this dirty place.

She washed the guano from the walls and swept the dry reeds which had broken under the feet of restless doves. She scrubbed their droppings from the altar and examined the broken saint and felt a little pleasure in seeing that the workmanship was poor. She carried it outside and lay it on the ground.

She watched the man carefully, hoping he would wake, but his breath was shallow. For hours she blew gently into his face. Each time Pablo went out, she feared the priest might die in his absence.

—Do not be gone long, she told Pablo. The priest may wake at any time and we must seek his blessing.

The next evening, she bade Pablo to sit with the man and she dared pass through the low doorway to the sacristy. It was cool and dim. She felt that the air was old, very old, and had not been stirred or even breathed for a long time. For its bareness, the room might have been granary, stable, or tomb. But a trace of the sacrosanct hung in the darkness, and she felt chilled in the presence of it. She crept to the rough table and found a broken chalice of wood, worn from handling and hewn by neophyte hands. Alongside, a cracked paten neither gold nor silver, awaiting holy moment. She picked up each one and wiped it carefully. When she finished, she washed the cupboard that once held flowered and hallowed finery, and the shelves still held the scent of garments.

When she came from the sacristy, Pablo was dripping water onto the priest's brow. The man's head lay in a pool of water.

—Be careful, she said. Do you want to drown him?

She put a hand on the man's chest and he coughed and shivered once and his feet twitched and then he lay still. Pablo held the little carved figures and looked anxiously at the priest, and Juana Antonia put her fingers to the man's nostrils.

—He lives, she said. But I do not know for how long.

Doves marched overhead in the thatch and she was quiet until they settled and fluffed themselves. They trilled to one another as she sat and thought.

—Do I dare, she asked them. Do I dare.

The doves fell silent and she listened to the man's labored breath.

—Pablo, come here, she said. Lean down.

She took the priest's rough hand, lifting it gently that she might not disturb him. She placed the hand upon Pablo's head and held it there.

—O mi Dios, she whispered. Hear this man's prayer that he cannot pray.

When she woke in the morning and turned toward the priest, he was so quiet and unmoving that she prepared herself to see that he had died. She sat up and put her hand to his cheek. Then the priest surprised her by opening his eyes. She leaned close and watched as his mind sought to anchor itself. His eyes rested on her face, and she wondered whether he saw a mother or sister, catechumen or beloved.

—Father, she said.

At the sound of the word, the man wept. The sunken cavity between the thin rows of ribs convulsed with pain or grief and she did not look away.

—Do not cry, she said. Now you will live.

Sickness had robbed the gaunt body of tears. Nothing spilled from the priest but sorrow, and Juana Antonia and Pablo were its witnesses. At last he quieted and looked about him. His hands moved under the blanket and felt his nakedness and he covered his face.

—We had to, Father, she said.

The priest tried to raise himself with shaking arms.

—Careful, she said. She helped him sit against the wall and pulled the blanket around him, and he drew his thin legs under it.

Then his eyes rested on Pablo. The priest tried to speak, and the voice was rough from disuse and he tried again.

—Who is this?

—My son, she said.

He stretched out a trembling hand. Juana Antonia, seeing it, scarcely dared to breathe. She steadied the hand toward Pablo, but the hand was not for her son. His eyes were fixed upon the figures, the man atop the burro.

—Who is this? he said again.

—It is only a toy, something I made. It is no one, just a man.

—I know this man.

Her brow furrowed. You were so ill, she said. Father? We thought you would die.

But the priest remained transfixed.

—It is only a toy, she said again. Pablo, show him.

Pablo held out the figures. The priest touched the man with tentative fingers, feeling the rough unfinished wood and the stripes of the adz, and he whispered, Deus meus.

Pablo let go of the figures and the priest pulled them to his breast. He pressed the man to his lips and his voice became high and small like a child and he cried, He has come to me.

All at once Juana Antonia saw what she had not seen before. She shook her head.

—El Santo Cristo, she whispered. You sly thing.

—He has come to me, the priest wept. Oh my Lord, he has come.

The priest did not see or hear them go. They left the olla of water and a little of the food and they went out quietly. Doves flapped upward as Juana Antonia pulled the door behind her.

They traveled slowly southward toward Loreto, begging the hospitality of the ranches along the way. One night, before the firelight, one of the ranch wives sat close to her, and in a moment of confidence asked: So did the priest give you his blessing?

—No, he was too ill. He could not give it.

—Ay, what a shame, you traveled so far to see him.

—Yes

Juana Antonia looked at Pablo lying before the hearth. He held three small goats of wood that she had made. He was oddly quiet; he had uttered no sound on their return or since. He looked up and smiled, and there was a knowing in the eyes. She dropped her tools and leaned close, for he looked so plainly as though he was about to speak. But Pablo held the goats to his chest and inhaled the smell of them, and turned once again toward the fire.

Dolores

La Mula Milagrosa

ARROYO PABELLÓN

— 1851 —

He was a man to whom nothing had ever been given. Alone upon the Arroyo Pabellón, he fashioned a droughted ranch: an adobe house and fences of cacti and round corrales of stone, built without the benefit of rain. By many drops of sweat he created it, from the very water within him. He raised a small plot of failing corn, and when all was finished he took a wife and brought her there, and for his diligence with the corn she called him Elote.

One night he rose from his pallet at the midnight hour and left Ana sleeping among the children too ill or feeble-minded to sleep alone. He stepped across the stronger ones, tossed over the ground as if some great battle had occurred there. None of the children his own.

He went out to check the corn. A cloud—just a pulling of corn-silk—covered the moon. He watched the cloud as a curiosity. Once a year a man might see a cloud. In wonderful years it hovered low with a misty grayness that fell all the way to the ground, but most often it was someone else's cloud and someone else's rain. In another year, or two years, his rain might come. But as he watched the moon, he smelled only dust and dry heat, and he hated the cloud which buoyed a man's hopes and passed indifferently through the sky.

The ground was a dry lattice, the arroyo dusty and impotent. He could smell a crackling death in the stunted rows, and everything knew of the coming necrosis except the poor green hopeful tips. The children knew and the workhand knew. The gray molly mule and the two john mules and the jack donkey knew. Even the goats now sold had known.

He was alone. He began speaking to Ana.

—I have done all I know, he said. Every last thing I know to do.

A girl stood in the moonlight watching him. She was Dolores-born-without-ears. She could hear nothing, but he was ashamed that she had seen his lips moving as he stood by himself.

—Go on, he said. He waved her off, but she kept watching.

Before he could dismiss her again, he heard a bellowing from the corral. Hooves thundering at the walls and a panicked whickering. He ran with the girl following and called for the workhand who lay somewhere in a haze of mezcal. He called again. He imagined the puma and the terrible bloody harvest, and at the gate he seized the machete. But he saw no león or coyote, no dog gone mad.

What stood there was a newborn foal. The impossible offspring of his molly mule, barren as every mule known to mankind until this moment. The foal was wet and kicking free from the membranes that tethered it to the mother. Straggling up beneath her legs, peering out and tottering.

The john mules kicked at the colt, and the molly hawed and showed her teeth. Elote scattered the johns and they flinched away, pawing the ground and shaking their heads. The molly crowded the wall. The foal ducked beneath her belly, and Elote roped the molly and pulled her into the yard, the son-of-a-donkey stumbling behind. Afterbirth spilling from the mother. Dogs slinking forward, hair bristling and challenging one another.

Elote stood faint in the moonlight, Dolores-born-without-ears beside him. Ana hurried out with an infant in arms. A bent-over boy followed. Little ones came stumbling out upon misshapen feet, whispering in languages known only to themselves. The workhand appeared, weaving from drink, blinking at the foal and trying to rub his eyes free of apparitions. He kissed his fingers.

Elote moved closer to Ana. There was a saying of such events, but he could not call it forth. A foretelling about the end of the world. The foal began to nurse as any ordinary foal, and when satiated it leaned into its mother. Some accidental equine mosaic, neither mule nor horse nor donkey, gangly and gray with a faint cross emerging over the withers. Elote stood dumbstruck and Ana blessed herself.

Dolores-born-without-ears was the first child discarded at the ranch. Elote did not see the father or mother or god-relative, but when he returned from the corn, Ana was holding an odd-looking child on her hip. He could not determine at first why it disturbed him, until he saw there were holes where the ears should be.

—Don't call her born-without-ears, Ana had said. So he simply called her Dolores, but in his mind he could not help adding born-without-ears, for that was what she was.

The ranch lay near the Camino Real, and soon other children were brought. A girl with clouded eyes. Two babies with turned-in feet. An infant neither boy nor girl but both, and it was a wonder no one had cast the bundle into a dry well.

For such children the ranch of Elote became known. The good Ana and Elote, people said, but Elote knew that only Ana was good. And what did it matter if one were good, for even a good person received no reward. Only once upon departing had a man pushed a blackened peso into Elote's hand. Burning with anger, Elote pressed it back. Ana looked at him and sighed, put a hand to her brow. She turned and went to the house. Later, Elote abandoned his tasks and looked through the window to see that Ana had not left, but she was there with the children around her. Dolores-born-without-ears saw him in the window, and he turned back to the corrales.

Elote pulled the molly and the newborn foal into the vacant goat pen. Ana persuaded the workhand back to his pallet and took the children to the house, Elote following. Dolores-born-without-ears watched their faces. The bent-over boy lay down on the floor. Elote looked at Ana. Neither was hungry, but they sat at the table.

—What do you think it is, Elote said.

—A mule. What else would it be? Or a burro. Mostly burro, I believe. You saw it for yourself. La cruz.

—Do you believe it will stay.

—Why shouldn't it?

—Perhaps it will go as quickly as it came.

In saying this, Elote frightened himself. He left Ana and went out to look. The molly huffed and lowered her head; the johns called from their corral and kicked the walls. In the moonlight the foal blinked at Elote, flicking its ears and blustering. He looked to the house, to the shadow of Ana in the window. He whispered to her in the darkness. What does it mean, he said.

He turned back to the foal. Tottering and unaware of what it was, coming over to him as mule and horse and donkey all. Some would say sent by God, but he was not some. Yet he did not know what the foal was, or even if a corral of stone could hold it. He felt very small, like a child, and something unknown was rising in his breast. He reached for the foal's head, but withdrew his hand and backed away.

He returned to the house and took some food, his loose lips working the emotion and the tortilla around his few teeth. Ana sat with him. After a moment she said that God had blessed them.

—We have been blessed enough, he said. A droughted ranch and perishing corn and not a single child of our own. A storehouse nearly empty and a salinous well.

He said that God, preoccupied with others, had looked away for a moment, which to a man was the span of a lifetime.

—God has given us many children, she said.

—Discarding a child and giving a child are two different things.

Ana looked down at the boy on the floor. He will hear you, she said. But the boy slept on.

—You are frightened by a gift, she said. You have always been so.

—I would not know. I hold no experience with gifts.

Ana looked away.

—I am only saying it is best to work for oneself, he said. That what a man tends with his own hand will not betray him. That the crop is faithful.

She said even now a crop lay in failure before him. He said must we continue in this vein every night. She said yes.

When Elote was a younger man, with his ranch newly established, he went to collect Ana. She cried in the yard with her mamá, and Elote waited until she had finished, and they rode together toward Pabellón.

He asked if she was afraid. She said she was not, but she cared to know about Elote's people. She wanted to know if Pabellón was his father's ranch.

Elote said no, that the ranch was of his own making. He said he was the son of someone else. That was what his father had told him. Elote looked at Ana and asked if this changed what had been arranged. She said it did not. He said if she intended to leave him, it would be better to turn around now, but Ana kept riding.

He told Ana how his father had said, Do you know what that means, to be the son of someone else?

—And did you know? Ana said.

—No. I was only a small boy at the time.

He told Ana that his father had to explain it to him, how Elote should look around and see all that there was, how everything belonged to the father and none of it to Elote. Not the smallest thing would be given him. Not this olla or the water in the olla. Not these animals or the land they stood upon.

—Do you remember your own father, Elote asked.

—Yes, Ana said.

—I imagine that even if your father was very poor, he gave something to you. A blanket or riata or a toy made from fragments of tin.

Ana rode quietly.

—My father lived a long life, Elote said. For such giving, there were many opportunities. But none were taken.

By the time of the foal's weaning, word had spread. A crowd from ranches around came to the stone corral to see the foal of a molly mule standing in the moonlight, the candlelight. The people shared their provisions with one another, though the most devout would not think of eating. They reached their hands to the foal and debated its constitution, whether mule or donkey or horse or a new design altogether. The men declared it a donkey, in respect to the sire, and the women held their peace.

The workhand, weaving from mezcal, set himself up at the gate as though he had wrought the miracle himself. He indicated the molly. Nunca estuvo preñada, he told the pilgrims. Skin and bones one day and a foal the next.

—Must I work for the whole world, Elote said to Ana. Feed them from the last remnants of our provisions and shelter them too? Those who feel free to walk the country on the charity of others.

Among the pilgrims came a man overtaken by tremors, a gaunt man with a dark birthmark covering half his face. He came first to the house, hat in quaking hand. He carried no pack or bundle.

—Where is your home, Elote said.

The man said he had none.

—For whom do you provide. For whom do you work?

—I cannot work, the man explained. I came only for the foal, I hear it has the touch of God.

He dropped his hat and Ana picked it up and dusted it. She brought a rolled tortilla and he struggled to press it into his mouth and she turned discreetly away. She gave him water, and the main of it splashed to the ground, and he handed the olla back to her.

—Elote will take you, Ana said. Que Dios le acompañe.

Ana looked at Elote and there was no refusing her. He followed the man out. When they were away from the house, Elote said, You will return just as you came.

The trembling man kept going.

—Just as you came, Elote said again.

The man passed through the crowd of pilgrims and with a shuddering hand he dipped into the trough where the foal had been drinking and sprinkled the dregs about his shoulders. The others did the same. They dared not enter that sacrosanct space, but they hung over and anointed themselves. The trembling man reached again for the water while Elote watched, silent and unprofessing.

That evening, a young couple came to Elote. The man had a care-worn blanket picked clean of straw, hastily mended. He held it out. His barren wife stood alongside, delivering the blanket a little with her hands toward Elote, who turned away.

Ana pleaded with Elote after they had gone. The gift is for the foal, she said. Not for you. But he refused every offering. A pair of teguas. Three good reatas and a blacksnake whip. Dried beef and a jar of mezcal. A cage with two gray doves. A few silver coins from some unknown time, worn from handling. Good ears of corn that lay there enraging him.

But in the night he went to where the pilgrims slept and took the offerings. He carried them to his storehouse, and the articles weighted his hands as no tack or tool or harvest ever did. Taken in payment for promised rain. For the promise of children who are born and not born correctly. For the promise of good when there is only suffering.

In the morning he could not look any person in the eye and he could not look at Ana. He drove the pilgrims out. They went protesting down the road and some dared to carry hairs they plucked from the ground or the walls or the foal itself. The trembling man was the last to go. He stood before Elote and shook like an epiléptico but said he was not. He asked if he must go. He said he had only just arrived.

Elote asked how many prayers were needed. The man pointed to the sky with a trembling hand, as if only the heavens knew.

Elote drove him out also. He waited until the man dipped beyond the ridge, and when the figure was only a small dark form lurching away on the horizon, Elote looked up at the sky.

He went to bed and woke without dreams and the moon had set. In the darkness he thought he heard pilgrims. He heard the molly groaning and pawing the ground, and when he came to the corral, he found her standing restless and alone.

The gate was fastened and the foal was gone. He looked about in dread. He ran to the storehouse and found the offerings as before, and he hurried to the house and woke Ana. She left the children and followed him. The molly circled the corral, eyes wild and grieving.

—And now you see, he said.

—What do I see, Elote.

He spoke of a changeable heaven, one that without fail rescinds what it offers. One that causes corn to grow into a world without rain. She said he was not speaking of corn.

Dolores-born-without-ears brought him one of the john mules and he mounted up and waved her away. He rode into the arroyo but saw no tracks and no man. He went into the draw and out again, and ascended the hill. He could see the molly below, circling the small corral, and in the largest of the corrales he saw that the second john mule was gone. And then he knew.

Ana was already at the tack room when he came. She gathered bottles now empty of mezcal and stood beside the vacant pallet of the workhand.

—He is gone, she said.

—And so he goes, with all that I have worked for in his keeping.

She placed a tired hand upon him. Tell me how you have worked, Elote. For the mula milagrosa.

He remained quiet, and when she could hold it no longer, she asked did he believe he was so special that every curse was for him alone.

For days they argued and Ana entreated him not to go.

—It is for you, he said. For the children.

Ana said she feared he would not return, that without him they would not live. He said they had corn and dried beef and even some coins. He said that if pilgrims came, she must implore them to give what they had, and seeing the children they would.

In the morning as he readied his gear, she said they did not need the foal. Was it not enough that they had caught the eye of God? He said he did not seek to be under any such eye. He wanted only what was rightfully his.

—For yourself you go, then, Ana said.

—Have you not been listening? For you. For these children.

He left Ana standing in the yard. He gave lead to the molly, who huffed the ground and set out toward the south. Dolores-born-without-ears ran as far as the gate, and Elote gestured at her to go back.

He went south toward the town of El Rosario; the workhand would take the foal wherever people resided, wherever offerings would be given. He felt a rush of anger as he rode. He saw the workhand's drunken red face, the stolen john, the foal so recently weaned. The pocketful of earnings.

He followed the arroyo, the best of desert roads, and the dry watercourse channeled him between low red hills and around stones dark with desert varnish. The sun like a great monstrance warmed the land. He looked back, feeling the nagging absence of something forgotten. He checked the gear again. He carried water and jerky and tobacco, and husks to roll the tobacco, and the machete and a few coins, and at last he realized the absence was Ana.

He followed the coast, riding past the stone ruins of someone else's dream. The adobes watched him pass with dark, windowless eyes; they were too old for anxiety.

At midmorning he heard coyotes singing. He remembered once, when he was a boy, an old passerby came to his father's ranch and said these were the dogs of God. The man told of a song to scold them:

You've followed me everywhere to no avail!
Your barking fills the whole world.
You bark from your arse as much as from your mouth!

Ever after, his father would often turn without warning when Elote was speaking. As much as from your mouth, his father would recite.

He rode on. The brush grew low toward the coast, and the arroyo fanned out and emptied him to the sandy flats. He saw the five volcanoes rising from the sea, and the shimmering white salt pans, and he did not stop until he came to Socorro.

It could not be called a town. A cluster of jacales and poor crops as dry as his own. A family sat in the shade: an old man and old mother, and three girls who could not be the children of these elderly ones. The woman got up and asked if Elote required refreshment, if he required rest.

Elote asked if they had seen a man with a young animal, not quite mule nor horse nor donkey, and the children laughed but fell silent when they saw his face.

—The foal was here, the woman said. With a man leading it and telling stories of its birth.

—A drunken man, Elote said. A man with a face red from drink.

—No, the old man said. Not that kind of man at all.

He said the man trembled from wonder. That he owned very little, nothing that could be carried. That he had renounced all worldly goods.

—A man trembling from wonder, Elote said.

—Yes.

—And where did this man acquire the animal.

—From the desert. From the wilderness itself.

—No, Elote said. The foal is property belonging to me. Stolen by my own workhand.

They did not know of any such workhand. They only knew of the trembling man, who did not labor as others did but shook with awe and brought the foal to those in need. The couple spoke to Elote slowly, as to a child or one mortally ill. Elote knew they looked upon him as a wretched pilgrim. He hated to find himself in such a category, and as he rode away he could not hold back from saying, Yet the man who leads the miracle has found no miracle himself.

He continued south and the molly resisted him, swinging her head in protest, and he spurred her hard and rode on. He thought of the trembling man who had come into possession of his property with no thought of returning it, no thought of payment or offering. He remembered the pilgrims, the storehouse of offerings given in kind, the couple who in decency had paid him a good blanket. He thought of the trembling man's face, how he stood jittering before them without bundle or pack. Elote despised him for that weakness, and more for the weakness which allowed him to travel upon the charity of others. His mouth watered and he reached for the last of the beef but realized that he salivated from anger, from thoughts of the trembling man.

He pushed the molly, and at every rise he scanned the horizon for a lurching figure. By late day the molly's head began to droop. He dismounted and lifted each foot until he found the thorn, deep in the hoof wall. He sat back on his heels.

—Must every last thing be taken from me, he said to Ana. Every last good thing.

He walked toward El Rosario with the molly plodding after. Anger bloomed. The molly pulled to the north and he whipped her with his hands and she bucked and defied him and in this way they came to the outskirts of the town.

He could see the old mission at a distance, graying in decay. Adobe houses lay in an alluvial plain that at any time might rage with floodwaters and raze the community entire. But people would live nonetheless where there is water, even in the center of the arroyo itself.

He walked into the zócalo, and upon the edge of a dry fountain sat a circle of men, their eyes in shadow under their hats. He went forward with the limping molly and a boy came from the side as if he had been waiting and offered to take the rope. Elote held it fast. He faced the elders.

The men asked where Elote resided. He said he had a ranch at Pabellón. He said he sought a trembling man with a young burro.

—Is there an alguacil in this town, Elote said. Or some such man who looks after the affairs of justice.

—What business have you with the alguacil, one of the elders said.

—My own business, Elote said.

The elders looked him over. One of them said that perhaps it was not the alguacil that Elote was seeking. Perhaps it was the priest of Santo Tomás, who was even now tarrying in town on his way south.

Elote felt a pounding anger rise within him. He said he wanted no priest, that he did not seek the foal for those reasons. He said the foal was not for himself, but for his wife and children.

The elder said he knew of the foal, that this was a marvel never seen before in the village. A girl was freed from a malevolent spirit. A speechless man now uttered words of love to both wife and lover. A twisted foot became right.

—So the man has but recently left, Elote said.

The elder looked at him and then to the others. He asked if Elote did not believe him. He said Elote could speak to these individuals if he liked. They could be summoned. Was Elote one to show no amazement at all.

Some children ran past and stopped when they saw the stranger called like a miscreant in front of the elders. The men motioned him to stand at a distance, and they conferred among themselves. The children conferred also. Elote looked about the zócalo, ringed with adobes that might be shops or talleres or homes. There was one low building that must be the jail, and a smaller dwelling for the office of the alguacil, which no matter how spare is the seat of power in the town.

—What is written upon me, he said to Ana. What is written upon me that the whole world opposes me.

The children whispered as though they had witnessed such a spectacle before, and they bore the solemnity of those watching a man go to his flogging. Elote felt fear begin to rise, and he edged away into the street, pulling the molly. When he looked back, every man had turned toward him, and they sat in a line silent and scowling.

He led the molly limping from house to house. To any person who would listen, he inquired of the trembling man. Finally a girl indicated a crumbling establo and said a man inside was snake-bitten, but she believed he was the man. Others had brought him to town because his woman was here.

—What of the animals, he asked.

The girl said the man rode no animal. Elote said there had been two animals, both belonging to him. The girl shook her head.

He secured the molly near the door and went in. A man lay askew in the corner, surrounded by bottles. His ankle was bandaged, black and twice the size of its mate. Overflowing the wrappings. The man's face was turned to the wall. Elote shook him.

—Oye, Elote said.

The face of the workhand turned toward him. The head lolled. Elote grasped the chin, and the clouded eyes looked at him without recognition. Elote reached for the man's pocket to find what earnings he had gained, but he saw a movement in the doorway. A woman stood there watching. He pulled his hand away.

—This man stole my property, Elote said.

She looked at him. He has no property, she said. With nothing they brought him to town.

—Did he come with money, Elote said. From the sale of what is mine.

—No, she said.

—And the epiléptico. Did you see him. He leads the foal of my molly mule.

The woman looked at him without surprise, as if every day one spoke of such marvels. She considered him for a moment. She said she knew of no epiléptico, but for a coin she would bring some food. She backed through the door without turning, as women do in the presence of unpredictable men.

—I am no thief, he called after her.

She returned with strips of deer meat. She apologized that she had neither bean nor tortilla, but she lived only on what was brought to her by the hand of God. Elote asked if God brought deer every day and she said no. He asked if God dried the meat. Did God himself scrape the hides. She looked at Elote with pity, and to cover himself he gave her a coin and said, Why would the world oppose a man who seeks only what is rightfully his?

—Was the foal not a gift to you, she said.

He did not answer. He took a swallow of drink from one of the fallen bottles. The woman stood quietly against the wall, watching him.

—I imagine you know all these things, he said.

She said she did not know, that she was not a prophetess as he supposed. That people say the desert itself is the prophet to the prophet.

He took another drink and said, What do you make of it, then? Is such a person accursed?

She said she could not answer, but a curse would not stay where it was not welcomed. She took his bowl and went out. He turned again to the workhand and knelt, drink burning within him. He slapped the man's face.

—Where is the foal. Did you sell it.

The workhand shook his head. His eyes shone with fever and venom.

—Me cuida esa mujer, he said. Esa buena mujer.

Elote said he did not care if the woman attended him or if anyone did. He only wished to know what had become of the foal. The workhand began to weep and said that while leading the foal he was bitten, and the john mule abandoned him, and did Elote himself send the serpent? He did not know what had become of the foal. The epiléptico had led it away. Did Elote remember him?

Elote stood and kicked the workhand once, twice, and a third time in the wound itself. The workhand writhed and Elote would have kicked him again but a female voice cried out. He startled and came back to himself, wiping his brow and looking around for the woman, but no one stood there at all. Sweating, he went outside and leaned against the wall. He ducked his head.

—Stay with me awhile, he said to Ana.

He tried to lead the molly into the street but she would not go. She reeled on three legs and he feared she was already ruined. He thought of the elders who looked at him with such malice and he was pulling the molly into the establo away from the eyes of the town when he saw the men already coming.

They surrounded him and he held to the rope and the men sprang forward and pulled it away. They bobbed their heads and called him a heretic. He did not deny that he was. They said they would not allow him to harm the trembling man or the foal. Elote tried to wrest free and said he must not be detained. He told them of the many children who lived under his roof. He said he had a wife. They said if such were true, then why did he abandon them? Elote was shouting as the men of the town led him away by the arms.

They forced him to the jail and unlocked the iron grate. The door was narrow and they dragged him sideways and pushed him through and closed the frame, and the wooden door sealed it over.

There was one high slit of a window and that was all. In the thin light he saw bodies against the walls. A hand sought him and he pulled away and stumbled toward the window. He looked out; people were passing on the street. A guard, scarcely more than a boy, stood rolling tobacco and fumbling with the husk as if new to it. Dried leaves were picked up by the wind.

—Listen, Elote called to the boy.

Voices laughed behind him in the gloom. The boy looked up. Elote thrust his fingers through the window. From behind, a man pulled him down. The man held up his own fingers, swollen and black.

—They wait for it, he said. For a new man who doesn't know . . .

Elote shook free. Listen, he called to the boy. I've done nothing. I am the man who has been wronged . . .

The boy turned away to smoke. The man pulled at Elote again.

—It's no good, he said. You make it worse for yourself . . .

The sun was setting and he dreaded the coming darkness. Bodies moved around him, and a woman crouched there with her skirt hitched up and he smelled sourness and turned away. The man held out his good hand to Elote.

—Gertrudis, he said.

Elote was afraid of the man. He was afraid of all of them, these dark forms that lined the walls like felled bats.

—How long have you been here, Elote said. What is the usual stay.

Laughter rose up from around the room. The usual stay, voices cried. Gertrudis shouted them down.

—Have you anyone on the outside, Gertrudis said.

—No, Elote said. He would not speak of Ana in such a place.

Darkness gave way to blackness. Someone beside him fumbled with a packet. Gertrudis pushed a bit of tortilla into Elote's hand.

—Take it, Gertrudis said. My woman will come again tomorrow.

At once hands were upon him. He pushed the tortilla into his mouth and voices rose up. They cried for bread.

—Quiet, Gertrudis said. Be quiet. This man is new, he comes with nothing.

Elote pressed into the wall. Sounds surrounded him—labored breathing and small cries and shifting. Someone eliminating, water spattering the earth. He began speaking to Ana.

—Perhaps you wish for the priest, Gertrudis whispered. That is one thing they will give you. They will send for him if you call.

—No, Elote said.

—Do not be afraid.

—I am not afraid.

He tried to move away, but speaking of fear had brought fear upon him, and he could not contain it. He whispered to Gertrudis of a wife abandoned. Infants malformed and a failing crop. He spoke of a world which forsook its sons.

Gertrudis was quiet. He took out a cigarillo, and Elote looked longingly at the tiny flame and Gertrudis allowed him a pull.

—Listen, Gertrudis said. Have you heard of the foal of a mule? Walking the country.

He reached into a pocket and took out six long tail hairs braided into a thin plait.

—I touched it myself, Gertrudis said. But I was too joyful, I had too much to drink . . .

The man leaned close and was about to speak again but Elote stopped him. He said that too many people had already spoken to him of miracles and he sought no such miracle.

His shadow had risen on the wall with the moon. Elote spoke again of the foal. He said that others believed he wished harm to it, but this was not so. He said he followed the foal at the risk of his very wife and children. That perhaps his wife would not forgive him, and to his children he would not be remembered. Perhaps this was best.

Gertrudis sat silently. Elote thought to speak again of Ana and the failing corn and the children but he could not. Instead he told Gertrudis of the birth of the foal. How out of nothing it appeared. How ordinary and odd. The kind of animal given to a boy or girl to own for a time, because no one expects the animal to live. And though the animal does not live, the good gesture of the giving is not lost upon the child.

In the night, he heard sounds upon the roof. A quick pattering as of animals passing. Claws or the scratch of batwings. He opened his eyes to the blackness and realized it was rain. He went to the window. There was no smell of a storm and he craned his neck along the slit and saw no clouds. He thrust out a hand. Into his palm fell one bead of rain and he licked it and reached for another. He heard quick steps along the wall and he pulled the hand away and slid down. The pattering ceased upon the roof, and he could hear its soft drumming moving away along the street.

In the morning the guard came, calling for Elote. Gertrudis pushed him up. Go quickly, Gertrudis said. He pressed a packet into Elote's hand. The guard jerked Elote out and he heard men cursing and the voice of Gertrudis scolding them. He was led to the office where the alguacil waited.

—The priest heard of your plight, the alguacil said. He made his case for you.

Elote looked around. The room was extraordinarily bright.

—I would see the priest to thank him if I were you. Before you make north.

—North.

—Yes, for that is where you are going. Back to your place. You are to leave this pursuit, do you understand? Do you know the second time no priest will save you. Do you know that.

Elote nodded. He would have said anything at all.

—When will my molly be returned to me? he said.

The alguacil shook his head. The guard took Elote by the arm and pushed him into the sunshine.

—The man Gertrudis, Elote called. Is there pardon for him? It was only a little drink.

The guard waved Elote away and watched as he went north along the street. Elote dared not turn. He kept going until he had passed from sight and it was only then he realized he still held the packet in his hand. He stopped to open it and thought of the cigarillo it contained. But instead, the tail hairs of the foal fell into his palm. The wind nearly caught them and he closed his hand.

At the edge of town, a man worked at shoeing a horse. Elote looked back and saw no official, and he hazarded to inquire if the man knew of the foal, and where the one who possessed it had gone.

The man said he could not say where they were bound, but they were known to follow the road to the east.

—Does he make money from this, Elote said.

The man looked off and whistled. Shall we profit from the hand of God, he said.

He went east and spent the night at the foot of Mesa la Sepultura, the grave. In the morning he drank at Agua Amarga, as bitter as its name, and he found the remnants of a hare dropped by a hawk or a coyote. He ate the raw remains and talked to Ana, and slept in a hot fretful wind among poor mesquite.

—For yourself you go, then, Ana said, and Elote did not deny it.

He was on foot, as one of no reputation. He carried only the plait of tail hairs, and without the benefit of a trail he walked through the rolling desert plain, the sharp summits of the sierras behind him. Mesas rose above him like coffins of stone, the flats with their tops blown off by once-volcanoes. The land ahead was unbounded, the sky taking the greater measure.

Near Agua Dulce he found a brackish waterhole and he knelt and made prints among those already impressed into the ground: deer and coyote and the large spread paw of a puma. On the opposite bank he saw the hoofprints of a young equine and those of a man. He got up quickly.

The sun was arcing downward and he followed the arroyo until he came to a cluster of reed-roofed adobes. Dogs came to warn of him and then to greet him. A family emerged from the house: a man and a boy, a woman and two girls who stayed in the doorway. All of them as well-tended as the grounds around, and unsmiling down to the smallest among them. He saw corrales and tinajas and animals and an orchard in fruit, every fence mended and the adobes clean and bright. He saw what he might have created if given half as much. What he had done a thousand times in his mind.

The boy came forward, but the father did not move to invite Elote. The boy froze like a person caught and looked shamefaced at the father. Then the man nodded, and the boy greeted Elote.

The man was older than himself. The woman was like Ana but without life in the eyes. She stood silent, and momentarily as if from some signal he could not perceive, the girls went into the house and Elote knew that food was forthcoming.

The man said he could see the travel had been difficult. He led Elote under the eaves to cane chairs recently mended. Elote looked toward the corrales and saw no foal or man. He began to inquire but thought of the elders at El Rosario and the dark chamber of the jail and he had no strength to withstand what might come.

The boy returned with an olla. He gave it to Elote and watched him drink, and shook Elote's hand and said they had water in all but the driest of times and Elote was welcome to it. The man waved him away. The boy went a short distance and stood watching them, the olla hanging from his hand.

—Where do you come from, the man asked.

—From Pabellón. Upon an arroyo such as this, but with little water.

The man said that was truly a difficulty. He had lived upon such ranches himself.

Elote looked up. The boy lingered near the corner of the house.

—Are you the only boy, Elote said to him.

—Sí.

—And you help your father, do you.

The man looked down to the arroyo as if something new might be viewed there. He cast down his half-finished cigarillo and indicated the boy.

—He is not much of a worker, the man said.

The boy stared away as if he had not heard. Elote said for the boy's benefit, He looks to be a good worker.

—More or less, the man said.

The woman came with plates. The man did not speak to her. She had not quite gone through the door when the man said that when he was younger, there were few people in this region to marry. That this woman was all there was at the time.

The sun and its heat began to wane. Elote closed his eyes. The sounds of the ranch surrounded him in a muted familiarity. Mules whickering and a dog alerting another of something in the brush. The woman's low voice and the girls stifling their laughter. Small birds calling in their languages. He sat listening. How easy to fly to Pabellón, he thought. How easy to go anywhere one wanted.

Ana and the children appeared before him, Dolores-born-without-ears and the bent-over boy and all of them. Softened in the dusk. There and now away. He realized he had slept.

The man sat looking across the arroyo. Elote could imagine him doing so every day of his life, and knew that he himself had a similar look in his own place. The man said Elote should sleep soon. Elote looked at him again, a person of his own kind, and he felt a confianza between them and dared to say, Perhaps you have heard of a foal of a mule. Walking the country.

—Yes, the man said. Two days ago it passed through. It seemed an ordinary burro to me. Taller perhaps. Perhaps not.

The boy took a step closer and bit his lip in thought, as if Elote were a priest or maestro or the only source of learning. The man looked at the boy. Do you have work to do, he said.

The boy went slowly to the corrales, and Elote saw the window curtain fall where the woman had been holding it. He heard the plates and the trastes and the woman speaking to the girls.

Elote asked if the one leading the foal had a tremor. The man said it was so, and he did not like to speak ill of others, but he was glad the man had not stayed.

—Where were they bound, Elote said.

—To the south, to the coast. To a ship, the capital, who knows.

Elote looked across the arroyo and asked what lay to the south.

—Nothing, the man said. Stones. Mal país.

Elote felt a weary emptiness, as empty as the wasteland the man had spoken of. As if the foal had passed into a void where men do not go.

They smoked, the ends of their cigarillos glowing in the dusk like the coals of small fires. Elote closed his eyes. He might have been under his own eaves. He would have spoken to Ana, but the man was beside him. He allowed Ana to feel his weariness, and from that weariness he hoped she understood that he would come. He had already gone to them. All that remained was for his body to follow.

When he opened his eyes, the boy stood again at the corner of the house. The man got up and wished Elote a good night with untroubled dreams. He told the boy not to bother Elote with much talk, that he should settle him and be about his business.

The boy led Elote to a lean-to with a cot of palm wood, and he sat beside Elote and whispered to him. He asked if Elote sought the foal for a boy like himself, a boy Elote had at home.

—There are many boys at home. And girls, Elote said.

The boy said Elote must truly care for them to travel such a distance, and he wished he could give Elote a horse. Elote closed his eyes. He said he wished it too.

He heard the father's voice and the flat voice of the woman answering. He heard the man calling gruffly to the boy. The boy looked up and pulled at his hair as if something had alighted there. Elote indicated that the boy should go.

From the doorway, Elote saw the father in the yard and the boy going over to him. The boy was speaking his reasons, and the man raised both hands to the sky as if to inquire why such a boy was ever created. The boy did not flinch or move. He tried to speak again and the man walked away from him.

For a long time the boy stood there, looking after the father. The woman appeared in the window like a ghost or a shadow or the crying woman of legend. She let the curtain fall. Finally the boy went inside.

Elote sat trembling on the cot. When he closed his eyes, he saw the yard as it had been, but instead of the man standing there, he saw himself. He saw Ana in the window, her eyes grown dull, and Dolores-born-without-ears downcast before him. He got up and looked out. The yard was empty. The birds slept in their hidden places and the animals leaned into one another. The wind had gone with the sun. The lamps in the house went out, and he saw the dark figure of the father pass through the door.

A chill came over him. How easy to go to Pabellón, he thought. But you return just as you came. As one who stands over a child, as one who crushes the spirit of a woman.

He lay down and tried not to think, but a thought rose of its own accord. He saw himself on the road, returning to Pabellón. He saw himself not as the man in the yard, but instead as the small, shameful boy, one who had stood too many times bereft before the father.

Elote rose at the zenith moon and went out. The sky held no clouds and he crept down to the arroyo. The dogs, now familiar, trailed him. When he looked back, he was surprised to find the boy following. He waited until they walked together and Elote stopped and grasped his hand. He passed the tail hairs of the foal to the boy, who shook his head, but Elote would not retake them.

They followed the curve of the hills until the ranch was no longer in sight. The boy wore a pack, and Elote thought he intended to accompany him. Instead, the boy gave Elote the meat of two doves and a botella filled with water. He said that Elote must first go east, and when he was well away from the ranch he should turn south until he came to the country of stones, for that was where the trembling man and the son of the molly had gone.

Elote went south into a wild place upon no trail at all. Vast boulders lay across the land. Tiraditas. Thrown from the hand of God. He became a tiny thing among the stones. Between them grew curious twisted trees without limbs, yet covered with leaves. Plants with no known relations. Everywhere he saw the tracks of correcaminos and hares and lizards, but no tracks of a man.

The night chilled him. With the skeletons of cholla he made a fire. He ate the last of his provisions and lay down to sleep.

He woke speaking to Ana. What shall I bring you, he said.

But Ana wanted nothing that could be purchased with a coin.

—Say to Dolores that she is good, Ana said.

—That she is good.

—Yes. That she is good.

—She cannot hear me.

—She will hear you.

The morning was very cold. When he came to a vast arroyo draining no water from waterless mountains, he walked along its dry course among short blue palms. He carried nothing; somewhere the empty botella had fallen from his hand. He found a place where coyotes had been digging, and he worked down to a small muddy slough and drank. The wind blew the crystalline sand about him and his eyes were red and weeping.

The sun rose above the country of stones. When he looked up, he saw the tracks of a man with hoofprints following. He got to his feet, but in the glare he could see no man or animal. He went on, following the tracks. His mouth was dry and he concocted the smallest amount of saliva but it brought him no relief. He could hear the rushing wings of zopilotes above, and he thought perhaps these dark birds were the prophets of which the woman at El Rosario had spoken.

Toward sunset, the arroyo fanned out into a sandy place. The cords of his shoes gave way and the leather split and he went on, shoeless and bleeding like a desertworn stigmatic. As he crossed, the tracks suddenly diverged. In the prints he saw the struggle and the breaking away. He saw the trail of a man who ran with a frenzied, lopsided gait, and the place where the foal shook free of its cargo. He did not know how long the man had tarried there, watching the foal as it fled without restraint, kicking away into the waste.

He sat down. Night was coming. There were no birds, no movement at all. The tracks of the man led away, heavier with the pack he must now carry, toward the western hills. A cloud passed the failing sun and he sat down. He tried to summon his anger, but saw in the staggering footsteps little left to serve as a vessel for his wrath. The light dipped below the horizon and he shivered.

At some point he lay down and slept. He dreamed of Dolores-born-without-ears, who appeared as a grown woman revealing her palm to him, covered in gold dust. When he opened his eyes, a figure stood among the stones. Stars swirled in his vision, the stars of hunger and pain and weariness, and he shook his head and looked again. The foal was watching him. Taller than he remembered, standing with ears alert and watching. It snorted and came blustering through the boulders to the plain where he lay. When he got up it shied away, but turned again to watch him from a distance. It looked at his hands.

He had nothing to offer, nothing with which to persuade it to come. He clicked his tongue and held an empty palm to the foal and it inclined its ears but remained where it was. He stayed very still. It took a step toward him. Then it turned and moved away, looking back once to regard him, and passed between the stones.

He stood for some time listening. When he heard nothing more, he found his shoes where they had fallen and tied them with strips from his tunic. He walked north under the moon. Through the night he went on, and Ana was with him.

He walked with her in silence. When the sun rose, he found the place of the coyotes and drank. He sat in the shade of a tall cardón, so like a man with its thick green arms raised to the sky, covered with the furry beginnings of flowers along the riblines. While he rested, Ana spoke to him. She inquired of the foal. He wiped his brow with a shaking hand. He looked at the ground so his face might not be seen.

—Elote, Ana said. But her words held no anger.

He looked up. Finally he said the foal was given to him. But it would not be possessed. He told Ana he was coming. Estoy de camino. He got up and followed his tracks, going slowly northward until he found the trail, along which families would receive him in the manner that people of all ranches do.

Dolores-Born-without-Ears

CALMALLÍ

—1883—

Sand arrives at the gold fields of Calmallí, blown across the desert on Pacific winds grain by grain, coming to rest against low interior hills where the mesquite, the brittlebush, the creosote, and the palo verde discover the moisture and slowly seize upon the mounds, anchoring them into place with their thirsty roots. The miners do the same. They seize upon the gold, riveting Calmallí into a settlement.

At Calmallí there is nothing to relieve the eye. Only the giant cardón and the Harris's hawk rise above the landscape, and the solitary windlass at the wooden house of don Tránsito, the one man who has made good in the gold diggings. To unburden the eye there is only the brief sight of don Tránsito's wife, who the miners must address as doña, though she will never hear anyone honoring her.

Every morning, in the house of don Tránsito, doña Dolores comes downstairs to the small store and stands behind a counter of ironwood and sells goods at four times their value: beans and chiles and café, dried beef, dates, tobacco, and water from the well. She pushes bottles of aguardiente upon the miners, who become drunk and careless, speaking love to her. But Dolores can hear nothing. She has no ears at all, or inner workings of ears. Her earholes are like exploratory mines, abandoned and leading nowhere. When the miners stumble away, she scrapes the cracks between the floorboards and retrieves the fallen gold, even the very dust. She amasses her own stash unknown to any man, even don Tránsito.

She has not lived with him long. Only the previous year did he pass her father's ranch at Pabellón, conducting business on the way to Calmallí. By the end of the visit, her father Elote was motioning for Dolores to go with him. She did not understand. She was not a young woman to be given, but don Tránsito gently took her arm. She kept looking at Elote and he would not meet her eye.

He did not come outside to watch her leave. Don Tránsito lifted her into the wagon and she kept looking back until they drove over the rise. Then she turned ahead and covered her eyes. But when she looked through her fingers, she saw for the first time what happened to the trail when it went over the hill. She saw the broad mouth of the arroyo and the sea. She had not known that water could gather in such amounts. At first she did not believe it was water; she did not know what it was. Don Tránsito took her to the shore and let her touch it and taste it, and then he touched and tasted her.

After he helped her back into the wagon, she rode with her face in her hands. They went south along the coast, and when they came to the village of El Rosario, don Tránsito bought two skirts and three blouses and took her to the house of a devout woman to bathe and dress her. Dolores did not want the woman to braid her hair, but the woman caught her and pulled two heavy handfuls away from her ears. The woman jumped back in surprise and blessed herself. Dolores made a rude gesture and took the skirts and blouses outside where don Tránsito waited.

He brought her to his house at Calmallí, where he became black with jealousy. He shot at miners, and miners shot at him in return. He taught Dolores that she must never turn her back on anyone who came into the store, and how to weigh gold dust on the scale with its tiny bowls of brass and counterweights, and how to put the earnings into a box of iron beside the bed. He taught her how to disable a man by kicking him in the groin. And he taught her what he liked in his own groin, before he became disabled by a bullet.

Now he lay upstairs in bed, beset by a wound that would not heal, listening to men in the store below and fretting. At night he clutched

Dolores and wept. She could smell death about him. Soon she would take her stake of gold and go home to Pabellón, where her father sat braiding rope all day under the eaves and talking to her mother Ana, long since gone. She recalled how her father's lips were always moving, until he fell asleep, when Dolores would wake him and help him to bed.

In the late afternoon, a falluquero—the traveling trader of goods and story and song—rode over the hill and saw the goldfields of Calmallí laid out before him. He sat atop his black mule with the pack-donkey tethered behind, and watched the miners laboring like ants below. He saw the dark circles of their cookfires, and the caves where they lived half-buried in their own tailings. The miners had carved the ground into a pitted grinding stone, dotted with shafts. Even a mule would stumble, even a donkey would be lost, but the miners went afoot. They carried only the horn spoon and the bucket, the bar of iron and the batea—the winnowing bowl. And their own breath.

The falluquero sat above them, watching. The mule and the donkey huffed and stamped. The sun was low and he shaded his eyes and spied a water well and a windlass, turning in the hot breeze, beside a solitary wooden house with two stories and true windows of glass. The house stood above any earthen home, any jacal in which he and all the men he knew were born and lived and died. It rose above the desert, which could not even supply wood for its own making. He wondered to whom the house belonged. He had seen such homes in prosperous towns, belonging to prosperous men, and though the people of the sierras esteemed him for his trade, the men of the towns overlooked him as they might a goat or a dog.

He imagined himself the owner of the house, looking out from the glass upon the gambusinos, those hand-miners laboring under the power of their dreams with gold dust leading them on. Following a vein, a dike, pulling earth from the ground without knowing what was there. Spinning and tossing their bowls, throwing the earth to the wind, aiding with their breath until the dust was winnowed away, their faces ashen from the soil. Digging beneath a white-hot sky while he looked on from the upper windows of the wooden house.

The miners straightened up to see him; some called a greeting to the new man. He lifted a hand. The mule shook its head and the donkey pulled at the tether, smelling water below. Then he heard someone curse. On the lee of the hill, in a small cemetery, he saw a dusty form struggling to dig a grave among some cairns of rock. The exhausted man stood beside a hole not yet big enough.

The falluquero rode over. A wrapped corpse lay on the ground, and a bit of blood had seeped through at the neck. The mule arched away. The digger pushed back a frayed sombrero and gazed up at him.

—I knew him from a boy, the old man said. Until don Tránsito shot him.

He wiped his eyes and pointed to the wooden house.

—He owns everything, the old man said. The house, the store. The woman.

At this the falluquero smiled.

—Put that thought away from you, the old man said. It's lucky don Tránsito doesn't shoot me, just for knowing this poor fellow.

He sat down beside the body and put a hand on the head and looked at the falluquero.

—I guess you're here to make it rich too, he said. What were you before?

—A falluquero.

—That's a good business, he said. Look at your animals. Look at your gear. Soon you'll be trading right down to your shirt, just to live. You're new here, you don't know how it is.

The falluquero grinned. Perhaps I don't know how it is, he said. But soon it will know how I am.

He secured the mule to a fencepost and took a shovel from his pack. He climbed into the grave and began digging. The sun was failing and the animals put down their heads. Cookfires began to appear on the flats, one after the other, red coals like open wounds. Disconsolate snatches of song rose up and fell away on the wind.

The old digger lifted the head and shoulders of the corpse, and the falluquero took the legs.

—Come on, hombre, the falluquero said. You won't dance here anymore. No use waiting for the ladies.

They lowered the body into the hole.

—May God remember the hour, the falluquero said, dusting his hands. And now, how about a drink?

—Have you any?

—The sweetest aguardiente flows from a woman, the falluquero said.

The old man shook his head.

—Isn't one man buried enough? I told you she is don Tránsito's woman.

—I thought you knew, the falluquero said. Every woman is the falluquero's woman!

Don Tránsito lay tangled in his blankets, sweating and bright-faced with fever. He held his revolver in hand. He wore no trousers because of the wound, and he pulled at the bandages. Dolores sat beside him on the rawhide bed. She felt nauseous; every day she felt nauseous. The man would not sleep. He took her hand and placed it on his chest and wept. She had never seen a man weep except her father Elote, who wept for Ana, her mother. Don Tránsito's hands were agitated, clutching her skirt. She looked at his eyes. The fearsome don Tránsito was himself afraid of dying.

She went to the window to watch the new man. He had a fine mule and a donkey, a pack of gear and good boots. He sat at his cookfire, full of talk and vigor and plans. He had come to Calmallí to grow rich, though he never would. The miners began poor and grew poorer.

They were badgers and coyotes ducking all day long into their dens, anxious and scurrying. Gesturing to her as she went to the well. They feared don Tránsito, but soon they would learn that he was dying, and another man would rise up to stake her as his wife. She thought of her father, alone at Pabellón. If she did not go home, the desert would overtake the ranch, and wild birds would snatch the corn. Coyotes would eat the chickens, and overcoming their fear, coyotes would eat the body of Elote.

She watched the trader gather branches for the mule and donkey. He kept looking at the house, moving easily, loping along like someone who would try to trick her. But she would not be tricked. That was something else don Tránsito had taught her—how to fire a pistol into a man's face. He had given her a gun of her own, small enough for a pocket. But she hoped it would not come to that. In not many days, when the trader did not grow rich, he would become tired and dispirited. Like others he would come to the store and surrender what little gold he had, his nuggets and even the very dust. When she had taken all he possessed, she would purchase his animals and go home to Elote.

She turned and don Tránsito was beckoning. He reached for her hair, twisting the heavy strands in his fingers and gesturing with the gun to the window. His mouth moved with worried talk. She took his hand and tried to free it but he pulled her close, his mouth moving all the while. He held the revolver to her cheek, as though he would take her into death with him, but she did not believe the intention was true. She saw something of Elote in him, only wanting his Ana, as husbands want their wives when they are afraid. She lay beside him, unmoving, until he grew tired and let loose. She watched until he fell asleep, and she took the gun from his hand.

The falluquero had caught two hares and was skinning and laying them over the coals. Some of the gambusinos had gathered, and the falluquero sat on a tin pail, a little above them, tending the meat. He handed around smoking pieces of flesh and gave a second portion to the old gravedigger. The men got up a song and passed the bottle.

—No one has ever seen her ears, a miner said.

—They say she has none.

—But beneath the hair . . .

—Ay, to lay wrapped in such hair.

—Don Tránsito traveled all the way to Pabellón for her.

—It wasn't his songs that won her—she can't hear a thing!

—He's singing his death song now.

—One can't kill a man like don Tránsito.

—For days no one has seen him.

—Yet his revolver sees you!

The men laughed. The falluquero looked out. Lights of cookfires lit the night. Songs rose across the land and flames flared where men were careless with the aguardiente.

—You say don Tránsito is dying, the falluquero said.

—Some say, but who wants to find out?

—Someone must take his place, the falluquero said. And who better than a falluquero with a keen mind for business? Who better than a falluquero with a keen hand for a lady?

—¡Ándale! cried the miners.

The old man looked up. You'll make use of her like all the rest, he said. Or else she'll use you, one or the other.

The falluquero handed him another scrap of meat. The miners shook their heads and said the falluquero was well-born and generous and he smiled to himself and passed the bottle to the next man. The old man pulled his hat low and the falluquero began to sing: Ay Dolores, Dolores, eres más bonita que las flores . . .

He looked toward the house and saw a candle extinguish in the lower window. A light appeared upstairs. A shadow came and went, a small form going by.

—That poor woman, the old man said. She'll never get back to her place.

—Is that what she wants? the falluquero said.

—Every woman wants to go home, the old man said. Husbands be damned.

The men talked over one another.

—One day she'll up and go.

—In what? Don Tránsito sent the wagon to the coast.

—I would take her!

—I would carry her!

—¡Oye, falluquero! Don't you have a woman?

The falluquero lowered his head and poked the coals.

—Somewhere, he said.

The men laughed.

—What does that matter? another said. Somewhere is not here!

She kept the store closed, and some of the miners began to gather beneath her window. When she looked out, they took off their hats and ran their hands through hair thick with dust, jostling one another. She kept the curtains drawn, but through a small rent in the fabric she watched the trader's comings and goings. In the morning she saw him walk with the old man into the ravine, and in the evening the two returned with a troubled gait that assured her they had found nothing. One evening she saw the falluquero go to another man's fire circle and trade his good boots for water and aguardiente and tortillas. Now he wore poor sandals too large for him, stumbling as he went back to the cookfire. He gave the tortillas to the old man. She kept watch until the sky grew dark and she could only see the red dot of him, illumined by the coals. His hands flashed as he talked. When the fire died, he disappeared.

Don Tránsito lay unmoving on his cot. His eyes were open. She put her fingers beneath his nostrils and felt a slight breath. She searched his face to foretell the hour or day of his passing but could read nothing there. She left him and went down to the store in the darkness and did not light a lamp. Kneeling beside the wall, she pulled a board from its place and took out a small bag. She felt its weight in her hand. She took a second bag, smaller than the first, and poured out a measure of dust, holding her breath so that not a single flake might be lost. She returned the larger stash to its place in the wall and kept watch at the window, holding the little bag in her hand. A man passed by and stopped to urinate, but it was not the trader. Perhaps he slept or perhaps he had gone out by night with the old man. Before dawn she hid the bag in her pocket and took the bucket and went out, though she needed no water.

The falluquero sat on the hill, keeping watch. The stars were bright, like countless miniature moons, and he smoked a cigarillo in the shining night and examined the house. The miners already looked to him as a juez or a magistrate, and in time he might construct a balcony on the house to which men would come and see him. He was lost in these thoughts when the woman came out with a bucket in her hand. She looked left and right, as though searching for someone, and went toward the gate and the windlass. Such was the length and blackness of her hair that when she turned, she disappeared into the dark. He heard the gate open and close, and he got up and picked his way down the hill in the near-dawn, hurrying, scattering pebbles as he went.

He stole to the wall that enclosed the water well. He meant to speak to her as a good man with a good manner, though he knew she could not hear him. But when the gate opened, he feared startling her and he stayed in the shadows. She set the bucket down, inhaling the morning air. She seemed small under the vastness of the sky, the world upon her too large. Perhaps he would take her home to Pabellón to visit her relations after all was settled.

The sun was coming up. She lifted the bucket to go back. He followed and did not know how she heard him, but she turned.

—I would talk to you, he said.

She stood examining him: the soiled trousers, the fraying sandals, the poor shirt he had traded for his good one. She set the bucket down and put her hand into the folds of her skirt and took out a small bag. She offered it to him, her flat palm like a shelf holding it. He opened the bag and tipped it toward the first light and looked inside.

—No, he said. I don't want your money.

She indicated with a nod that he should take it. She pointed to where his animals were standing. The mule lifted its head, and the donkey shifted in half sleep.

—I don't intend to sell my animals, he said. But I intend to stay.

He said the common opinion held that don Tránsito was dying. That she should not worry because he was here to care for the house and the store and for her. For this he needed his animals. He said he knew he had not yet succeeded in the gold fields but he was a man adept at business and had much to offer. He stepped closer.

She looked at him darkly and he saw that she did not want another man loving her. But he was not another man. He put a hand upon his heart and held out the bag and she took it and turned to go. He caught her arm and she shook free and he moved back, holding up his hands.

—I want to help you, he said. He reached for her again.

She took the bucket and brushed his hand away, and at the door of the house she paused to make a gesture which he well understood.

Dolores pulled the dressing from don Tránsito's wound. The shredded tissues were darkening; his flesh was preceding him in death. She brought the basin and washed his face and neck. He lay without expression, his hooded eyes half-closed and his breathing shallow.

The trader had wanted to speak love to her, and now that course was ruined. Even if he sold the animals to her, he would want to go along. She knew the kind of man he was, one to want what other men wanted simply because they wanted it more.

She would go on foot; in the night she would take the road and at every ranch she would ask to purchase an animal to carry her to

Pabellón, even an old mount so she would not spend much of what she had saved for Elote.

Don Tránsito blinked and blinked again and she glanced up. A tiny stone hit the window. And another. She got up and looked out. Two men stood below, calling to her. One held a pouch. She did not know if the bag contained gold, or whether the man only sought to draw her out. She covered don Tránsito's legs with the blanket and took the little pistol and went down the stairs.

She stood at the closed door, her hand on the frame. She could feel the knocking and she turned away, but at the stairs she thought of obtaining one final bag of earnings for Elote and she went to the door and opened it.

The two men came inside. They nodded to her, talking all the while. One wore the boots of the trader. The other removed his hat and kept it in hand. The booted man smiled and she did not like the look of his fingers, which would not stop moving. She stepped behind the counter and indicated that the man should show her what he carried.

The booted man came boldly around the counter and took a bottle of aguardiente. She put her hand on the container but he eased it away and poured himself a drink. The hatless man nudged him and leaned over the counter, murmuring and blinking his sad eyes. The booted man took a sip and edged the bottle toward her. He put his hand over hers, and in a moment her pistol was out.

She pulled back the hammer and the men backed up. With the pistol she pointed to the door, but they came slowly forward, gesturing as men do to animals to calm them. The man with the sad eyes held a hand to her. The other was shaking the little pouch and he took two quick strides and she raised the pistol and pulled the trigger. She saw the men duck and the wallboard behind them split with a puff of dust rising into the air. The booted man came at her and she raised the pistol again and this time he flew backward, falling against the wall with a ragged hole through his cheek. She saw his surprised eyes as he went down. He lay twitching, a dark pool beneath his head, and the other man stood gaping only for a moment before making for the door. She ran to shut it behind him and stood trembling, shaking out her hand and walking the room. The man on the floor lay still. She pushed him with a foot and covered her eyes. Then she knelt beside him, taking the pouch from where it had fallen. She emptied the bag into her hand. Small stones of the most ordinary kind, without any color at all.

The falluquero heard a shot from the house. He looked up and heard another and it seemed but a moment before he found himself at the door and did not remember crossing the yard. A miner stood outside, wiping his brow, and spoke some kind of warning but the falluquero went past. Dolores was half-sitting on the stairs as though she might flee. She held a pistol and a man lay on the floor.

The falluquero held up his hands.

—I've come to help, he said. He took a step and she shook the pistol and he ducked without thinking and straightened up again. There were other men behind him. They crowded the doorway, and Dolores' eyes flicked from one to another. One of the miners said he had a gun and the falluquero told him to put it away.

—Stay out, he said. Váyanse, todos.

The men did not go. Dolores kept the weapon raised and he knew she was watching his eyes and hands and he was careful to look at her face alone. He heard the murmuring of those behind him and he did not move. She kept the pistol on him and watched his mouth and he did not know what she might understand. Perhaps her own name.

—Dolores.

He started forward and something spun him and threw him down with a whipcrack and he lay breathless on the floor inside the four wooden walls with the ceiling turning above him. His vision washed red and he was confused, imagining that he looked into the fire. Somewhere a woman was keening but it was not quite the sound of a woman. A fox or young rabbit caught. He lay pinned, ears ringing, blood decanting from his shoulder and the thirsty wood beneath him taking it up. When he opened his eyes, time had leapt again and the feet of men thundered around him and he put his hand to the shoulder where the bullet had passed through. His palm came away bloody and the world took a turn and he found himself standing inexplicably in the graveyard, high above the valley floor, the miners like tiny men with their eyes raised to watch him. A wooden bowl was in his hand. He threw earth into the air, winnowing and catching, and gave a loud huh! when it landed.

Las Flechas

SIERRA DE SAN FRANCISCO

— 1883 —

The cattle of the Sierra de San Francisco have no memory of their grandfathers. They do not recall the priests who sailed their long-horned ancestors across the Vermilion Sea, along with soldiers and wives and children, to build a mission. They have no tales of men who tended the first cattle, men who called themselves gente de razón—people of reason—and how in this lonely frontier every poor man at once became a don, and every woman a lady. The gente de razón settled below the sierras and built a town called San Ignacio. They fashioned a small church of thatch, and the thatch gave way to adobe, and the adobe at last to the great church of stone, built by the Cochimí. When the soldiers retired from service, they became mayordomos—foremen who watched the Indians work the mission ranches, high in the sierras upon the Spine of the World.

Before the cattle and before the Jesuits, before the gente de razón, even before the Cochimí, there were the painters. They painted vast murals upon the canvas of rock. They re-created the world. They painted and overpainted with slurries of hematite, of manganese. They harvested paint from the rock, and to the rock it returned. The painters rendered giant things upon the canyon walls: the mountain sheep and the deer, the turtle and the whale, the shaman and the ordinary man and woman. They painted their longing for the time of the gigantes, the revered ones who had come before them. An individual hand, an individual artist did not matter. Every person added to the whole. And what became of the painters no one knows.

On the feast day of San Carlos Borromeo, the falluquero rode through the Sierra de San Francisco on his way to Rancho La Falda, coaxing the string of mules over the dry tablelands. Their bells went ringing down through the arroyos and to the heights again, and the mules snatched little leaves from the scrub as they went along.

The falluquero cricked his sore shoulder and looked down into the gorge. Rancho La Falda—the Ranch of the Slope—was not the kind of ranch with vast grasslands for cattle. It lay below cliffs of red, russet, and black, dotted with scrub and cacti and the branches of leguminous trees. But cattle lived there still. The ranch was a tiny thing buried in the bowl of the earth, as if the people had fallen into the chasm with it.

The falluquero had not come to Rancho La Falda in four years. Even so, his conscience pricked him, for the people of the sierras were his own people, and to make a living he must charge them a high price for every item he carried—tin and kerosene and coffee and all that could not be raised or fashioned or grown on a ranch. In exchange he took the art of their hands: saddles and teguas and gloves and reatas and goat cheese and embroidered cloths to cover the cheese. For a time, the falluquero gave up the trade. But he could not escape it. He had a way with people, as other men had a way with horses or mules. He cajoled them with story and charm, and carried away what little they had.

Now he could see the brown line of goats going up the trail on the other side, and the white speck of a woman's skirt. It must be Noni below, driving the animals out to graze. Poor Noni still at the ranch. Se quedará para vestir santos. Forever a saint-dresser, an old maid. He looked again. The boy was not with her. He heard the goat bells and the woman's cry: Ya! Chiva! The goats funneled up the trail and the white skirt followed. The mules lifted up their ears.

His train of animals began their descent and they went more quickly now. La caponera—the bell jennet—led the way, and their hooves sent loose stones tumbling. If he had wanted to, he could have started a little avalanche, just a small one of pebbles, to let the family know he was coming. But he went on in silence.

He thought about the gold mines of Calmallí, where nothing had worked out. Those wild hand-miners, those gambusinos—in the end they found only adarme. A whit. A speck of nothing. Something conspires to keep things from working out, he thought. The one that is born to be hanged shall never be drowned. Something conspires.

Noni stood on the trail above the ranch and spied a rider on the other side, a dark form descending. She shaded her eyes, and at once she knew the man. She stood forgetting the goats as they trotted up the trail by themselves. There was not one thing about the man that she liked. Yet she turned and went down toward the house.

Not long ago, her brothers spoke of the falluquero: I saw him in town. He's the same old tale-teller, he really had us going. Now he's at Calmallí, did you know there's gold there? He won't come trading to us anymore. He'll be rich. To the bold man, fortune gives her hand.

The family gathered in the shade under the thatched eaves: Noni's father Old Tino and her mother Ignacia; the elder brothers Juan Nepomuceno and Tomás, come from their own ranches; and the brothers still at home, who traveled two mule days to visit their novias in San Ignacio where Noni had never been. She kept to the kitchen and heard the animals and the bells of the animals, the shout of the falluquero, and Ignacia calling: Well, lucky the eyes that see you!

Noni looked out. The younger brothers took the mules and went hurrying so they wouldn't miss any of the news. Old Tino struggled up from his seat to shake the falluquero's hand, and Juan Nepomuceno and Tomás greeted him too. Noni ducked inside, and when she looked again, little Carlitos was sitting on the falluquero's lap.

—Come here, mijo, she said.

Carlitos wouldn't come. The falluquero looked at her and away.

—¿De dónde has venido? Tino asked.

The falluquero gestured expansively. All over, he said. To the coast. Eye of the Hare. Malarrimo.

He leaned forward, tipping his head like a bird listening to the ground. Noni could never recall him making such a gesture. He squeezed Carlitos and said, You can't imagine the things that wash up at Malarrimo. Bottles, a mound of glass bottles let loose from the hands of drunken sailors all over the world. Red trees, giant trees. And whale bones, enough to make a whole new whale out of them.

—No me digas, Ignacia said with wonder.

—The tide brings them. Piles of china. Glass globes the japoneses use for fishing.

Noni did not want to listen, but she could not stop imagining the mountain of bottles, and the globes, and the whale. The falluquero looked at her and winked. He put a bean on the back of his hand and slap! The bean jumped into his mouth.

—Again! Carlitos cried.

Tomás tried a bean on the back of his hand. The brothers called their encouragement, and Noni saw the falluquero turn away. His face became like other weary men she knew, the folds and crevices worn into deep arroyos around his mouth and on his brow. She could see in his face how Carlitos would look as an old man, sad and serious. She saw anguish behind the falluquero's gesturing hands and bright eyes, and she did not know what it was.

—Today is Carlitos' saint day, she said.

—He knows that, Ignacia said.

The falluquero's eyes turned bright again and he said to Carlitos: That is why I brought you something.

He pulled from his satchel a tiny blue bottle and blew across the top and produced a note. Noni went back to the kitchen. She stood by the fire, a tin cup hanging from her hand, and she felt the ache of sorrow rising. She didn't move or say a single thing to spoil it.

—What's wrong with you? her mother asked.

In the darkness of predawn, Noni left Carlitos sleeping and went out under the half-moon. The night sang with frogs. With no light she stole along the arroyo, and she knew every pool and palm and stone.

She came to a dry spillway in the rock, worn smooth from eons of stormwater tumbling down from the mesas. She climbed the spillway and went carefully along the high trail, above the canyon and the trembling green heads of the palms. She could hear goat bells and the echo of bells, as if from a herd of goat spirits answering.

The paintings lay upon the canvas of the rock: vultures with spread wings, and deer bucking and running with hooved feet and even the little dewclaws painted on. Borregos with fat curved horns. A whale of the kind the falluquero spoke of. There were outlines of rabbits half-done, as though the painters had never gotten back to finishing. Where the rock curved upward, the animals went scurrying on the ceiling over her head.

Giant men towered on the wall above, black and red and some half of each. None had a face. They were only outlines of men filled in, with their arms raised. In the middle stood a red man in a dark cap, pierced by arrows all over his body. The man of Las Flechas. Darts shot through his head and shoulders and even through his middle.

She carried a votive from her mother's altar. She placed it in a circle of stones, and when the wind quieted, she lit the wick. She told the man of arrows about a place where tides brought curious things. She spoke of japoneses who labored in the sea with globes of glass. She talked of red trees and a mountain of bottles. At last there was no more to say. She sat beside the man of arrows and stroked her arms against the morning chill.

In the evening when work was finished, the men gathered under the eaves. They ate their supper, and the women ate after them, and all settled in to hear the falluquero. Noni stood in the doorway and held Carlitos close.

—Tell about the mines of Calmallí, Tomás said.

The falluquero put a cigarillo to his lips and said, There is nothing much interesting to say about Calmallí.

Tomás looked disappointed. The falluquero looked at Noni and said, Unless getting shot is something interesting.

The younger brothers crowded in. The falluquero pulled his shirt aside. On the lean shoulder lay a dark wound, old and dry and pulling inward toward itself. Noni stood half in the doorway, looking at the wound.

—What do you think, Noni? the falluquero asked. Yo soy bandido.

—I'm a bandit, Carlitos said. The falluquero shaped his hand like a gun and pointed it to Carlitos' shoulder and cried, Pum! The boy fell to the ground and kicked his legs.

—Who shot you? Juan Nepomuceno asked.

The falluquero looked from face to face with a half smile. Noni saw the way he turned his head, and she knew then that he could not hear from one ear but would not say so. She saw a flicker of torment pass his face. He looked at her and she at him. He seemed as one needing absolution, who cannot bear to ask and hopes the other will know, and that will be enough.

Noni did not sleep. The falluquero lay just on the other side of the wall, perhaps also not sleeping. She got up. A dog came lonely and wagging into the room and she pushed it aside. Quietly she went through the orchard and down to the arroyo, a road of white under the moon. Palms rustled in the night. Bats flitted down and flew again into the stars.

She climbed the spillway. She had guarded many thoughts to share with the man of arrows, but could not recall a single one. What appeared instead were animated hands, worn from work and ropes and tanning hides. Eyes the color of brown sugar and cigarillos on the wind. A warm evening in an orchard long ago, and words that were spoken and not spoken.

In the moonlight Noni examined the man of arrows. The rockface was cracking, white with guano where the tiny feet of bats had found purchase. She feared one day she might find the man fallen, broken on the ground in fragments. But there he remained with his hands in the air, surrounded by animals that were somehow free of arrows. She thought the man had taken all the arrows into himself.

—Don't be so somber, Ignacia said to Noni. Laugh a little at his stories. He has been away a long time. Don't you want him to come back?

Old Tino came into the kitchen and poked the coals. The brothers came to take some fruit. Juan Nepomuceno looked out to where the falluquero was sitting.

—It is a good night for a walk, he said to Noni.

Tomás chuckled. A lucky night, he said.

—Déjenla, her father said, and shooed them out.

Noni put out the fire. She finished washing and went down to the arroyo. The sun had fallen and all was in shadow. Water slipped over the rocks, and brown beetles spun in the pool like tiny turtles. It was the season for harvestmen; the spiders marched over the stones like little beans on legs. Noni could hear laughter from the house, the voice of the falluquero telling his stories, the brothers adding their embellishments. She could smell the smoke of his cigarillo, drifting down to her like fingers on the warm wind. She stayed in the clearing, where anyone from the house could easily see that she was in the moonlight all by herself.

They met in the orchard among the date palms. The hairs on Noni's arm stood on end, as before a storm. He helped her lie down. One of the dogs padded near, and the falluquero raised his hand and it darted away. He smelled of tobacco and his hands were light and moving, as if telling one of his tales.

Her hand slipped beneath his shirt, over the wound. The air was alive with the pulse of frogs. She heard the caw of the huitlacoche, ugly and shrill, and the barking of dogs. She heard the cry of a young goat, so like the cry of a child, and burro bells and the rushing of palms. She dared not move. He did not hurry away. He lay back and blew a breath of smoke, and Noni watched it weave among the stars.

There is no sunrise in the bowl of the earth. Only a gradual blush over the jagged black line of the rim, and then the stars disappear. Noni woke before the falluquero, and the moon hung low over the ridge. The family rooster was not fooled by the moon. It began to crow, and little birds began their songs in the half-light.

They lay under palm trees with dead leaves hanging about the trunks like gray beards. The trees dropped their small fruits like rain. Noni did not look at him. The falluquero opened his eyes.

—Was there something you wanted to say, he said.

She kept silent. He had a cholla thorn through the fabric of his sleeve, both ends showing, straight as a needle. She pulled out the thorn and held it.

—This kind clings, she said. Hurting you over and over.

He put his face in his hands. Finally he said that yes, it was so. He sat up and took a cigarillo and smoked it and looked for another.

—You found no fortune, Noni said.

—No.

—Who shot you, Noni asked.

The falluquero said only that he might have been killed. How he had known many men who had died, of old age or accidents. Men of the sierras. They had died in their own place and had known all of their lives that they would die there, and that was a kind of peace. He said how this thinking had frightened him, because even at the very moment when he lay on the ground with the blood spilling from his body, there was pleasure in knowing that if the pistol did indeed kill him, he would die in that place and not this one. A story would be told of him, and thus he would be remembered.

He sat as a man of stone, as a man riveted before the pistol that had thrown him down. Noni leaned close. She spoke to him of Adam's branch that looks dead to the eye, no different than a twig cut off, lying on the ground alone. But it is not dead. It is only waiting for its chance. And should a little rain come, even just a little, it seizes the chance and bursts into flower.

At midmorning the falluquero rounded his animals, and the brothers helped load his things. Old Tino shook his hand. Noni watched from the doorway.

—Stay away from those violentos, Ignacia said. Y que Dios le acompañe.

The falluquero said that God would indeed accompany him. He thanked her for the blessing and patted Carlitos.

—This time you'll hit it big, Tomás said.

The falluquero raised his hand to them, but his eyes were on Noni.

—Que Dios le acompañe, she said. She raised a hand to him so that he might know.

He went riding off through the brush. A dog from the ranch followed until he took the trail out of the canyon, and then it turned back and the falluquero began to sing.

Noni rode with Carlitos along the canyon bottom under striped cliffs, around boulders swept down the arroyo in terrible rains, boulders as large as the ranch house. Tiny bushes grew in the shade of their broad bottoms like chicks around the skirt of a mother hen.

—Vamos a las pinturas?

—Yes, to the paintings, Noni said.

—I'm a bandit, Carlitos said.

The gait of the mule was easy. It rattled over stones upon hard hooves that were like stones themselves. Running water sang in the depressions, and the pools were green with algae. Palms stretched upward on their skinny necks.

Noni lifted Carlitos from the mule and tied the lead rope around the brush. They climbed the spillway.

—We will go como andan las chivas, she said. Like goats.

They sat before the man of Las Flechas. His hands reached to the skies, and the animals ran past. Carlitos yawned and his eyelids drooped. He lay back against Noni's breast and sighed. She heard the hoot of an owl that sounded just like its name, búho. She heard slow-moving water and the chirp of a cricket. Carlitos stirred and she soothed him until he quieted.

She told the boy of a mystery. Why someone full of arrows does not fall. Why such a person might even stand with hands in the air. How this kind of power is nothing to despise. How one pierced with arrows, with many arrows, can live.

La Pistolera

CALMALLÍ

— 1883 —

The falluquero had sold the mule train and came from the high sierras with only the wild-eyed sorrel who had been the strongest of the lot and the wheat-colored mule who was prone to kick. The trail was a narrow scar on the western hill and they came switchbacking down in the heat, the mules jutting over the canyon at the narrow bends and pivoting the four cautious hooves which seemed to have sensibilities of their own. He carried a leather pouch of coins that he checked and rechecked until he poured the coins into his shirt pocket and felt the heat of them against his breast.

He stretched his arm in its painful socket. He told himself Dolores would not be there, that she would not see him even if she were. But he urged the mules along at a pace faster than a man who carries no intention.

From atop the hill at Calmallí, he saw the gold camp as he had known it only a short month before. Miners labored under the sun beneath broad hats, pitting the land with their tools and tossing dust to the wind. There were more men than he remembered, and some straightened to watch him. He nodded and touched his hat brim as a mayordomo might greet his workers, and he lifted a hand.

In the far corner of the cemetery lay a sizeable cairn of stones with a lettered cross of wood. The tomb of don Tránsito. The falluquero smiled but caught himself and removed his hat. Then he noticed a new grave, a mound of turned earth with a smaller wooden cross exhibiting some scratching he could not make out. He dismounted quickly and knelt, but the grave was not hers.

He replaced his hat and looked down at the wooden house. Three horses circled in the corral, and a wagon stood where none had been before. He saw a pen of goats, curtains at the windows, and a cage of doves, swinging under the eaves. It was the same house, made grander in his absence and adorned with comforts perhaps purchased with the inheritance of a deceased husband. Or perhaps purchased by a new bridegroom.

The sun suddenly sickened him. He urged the animals down, coming into the yard and securing the lead ropes to the amarradero in front of the house. He had no courage to try the door. He recalled how Dolores, out of fear and misunderstanding, had leveled the pistol at him and let it fire. Now a rope latch hung at the door, dangling outside in what seemed a gesture of welcome. He pulled the rope and stepped inside.

She was working at the counter with her back to him. He saw that her hair had been cut and he felt a pang of grief until she turned. This woman was older than Dolores, and had the round face of one well-fed. She wiped down a bottle and looked at him not unkindly. There was one caneback chair by the wall and he took it and she brought him a dipper of water.

—I was looking for a woman who used to live here, he said.

—You and the world entire.

He looked around. Goods hung from the walls: sacks of beans and chiles and corn, clothing traded and now laundered, hats in mid-repair. Bottles of aguardiente stood on the counter beside a photograph of the new proprietor, a suited figure preserved upon a legacy of tin, reposing in an attitude of leisure with chin upon hand.

—My husband, she said. The brother of don Tránsito, que en paz descanse.

He got up and paced the room. He looked at the bottles and the small shining tumblers and he wanted a drink but did not want the woman to suppose he was careless.

—So you have come to find La Pistolera, the woman said.

—La Pistolera?

—So they call her. But I do not believe the stories men tell about what women do.

She said the whole territory now talked of a woman who had killed three men or perhaps more. Such stories had a way of growing, and soon there might be ten or twenty men dead in the telling. It was said La Pistolera could hear nothing from the world of men but other forces spoke to her from beyond. Had he not heard the songs? Of pounding hearts and slain lovers and a great mane of hair that encircled the unwary. She said something else the falluquero did not catch and he inclined his head.

—Are you deaf too? she said.

—I had a hard fall.

Her brow furrowed with concern and he glanced away.

—She shot me, he said.

—That is a surprise.

—It was to me.

She laughed. He said he had little memory of what happened after he fell, of who had taken him to another village and tended him.

—So you are one of the men in the stories, the woman said. In the songs.

He looked at her in surprise. Then he smiled. He said he did not believe he was. But he asked what the songs said, how widely they were known. The woman waved an indifferent hand.

He looked around at the shop, at the wares and the well-apportioned woman so established and the new inheritor of Calmallí in his wooden frame. He thought for a moment. He asked again about the songs, and the newfound notoriety of Dolores who he said was a friend. Before the woman could answer, he asked if he might trade one of his unruly mules for the smallest horse in the yard.

—I came to accompany Dolores home, he said. To Pabellón.

—You came to take her home, bringing animals she cannot ride?

He swallowed and passed a hand over his face.

—She has gone her way without the assistance of any man. With her own stake of gold.

—For my help I would not need to be paid.

She said he should not speak of payment and a woman in the same utterance and he apologized.

—I wonder why a man would pursue La Pistolera, she said, unless he wished to attach himself to a renown that does not belong to him.

He started to protest but she was already taking a tin of beans from beneath the counter, and a bag of machaca and a clean handkerchief with loose tobacco. She pushed the items toward him, and he handed her some coins which she counted. He went to the door and she followed, putting a hand on his arm.

—Oye, hijo, the woman said. She does not want to be conquered.

—Weren't you yourself conquered? he asked.

—No, she said. I am the conqueror!

Had he traveled for himself he would have passed through Calmallí Viejo where the spring lay, through San Sebastián and Paraíso along the old Camino Real into the sierras which was the more arduous route but held a greater share of water. But he went west toward the coast, the way don Tránsito had come with Dolores from Pabellón, along the road she would have remembered. He crossed the field of abandoned mines: La Esperanza, Victoria, Ascensión. He passed sleeping circles the Cochimí had made, rings of red rock standing on end, and he searched each one in hopes of seeing the shoeprint of a woman.

The ranches were few and he stopped at each to inquire. All had heard of La Pistolera but none had seen her. They gathered around and asked what he knew. He said La Pistolera had sought to do business with him. He had held the gold stake in his own hand. Had they not heard the songs . . .

At one ranch they asked to see the wound. The men admired it, and the women said he was fortunate, for many had fallen under the bullets of La Pistolera. He said he was not afraid, that perhaps he was the only man from whom she would accept help. He took their offerings of tortillas and goat meat, and as he departed, children ran with him until the path met the trail and they were permitted no farther. But he remembered how they had looked to him.

Now he recalled a young man and his sister who had a ranch beneath a dark mesa along an arroyo draining water from the sierras, good people with whom he had enjoyed a shared esteem. He followed the arroyo until he came upon the house, a square of palm-roofed adobe with an open kitchen in the shade of its ramada. He saw the brother working in a corral where mules milled about, and the sister sitting in the shadow of the palo San Juan tree with a washtub before her. The man waved and called to the sister and they came out to meet him.

The brother clapped his arm and shook his hand.

—Falluquero! How goes the trade?

—I am no longer a trader, the falluquero said.

—A pity, the brother said. The world needs respectable men in that profession.

The falluquero said he had gone to Calmallí for a time. He sought a woman with no one to help her, a woman who had gone walking.

The sister looked to the house and back again. She asked who was inquiring and for what reason. The brother silenced her with a frown and apologized. He invited the falluquero to the house.

The doorway was narrow and the lintel nearly at eye level, as if to accommodate some smaller people of the past. The falluquero ducked under and stepped inside. The only light came from the door and it took a moment for his eyes to adjust and there on a rawhide cot in the corner sat Dolores. One foot was elevated, bare and swollen. She had already recognized him and her face displayed a disappointed weariness. She put her head to the wall where curled and faded pictures of saints were hanging, and she looked away.

Her brow bore the dark patches of a sunburn some days gone, and her face was drawn with pain and trouble. He did not know how she had become so gaunt in a short time. He took off his hat.

—She had a cholla thorn, the brother said. We got it out.

The sister took the falluquero's arm and held it close in confidence. He leaned in to hear.

—La Pistolera, she whispered.

Dolores struggled up, holding the wall. She hopped once on the swollen foot, and the falluquero offered a hand, but she skirted around him and hobbled outside.

—I guess if you don't hear, you don't have to listen, the brother said.

The falluquero followed her out. She sat in a chair at the edge of the eaves, braiding and unbraiding the ends of her hair, and a dog settled at her feet. The falluquero took the chair beside her, and the dog looked up but she didn't.

He wanted to tell her that he understood she had not meant to hurt him. That the world knew him as a man surpassing the station God had granted him, and the accusation was not unfounded. He said that perhaps he had harbored some idea of glory when he first arrived, but now he had no pretense other than to fulfill her wish of going home.

She stared off. He plucked her sleeve and this time she gave a single angry utterance. The dog got up and slunk around the corner of the house. With a small motion the falluquero gestured north, and pointed at himself and at her, and with a quick hand she silenced him though he had not said a thing. She got up and went slowly down toward the corrales.

The brother had been standing there. The sister came with cups and two squares of dates wrapped in brown paper.

—My brother does not care that we are soon to be made infamous by this association, she said.

The man turned to the falluquero.

—What has she against you? he said.

—I do not know. I came from the sierras with the intention of bringing her home.

The brother looked at him for a moment. He said there was no need for the falluquero to trouble himself because he knew the district of Pabellón well and would deliver the woman safely, as hospitality required.

—You wear me out, the sister said. Your Samaritan ways.

—You would send her away by herself? the brother said.

—Por el amor de Dios, she said. Then let this other man go.

She pointed to the corral where Dolores was standing.

—You see that little red mule, she said to the falluquero. The hinny.

She said the mule was hers and hers alone. She said La Pistolera had approached her with coins, and she would have sold the animal on the spot if not for her brother. She gave the falluquero a look of gravity.

The brother turned to her.

—Will you prepare supper, he said.

In the morning, the falluquero found the red hinny saddled in front of the house. The brother leaned silent and grim in the doorway and the sister bustled about. Dolores waited in a chair, wearing a man's hat and holding a satchel and some foodstuffs the sister had prepared.

The sorrel mule was already saddled, and the sister handed the falluquero a packet like the one Dolores held. He said his thanks and Dolores stood up but would not look at him. He laced his fingers and she put her good foot into his hands and he lifted her into the saddle. She gazed straight ahead.

—Que Dios le acompañe, the sister said. See that you make her eat.

—I will.

Down at the corral, his wheat-colored mule shook its head and called a mournful cry, but the falluquero was already setting out with Dolores following. He looked back as they rode into the arroyo, but the brother had gone inside and offered no hand of farewell.

They passed through stands of green cirios, set in the ground like taper candles in leaf, and these gave way to creosote and at last to low gray brush near the coast. At every rise, Dolores' mule tried to turn around until the falluquero dismounted and tethered the animals together. They set out again under a cloudless sky. He thought of the villages they would eventually pass, the people who might receive them. He started to whistle but stopped until he remembered that Dolores could not hear him.

He talked to her as they rode. He told of his travels, of Malarrimo and the whale bones, and bottles that sailed the world like seagoing ships. He spoke of the Vermilion Sea, and the heights of the Sierra de San Francisco, and the great volcano of the Three Virgins. Toward evening he looked back and she was asleep. When he stopped the animals, she opened her eyes.

—We are on the road, he said. As I promised.

Another woman would have smiled at him, but her gaze was fixed on the trail ahead as if he were not leading her at all. The wind had come up. She twisted her hair into a low thick braid that did not reveal her ears. When she looked up, he smiled. She put on her hat and pulled the brim low.

At sunset they stopped on a rise overlooking the sea, the red palisades of the sierras distant behind them. He halted the animals.

—Let's get down, he said. Let's have something to eat.

She made no move of agreement but he dismounted anyway and waited beside the little red mule until Dolores slid down. He steadied her and took his hands away quickly. She began gathering what branches lay near for a fire.

After they had eaten, she sat with her chin upon her knees, watching the moon flow up from the sea. She brushed her cheek and he looked closer but she was not crying. He wished he might sing something that would ease her mind. Instead he talked of the shop woman of Calmallí, and the brother and sister, and how none of them had viewed him as a man of principle but here he was doing what he had promised.

The wind kicked up and sand peppered their faces. Her ankle had swelled and she pulled off the shoe, turning her foot to examine it, and the falluquero saw that the wound was red at the edges but not dangerously so. She took a cloth from her satchel and wrapped her foot. He offered a hand but she got up and moved to the other side of the fire.

—Why will you not take a man's hand, he said. What is the harm?

He crouched in front of her and pulled his shirt to the side, exposing the wound, the whole of his shoulder red in the firelight.

—Está bien, he said. No trouble at all.

She noted the scar without regard, as though she had not been the one to throw him down. She brushed off her dress and made a slow path to the water.

He took two steps after her and asked had he not been honorable. Was he not doing what she wanted. She kept going, and he shouted into the wind. The sand needled him. His hands fell to his sides. She had left her satchel beside the dying fire, its top cord pulled shut like the pucker of a mouth. He picked it up and put his hand inside.

The bag held a store of dried beef which she had not shown him. A ribbon which he had never seen her wear. A head covering of worn lace and a comb carved of bone. A smaller bag. He poured a measure of corn into his hand and poured it back.

She had seen him. She minced toward him on the wounded foot, hurrying, and he pulled out a thin piece of wood with burned edges and a small drawing in ink of an old man seated against the wall of a house, holding a riata or a cord. Braiding as old men do.

She came at him and snatched the sketch, turning it over and over as if he might have harmed it. She sliced the air with a finger. Repudiating or excising him. Her eyes were half-closed against the blowing sand and he could see her chest rise and fall. He stood right before her and still she would not meet his eye.

—I have done you no wrong, he said. None that I know of.

He laid hold of her wrist. She snapped free and stepped back and nearly stumbled, speech pouring from her lips, haranguing him in an unknown tongue. She went a distance off and lay down with the satchel beneath her head, putting an arm over her eyes.

—No wrong that I know, he said again.

He lay near the cooling fire and sang a ballad to himself. He must have slept, for when the sun had scarcely risen she was already mounted on the red mule without his help and she did not wait for him. He hurried to pack the gear, calling after her, and league upon league he followed and not once did she turn.

They kept to the road for the days that followed. Once, he stopped at a ranch to purchase provisions. The couple there inquired of the curious woman in a man's hat who rode on without the man she traveled with. The falluquero said that she was greatly admired for her many deeds, known throughout the district, and he was her guardian. When he caught up to Dolores, he tried to ride abreast but she spurred the mule with her heels.

They were coming to El Rosario and the mud houses began to multiply, set back from the road, small homesteads with cattle reclining in the shade of the mesquite. They passed the old mission of El Rosario de Abajo, the ancient place called Viñatacót of the Cochimí. Bells hung from their memorial tree before the ruins, and the chapel interior was flayed open to the sky.

They came to a crossing and a street more populous. The falluquero recalled how in a former year the men of this village had slighted him, though he came with goods and animals of his own. Now a man came walking alongside and asked where they'd come from.

The falluquero returned the greeting and said he was not at liberty to say. Only that he was taking this woman home. The man drifted back and the falluquero saw him conversing with two women on the stoop of a house. Dolores watched them.

—You'll be all right, he said. Stay close.

She rode ahead. He spurred forward and caught the rein. She tried to pull away but the mule was weary and would not obey. They sat on their mounts in the street. At the corner the falluquero saw a house with a lettered sign. A place to eat, a place where people gathered. Dolores held her mouth in a hard line and he extended an empty hand.

—We have no more provisions, he said.

She studied the house. She took three coins from her pocket and indicated that he should go himself, but he prompted the animals and they went willingly to the signpost where he secured them. She looked to the end of the street, and the dry mesas beyond, and finally she slid down by herself.

The cantina was an ample room with a good roof of woven palm and a wooden counter with a mirror behind. A curtain of braided ribbon separated off a patio where the cooking was done. A sofa of threadbare velvet sat in the corner with sunken impressions in the cushions as if to mark the places of previous occupants. The whole place struck the falluquero as though it might have once been the home of a person of means.

A group of men were seated at a table in the center and they glanced up to assess him. They were councilmen or prominent men and he saw they were at business with receipts spread out before them.

He put a gentle hand to Dolores' elbow and she took the first chair near the door. He saw her reading the faces. The men glanced up again and the falluquero paused in expectation of a word, a nod from one man of consequence to another. But they returned to their glasses of aguardiente, speaking in low voices as if any kind of talk was not for him to hear.

A stout woman who the falluquero took to be the cocinera emerged from behind the curtain, and when she saw Dolores she registered some surprise. Dolores got up and the cocinera came over to put a hand on her arm.

—I owe this woman an apology, the cocinera said.

She told the falluquero she had treated Dolores poorly on another occasion, that the woman's husband paid for bathing and dressing and she had handled Dolores in a rough manner. She said no person deserved such treatment no matter who she is. Or would become. Around the woman's neck hung a wooden cross, and she held it with an earnest hand and placed the other hand upon her heart. Dolores looked at her and nodded and sat down.

The falluquero was watching the other table. Some aguardiente for those men, he said.

The cocinera looked over. Hijo, she said. Leave those men be.

—Aguardiente, he said again. He fished some coins from his pocket, and the cocinera glanced once at Dolores and went to the back. She came out with tortillas and venison and a bowl of caldo which she set before Dolores, and a bottle which she took to the men. One of them asked who was buying. Another looked at the falluquero and said in a loud voice that the matrero—the wild thing in the corner—was the one.

The falluquero started over and one of the men waved him off and said something he could not hear. He lingered at the table's edge while they drank, and none so much as raised a glass to his health.

—I am no matrero, the falluquero said.

One of the men smiled. Bueno, he said. So you are no matrero.

The falluquero asked what business occupied them, saying he was a businessman himself. The man pushed back his chair in a clatter of annoyance.

—What is it you want?

—Where I am from, the falluquero said, one man thanks another.

—And where is that.

The falluquero hesitated. He said he had come from Calmallí.

—Not a matrero then, the man said. Un tejón. A digger.

The falluquero turned to Dolores. She was watching, sitting halfway on her seat. The eyes of the man followed the falluquero's gaze, taking in Dolores' travel-worn dress and the swollen ankle and the voluminous hair beneath the broad hat. The man stood.

—Can that woman speak?

The falluquero said she could, but was not inclined to. He said they traveled together, and they might have been wealthy but had left those concerns behind in favor of her dearest wish and he was taking her home.

The man came over to Dolores and the others gathered behind him. She rose from her chair and looked from one face to another.

—Señora, the man said. He snapped his fingers. He reached for her hair and she ducked back and her hand went to the pocket of her dress but found no weapon there and the man smiled. The cocinera stepped between them.

—You have drunk yourself blind, the cocinera said. This woman is not of interest to you.

The falluquero put himself forward and said there were stories of this woman that were beyond belief, yet he himself was part of those stories. He bore a wound now the subject of song. The cocinera put a hand on him. She turned to the men.

—For years I have known this woman. She is quiet as they say.

The falluquero shook free but the cocinera was already leading the men back to their table and filling the glasses. The falluquero followed and stood holding the crossrail of a vacant seat. He told them he alone knew the truth of what had occurred. The cocinera stepped around him with a new bottle and the men raised shaking glasses to her and returned to the shuffling of their receipts and the low talk which the falluquero could not hear.

The cocinera pulled his sleeve. Come, hijo.

He looked back and Dolores had gone. He scattered a handful of uncounted coins to the table and burst through the swinging doors and out to the street. She was at the mules, struggling with the knots that tied them. Her hat lay on the ground. He caught her arm. A wind came up, channeling along the street, lifting her hair. It was true that she had no outer ears at all and he had imagined that the apertures themselves would be larger but they were only the breadth of something bored by the smallest of awls.

She looked him full in the face. Her eyes were utterly dark even in the midday sun, and her eyes told him everything he was. He was vaguely aware of people passing, men and women and children, he did not know. If they were children he was reduced to one of them. He was uncertain how long she held him there. Later he would imagine it was merely the breath of a moment. She pulled the rope free and took the mule that was hers and mounted up and rode on. He stood in the street, spent and sweating, and she did not look back.

She kept to the coast along the road she remembered, going north. At Valle Tranquilo she saw riders and ducked her head and kept going. From time to time she saw a flash of brown wings, and she watched the Tapacamino flush upward and light upon the trail ahead.

Near Socorro she passed the place where don Tránsito had taken her, down by the sea. She reined the mule. The shore was wide and windswept, and she dismounted and climbed a small rise, looking out to the gray horizon and the waves. She thought of don Tránsito on his deathbed, weeping and gripping her by the hair, and the falluquero who tracked and pursued her and dared to grasp her by the wrist. Now she stood alone. She breathed deeply and knelt and took a handful of sand and released it into the gale. Her hair rose and fell behind her like a dark cope and she gathered it around her against the wind.

She mounted up and went on. In the distance she saw the shining white salt pans and the Bay of Five Hills. She thought of her father and kicked the mule with her heels, turning east into the Arroyo

Pabellón. When she came over the rise, she saw the ranch below and she stopped and drew from her pocket a small weighted bag. At the sight of the corral the mule started down, shaking its head and calling to other animals that might be present.

But there were no animals. Pieces of roof thatch lifted in the breeze and lay back down. Some of the rafters had fallen and the door was missing. The corn was gone. A raven wheeled above as though remembering the field of former years; it dipped and flew on. She got down and went to the door. A half-plaited rope lay on the ground and she picked it up, wondering how long ago his hands had held it. She crouched on the ground under the eaves, holding the rope and putting a hand to her throat.

A shadow passed on the hill. She dried her eyes and got up. She believed a man had been there and she stepped into the sun but saw no one. She looked again to see if her father had come, and when no one appeared, she went into the house.

All had been carried away. The cot where she slept as a child. The table at which her mother sat for supper. The tack her father guarded in the kitchen for fear of loss. She knelt in the corner and began digging. Once, she glanced up, certain that someone watched. She went to the window and saw no one but the mule, crowding into the shade of the house. She returned to the hole and laid down the little bag of gold, covering it with earth, and she trod on the place until there was no sign of it left to be seen.

El Boleo

SANTA ROSALÍA

—1913—

Down in the broad arroyo where the air does not stir, the copper miners of El Boleo company lined up in the barracks yard. They stood in front of the water tank on its tall wooden legs, surrounded by a fence of wire. The afternoon was so hot that everything appeared to be under water. The golden dry hills rippled; the fancy wooden houses on the French Mesa wavered in the heat. On the opposite side of the arroyo, on the Mexican Mesa, wives of government workers lingered outside their homes, fanning themselves. A merchant ship was drawing along the blue line of the sea, nearly lost in a hot white mist.

Men shaded their eyes and looked up. The water truck was coming in a billow of dust, rolling along the road from the solitary spring at Santa Agueda. The overseer Topetes rode ahead on his red horse with its tooled saddle and silver conchos winking in the sun. The miners shuddered in the heat as though in fever: Yaquis and Chinese and Mexican men from Mazatlán and Guaymas and Topolobampo, men who answered the advertisements and believed the promises. Seeing the truck, they edged their metal cans forward with their sandals, wary of the hot handles. Dogs stood with their tongues hanging out, lifting their noses to smell the water.

At the end of the line stood an old woman, a water can before her on the ground. She held her shawl over her head for shade. She watched Topetes giving orders, just a minor Mexican official gesturing grandly this way and that, like a general. When he looked her way, she turned to the soot-covered hat of the man in front of her.

The Yaqui workers got down from the truck, carrying the first of the water barrels. One of them climbed the ladder, and two others passed up the barrels, one man to another, and the man on top emptied the water into the wide mouth of the tank. Topetes dismounted the horse and gave a half-hearted kick at one of the dogs, and with a flourish he opened the spout.

The first man ran forward. Topetes would not turn off the spigot and he clapped and encouraged the miners as though it were some great relay as men jostled and pushed one another so not a drop would fall to the ground. Topetes heckled them with jovial talk, and when it was her turn, doña Dolores thrust her can under the spout and half-filled it, as much as she could carry. He was saying something to her, she knew, but she did not look at him. He kept gesturing and she ducked away and saw him lean down for a long drink, wiping his mouth before turning off the tap. Dogs rushed at the muddy pool, snapping at one another, and Dolores went along the fence, pulling the can behind her, stopping to rest, and going on. Topetes waited for her at the gate. He made the form of a little house with his hands and pantomimed in ridiculous signs: *Your house, it is good, is it not? Is it a good house?*

She had one gesture of hatred and she used it. Topetes was delighted. Ho! he cried, holding up his hands. He pantomimed again: *I am happy for you, happy for you.* She went around him, dragging the can, and made the gesture again when she had gone well past.

She woke in the predawn darkness in her tiny shack at the edge of the barracks. She did not like the house, leaning and windowless, with its small square of dirt in back where no animal could be kept—not even one chicken—because workers must buy all they needed from the company store at company prices.

She braided her hair without light or mirror, feeling for loose gray strands and covering the place where her ears should have been. She sniffed her hands. Her skin smelled of sea turtle meat. She thought of her son, a fisherman who once caught turtles for the French hotel, and her daughter who had helped him. The twin children of don Tránsito of Calmallí. Both children now grown, neither of whom would ever come home again.

She went out without breakfast, going past the barracks and along the wooden sidewalk at the quarter of town where shops lined the street, passing the shuttered doors of the drugstore and the general store, the cantinas and the butcher and the Trianón theater where the French enjoyed their plays and operas. The only light on the street came from the bakery window, casting a bright square on the sidewalk, and she knocked and waited.

Mme. Moulin opened the door. She had a sharp chin and sharp elbows and a sharp look. She pointed to the bucket where Dolores should wash. *Go on, go on.* The fans were already turning on the high wooden ceiling, and women with flushed faces were at the ovens. Dolores took her apron from the wall and went to her table and set to work, pushing the dough with bony hands, cutting and shaping the floured mass into rolls and buns and boules for the French families and the Mexican authorities. She kept count, and when she had rolled the hundredth boule, she took a pebble from her pocket and pushed it into the bun. Later Topetes would come, as he always did, to wink at Mme. Moulin and buy the boules, and one day he would draw the lottery and swallow the stone, or better, crack a tooth in his broad grinning mouth.

He had been there, in the company of the federales and rural police, the day the revolutionaries rode into Santa Rosalía to take the mines away from the French. The rebels came a hundred strong, their faces glorified by the sunrise, kicking up dust and shooting their rifles with bursts of white smoke, shouting the names of this general and that one. Dolores and her son and daughter had watched from the door of the bakery, ducking back as the rebels rode past with powder-blackened faces, their shining cartuchos crossed on their chests like rosaries of brass. Dolores saw Topetes go by, his shirt stained not with blood but with brown tobacco, firing his pistol into the air at nothing.

The rural guard flashed by. She saw men fall in the street as though the bones had been pulled from their legs. One man stopped right in front of them, holding his side like a pose painting in one of the great haciendas, and then he went down. Among the corpses lay a boy whose rifle had been too heavy for him to lift.

Then her son flailed back, and drops of blood fell from his face onto the stoop. He scrambled up; he signed that he was all right. He held a sleeve to his cheek. Dolores got to him first and her hands were trembling but she scolded him, pulling him away from the door. Her daughter jerked the curtain across the window and took her brother's arm and led him to the back, cursing in words and signs, cursing the French and the federales. Dolores brought a damp cloth. Her son said again that he was all right.

By afternoon the revolutionaries were defeated. The federales rode down the street with their rifles, making sure of the dead, and they rounded up the living—whatever rebel they could catch. When a federal man caught sight of her son's bullet-scratched face, they took him too. Dolores could not defend him; she could not say he was not a rebel or a revolucionario. He was not even a miner. He liked to fish, and braided his sister's hair very poorly each morning, and was too thin because he had been ill as a boy.

The federales marched the rebels to the high smokestack on the hill, lining them up along the flue of stone that carried smoke away from the town. The sky was dark with ash, the air metallic and sweet. Men covered their mouths with their sleeves. The soldiers were grave, and the miners were lost in grief, gripping their hats to their chests, their eyes cast down. Dolores' daughter went to the captain, imploring him, berating him, daring to put a hand on him until a federal man blocked her with the stock of his rifle.

Dolores could not make her voice cry out, could not will herself to move. Her hands hung at her sides and her throat had closed upon itself. Her son was at the wall. One of the guardsmen ordered every prisoner to sing a love song, and the ugliest voice—Dolores' daughter told her in shaking signs—would be shot. The captain said no; he cut the air with his finger and not a person dared to taunt the prisoners after that. But Dolores saw her son look at the rebels beside him, their heads bowed with fear, and he stepped forward and sang:

> If to thy window shall come Porfirio Díaz
> give him for charity some cold tortillas;
> If to thy window shall come General Huerta,
> spit in his face and slam the puerta.

Hearing this, the revolutionaries raised a cry of joy and all were shot down as one. Dolores did not see her son fall. She saw the rifles jerk in unison, and the white breath of smoke against the dark sky, and she must have fallen herself, for when she opened her eyes she saw her daughter above, standing firm, chin lifted, shaking the tears from her eyes. Her daughter took her by the arm and got her up. The miners lowered their heads. The federal men stayed at attention, holding their rifles. And Dolores saw Topetes there, a man of meager authority, ambling around in his white pantalones. He had only come to watch. He examined the corpses and then looked down toward the town, as a working man wonders when he shall go to supper. He yawned. Yawned as a man before siesta, or in the heat of a tiresome day. Yawned in the presence of the dead body of her son. When he had seen everything he wanted to see, he picked his way down the hill. Dolores could not forget how he had yawned.

For three days she went to the wall to visit her son. He had died singing. He lay with his mouth still open and his fingers on the ground, severed for the rings of copper. Dolores picked up the fingers and kissed them.

On the fourth day, the director of El Boleo ordered the rural guard to bury the bodies. He must have learned that her son was not a rebel after all, because he gave Dolores a little broken house that no one wanted, and paid for an iron placard to be placed at the grave. Her daughter had read the inscription to her, and there they had argued.

Her daughter said in sharp signs that they could not stay in a town owned by foreigners, much less live in the company of those who had killed her brother. Dolores would not leave the grave of her son. The daughter said Dolores did not love her, that Dolores could not love. But this was not true. She did love, but she was not one given to laugh, not one given to touch. She was harsh with her children when she felt love for them. The more she loved, the more reserved she became, treating them the same as people she did not like. Only after her son had died could she kiss him.

She had not always been so. As a girl, she loved her mother Ana, and her father Elote, and all the children who lived in their house: the lame and the blind and the little ones, and bigger ones who were still small in their minds. Then her mother died, and her father gave the children to passersby, one by one as Dolores cried, and he kept Dolores until she was grown and then gave her away too.

As soon as the placard was placed at her son's grave, her daughter left to join the revolution without saying goodbye. Dolores did not know whether she lived or died. Each night Dolores set out two bowls and filled them with turtle meat, eating one bowl but never touching her daughter's portion, even if she were very hungry. Every evening, she poured out half the water ration behind the house, and the next day she would stand under the hot sun in the water line and drag another heavy can home. That was what she must do, because she had driven her daughter away.

Now the sun was coming up. She worked at her table in the bakery, shaping the breads and watching for Topetes. At midmorning he came, pausing at the window to peer inside, steaming up the glass, coming through the door. He stood at the counter, smiling broadly while Mme. Moulin briskly took three boules from the rack and put them into a bag. She made a mark in her booklet of accounts, and she turned away and Topetes was still talking.

His son came through the door, just a little boy with a bright face under a broad straw hat. Dolores could see him through the glass counter. He had a braided string around one ankle and his feet were bare. He jumped up, trying to see. Topetes handed him a bun. Until today the boy had never eaten a boule; he always preferred the sweet bread. She watched him take a bite and another, and she was just going to exchange him a gingerbread but he ate the boule and was done. Topetes took his own boule whole, stuffing it into his wide mouth, and he winked at Mme. Moulin. He put a hand to his son's back, and they went out.

When they had gone, Dolores upset two trays—one of which contained the hundredth boule—and Mme. Moulin kept haranguing Dolores until she looked away.

In the late afternoon she set out for the cemetery, going slowly up the steep hill to the Mexican Mesa. She wore no shawl or hat, a slow pilgrimage in the final punishing heat of the day. Pausing at each switchback, she looked down at the company barracks of Providencia Camp. Far below, a brown donkey circled a mill, a dusty beast of burden. She saw the hot roof of the metal Eiffel church, the smelter and foundry. The straight lines of the railroad stretching away to the camps of Soledad and Purgatorio. She surveyed the electric plant and the iron machines and the wheels and wooden towers, the golden rock hills where nothing could grow. The harbor with its square-rigged ships and the blue waters of the gulf. She kept climbing, passing the homes of government men.

In front of Topetes' house—not as large as the houses of the French, but a good house with a spacious patio—the little boy sat cross-legged in the yard. He had a string on the ground, laid in a circle, with three small stones inside it. One pebble he held in his hand. He tossed a dark pebble into the air and snatched another from the ground. He kept tossing and snatching, and when he saw Dolores he became serious, showing what he could do. He said something to her and she pointed to her ear and shook her head.

The door of the house was ajar. She did not know if Topetes was home, or the woman who kept his house, and she waited a moment before walking over to the boy. He offered her a pebble but she motioned for him to do it again and he set to throwing. He grabbed all three stones before the tossed one fell, and he was quick and bright. She clapped for him. He scattered the stones with a flourish and threw the dark stone again. The sun was already halfway down to the sea. The boy was getting tired; his eyelids looked heavy and the day was mostly gone. He shook his head and yawned.

In the small stretched face she saw his father Topetes, the same wrinkled brow with the hairline growing nearly to the eyebrows, the same squinting eyes. Topetes of all the men, acting that day as though it did not matter whose son fell, as long as it was not his own. Sons of no consequence, dried-up leaves dropping and blowing away in the wind. Then the boy rubbed the sleep from his eyes and turned into himself again, a boy who might have been any boy, except he was Topetes' son.

A woman came out and brushed her apron and called. She saw Dolores and frowned. She came over and shepherded the boy toward the house, guarding his back with her hand. The boy looked back and the woman scolded him, and she closed the door.

Dolores went slowly on. At the top of the hill she came to the cemetery, a small town unto itself. Markers of copper and iron, some green with age, stood among simple stone memorials and full-size tombs of white surrounded by iron railings, as a house might have. On the opposite hill, she saw the other graveyard where the French were buried; the dead looked at one another across the arroyo that separated them. She walked to the farthest edge to a new grave with a curling metal placard on a spike, so close to the cliff that she feared one day it might tumble down into the sea.

In her pocket she carried one short candle, the kind miners fasten to the metal dishes on their hats, and she struck a matchstick against the headstone and lit the wick, sheltering the flame with her hand against the hot evening breeze. Beneath the ground lay the body of her son, and she placed her hand there.

She looked again to the opposite hill. She could see the long flue of stone, climbing the hill like a rectangular snake. She was too far away to see the dark bloom of blood on the bricks, though she knew the blood was still there. She wished she had not buried her son in sight of the place of his own death. She did not know why she had not defended him, why she had not moved or cried out. She did not know why she had not begged her daughter to stay.

The candle went out and she set it down. A coal vessel was coming into the harbor. She could see officers from the company headquarters going down the road to meet it, and dots of men on the deck. There was no woman among them, and of course her daughter would not come on a coal ship, if she were to come. But she would not come.

Dolores fingered the letters on the metal placard and recalled what her daughter had read to her, the last words she offered before she went away:

nació el 23 de abril de 1884 fallació el 1913 de octubre su madre
y su hermana y sus compañeros le dedican este humilde recuerdo

They had killed her son for nothing. They all killed for nothing. Rebels killed federales, and federal men shot them in return. General striking down general, another one rising up. It meant nothing to be shot; it meant nothing to die. A corpse was a mere footstool. Federales, rebels, pacíficos—it did not matter which side one fought for, or none. The world went on, and no one accounted for the dead, and nothing was ever paid.

She took a handful of pebbles from the grave and put them in her pocket. Then she poured them out and took three rocks of larger size, and these she carried down the hill in the fold of her skirt, passing the house of Topetes and the empty yard where the boy had been playing.

That night, she went out under the scant light of the new moon, going past the wooden barracks where miners had fallen onto their cots in rows like dead men, their sooty clothes still on, some drunk with tequila and others sick and spent. Each window stood open to allow a breath off the sea and she walked carefully past, making her way along the laundry lines, ducking beneath forgotten shirts and torn pantalones suspended like flapping effigies. She passed the metal church, saw the flame of presence in its red globe above the altar, swinging slightly in the breeze from the open door. She spied two men on their knees in the aisle, their arms outstretched in the form of a cross. She wondered what wrong they had committed, and how long the priest said they must suffer.

She went on. She met no one on the road, and when she came to the top of the French Mesa, she paused for a moment in the shadow of the high clocktower of the company headquarters, where the French directors had their offices and maps and telephones and counting machines.

She pulled her shawl tight and kept on. On a rise above the harbor sat the French hotel, a two-story building of wood with fine dark doors to rooms that faced outside, and a verandah where guests could sit and look down to the sea. The room lamps were out; only the entry was lit with a weak electric light. Dolores could see the dim foyer with its mahogany ceiling and the red brocade on the walls. She stood panting from the climb. She took a stone from her pocket and hefted it in her hand.

Something caught her eye and she turned, but it was only a pulley wheel down at the harbor, swinging in the wind and catching the moon. She turned and faced the hotel. Nothing stirred.

The windows were dark, but in the rooms slept distinguished guests of the company, businessmen who came to see the grand enterprise that was the town. In the room at the northern corner lay Topetes with one of the brothel girls, every time the same room, which she knew because when she made deliveries of bread to the hotel she had seen him, even in the afternoon. He was rumored to be generous, and the women asked to go with him, or so Dolores' daughter had said.

She studied the window but no one appeared. The evening watchman had left. The street was still. She threw the rock. It struck the newel post and skittered along the rail. She took another stone from her pocket and threw it and missed and took one more. She threw with all her strength, and this one broke the corner window. A light went on in the hotel, and another, and she saw the frantic shadows of men. She hurried down the hill in darkness, avoiding the road, and when she got to the harbor she hid in the dark of the train house, behind the high wheels. She was breathless, and she covered her mouth and smiled, and then she began to cry.

In the morning when Dolores brought a sack of bread in a handcart to the hotel, the officials were on the second story verandah in front of the very room with its broken window, and Topetes was there. She could see him recounting what happened, telling and retelling the story, imitating himself in bed and sitting suddenly upright, shielding his face from the broken glass, checking himself for injury, hurrying to the window. Grandiose and postulating on who it might have been. Blaming perhaps the miners who painted ¡Viva Madero! on the narrow-gauge railroad cars, those humble guerrillas the federales could never catch, those who read opposition newspapers which came in the backpacks of sailors from the merchant ships.

She lifted the handles of the cart, but Topetes saw her and gestured, and the federal men turned. Now Topetes was coming down the stairs. She couldn't move, she couldn't hide. He was at the cart and he put a hand on the prow. She looked up. He reached into the sack and pulled out a boule, and tucked it under his arm and reached for another. He was talking and gesturing all the while, never solemn, never one for gravity. *You brought this all for me? For me?*

Topetes' boy had come down the stairs. He stood windmilling his arms and looking at the ships in the harbor. Her throat caught. Topetes' son, who would grow and live to a golden age, to see his own children, to take care of his father when he became feeble, while her own son lay as dry bones in the ground.

Topetes was thanking her for the bread. He handed her a coin. *For you, just for you. Hide it, put it in your pocket.* He thought only of bread. For her son he had not paid and would never pay. A shabby house, a coin, a yawn—that was all that was given for the life of her boy.

He was already going off with the federal men toward the company office, telling and retelling. Topetes' boy was still there, looking down to the harbor. She watched him, a thin figure in short pants, barefoot, with knees dry and gray from kneeling, lost in his own dreams as he looked out to sea. He knew nothing of her son, of all that had occurred. But he was the son of Topetes and he must do.

She beckoned him to the rear of the hotel and he followed. The cook took the sack of bread from the cart and wrote in his account book, holding the stub of a pencil with fat fingers, and she mimed that he should give the boy something. The cook brought three hard-candies wrapped in red papers. She gave the boy one and pocketed the two. The cook waved her off and she left the cart there.

Now the boy came along, talking as they walked down the hill. He pretended to toss a pebble into the air, practicing, and looked to see if she was watching. She nodded to encourage him. When he started to skip away, she held out a candy and he took it.

It's good, good, he said.

He kept along with her, through Providencia Camp and past the shops and all the way to the foot of the Mexican Mesa, to the switchback road, and she imagined he believed she was taking him home. Some stones were heaped in a pile where they had slid down from the heights. She picked among the rocks and selected one of medium size and she said with signs: *You are a strong boy.*

He made two fists to show how strong he was.

Carry it, can you carry it?

She gave him the stone and he struggled to hold it, nearly dropping it. Finally he clutched it to his chest, resting his chin upon it, weaving a little. They started slowly up the hill. He was smiling, talking, his head bobbing. *I am very strong, very strong*. He blinked the sweat from his eyes.

Three times they had to stop and rest. She gave him the last candy and he ate it and got up and this time he couldn't lift the stone. She handed it to him but did not offer to carry it.

Keep going, she said. *Keep on.*

She was afraid he would not go. But he marched with small planted feet that puffed up the dust of the road. At the top, they came to his house. He looked to see if the house-woman was there, to show what he could do, but the door was closed and the curtains drawn.

Come on, come on.

He nearly gave out before the cemetery. She waited while he rested, and gave him the stone again. His arms hung down. He gripped the stone above his knees. His legs were trembling.

I can, I can, he said.

At the far edge of the cemetery, they stopped at the grave. She gestured that the boy should place the stone there. *Here, on top. Just like that.*

He had carried it all the way. He made two fists again to show her his strength. She made the sign of the cross, and signaled the boy to do the same. He wiped his brow and gestured to her.

That is heavy, heavy.

Yes. Are you tired?

Yes. Are you?

And she was tired, as weary as though she had carried the stone herself. Weary as though the stone still lay in her arms.

She sat down beside the grave and looked out to sea. Pelicans flew in formation and dove into the waves, and pilot birds wheeled overhead. She saw a small school of fish driven to the surface by larger ones. Company men were at the harbor, directing the throng of stevedores. Older men sat on the pilings to observe and comment. Down at Providencia Camp she saw Topetes on his horse, high-stepping around the yard, stopping to talk to this miner and that one, and the world went on as it was.

With one hand she covered her eyes, and with the other she waved the boy off. *Go on, go along.*

The sun was burning her neck. When she uncovered her eyes, she saw the boy had not gone. He studied her face and made a sad face too. He sat down, pushing his feet in the dust as if he did not know what to do. He sat without speaking, without gesturing, and watched her face. He took the edge of her skirt in his hand and held on to it.

A breeze had come up and the sky was clearing. She wiped her eyes. She saw the garden truck coming over the hill from Santa Agueda, and a donkey cart passed below, driven by children. The white tombs of the cemetery were gleaming all around her, and far in the distance, from the direction of Mulegé, came a falluquero driving his animals along the road.

The Roof of San Xavier

SAN FRANCISCO XAVIER DE VIGGÉ-BIAUNDÓ

—1923—

At dawn the old falluquero carries the woman—light as the bones of a bird—up the spiral stone stairway of the mission church, bears her on his back into the choir loft with its tender wooden rail. He pauses so she can look down to the nave, to the worn flagstones and the long aisle of wooden benches and the stone fonts with their annular mirrors of water, so she might call to those standing in the sotacoro or kneeling at the altar before the golden retablo that stretches to the roof with its garrison of saints. She calls to see who might turn, but if they call back, she cannot hear them. They seldom turn.

He carries her across the loft to the second spiral staircase of splintered mesquite, up into the single tower where the green copper bells hang gravely in their open portals, and sets her on the bench where she might rest a moment.

She does not want to sit. She strikes his arm and hobbles to the northern bay and stands beneath the bell, looking down to the one street of the village, the homes of adobe and thatch. She searches for any unknown man, any new man passing through the town, and calls to him in a frightful voice, a crow's voice, louder and louder until he looks to the bell tower. She will not relent until the passerby comes up, smiling with bemused wondering, for the people of the town have already warned him of this ritual that every visitor must undergo. When the old woman looks carefully into the man's face, she dismisses him in a violent storm of pantomime.

Every morning the falluquero carries her. At sunrise he sits trembling on the top step. His days of vigor are done; his old heart pounds from the climb.

—Ay, Dolores, he says.

She had a room in the old storehouse behind the mission church. Sometimes in the evening after she had fallen asleep, the falluquero held her hand as she never permitted in all the years he had known her. He had followed her to every town and place. Once he had even accompanied her on the road to her father's house at Pabellón, just because it was what she wanted. In the end, she abandoned him and rode the final leagues to Pabellón alone, but still he kept watch. He had always kept watch.

She had been married to a storekeeper, and he felt ashamed to remember his gladness when that man died. The husband passed without knowing she carried a son and daughter in her womb. The falluquero would have been a father to those children, a greater father than he had been to his own child, born on a small ranch high in the sierras. But Dolores did not want the falluquero. Like a stricken sea-widow she walked the perimeter of the cross-shaped roof of the mission—the stipes and the patibulum, the pillory and the arms—surveying the street below. Her vision was keen and her pockets hung heavy with olive pits to hurl at those who did not answer when she called. The townspeople of San Xavier were a little afraid of her, this supposed wife of the falluquero, this lone gargoyle in black dress with unbound hair of white, standing atop the dark castle of the mission church, wandering among the twisted finials, her face suddenly appearing above the stone waterspouts that jutted like cannons from the upper ramparts, looking for the son who had long since fallen to the revolution and would never come home.

The falluquero cared for her, year after year, even as she pinched and struck him. He feared that if he left, she would die in the company of those who did not love her. But she had worn him out. He often stood looking at the high hills around the mission, remembering his own sierras and the familiar peaks and red canyons, the ranches hidden along narrow arroyos with scant water, the people he had not wanted and the son he had left behind. Sometimes his thoughts carried him there as he slept. He had been a dandy in those years, a man of songs and tall tales and news. He recalled the people eagerly awaiting him, the stories told and told again after a meal in the shade of a ramada. In the dream he often believed he had died, and heaven itself was the circle of those people. Old Tino and Ignacia. Noni. His own little son Carlitos.

Now the falluquero lived in a small jacal beside the orchard of ancient olive trees, close to the storeroom where Dolores lived. He cooked for her, carrying a tray with warm broth or goat meat or tortillas, going slowly across the shadowed yard, nodding to neighbors who watched from their doorways. Once he had believed she would look upon him with kindness, but all he had earned from her was a bullet through the shoulder when he was a younger man. At times he found himself fingering the scar. Every night he helped her into bed. With sharp fingers she pinched his arm if she saw his lips moving. Some nights he slept in a chair beside the bed. Always he was careful to let go of her hand before she woke.

One dark morning, his legs would not carry him up the stairs to the roof. Dolores, on his back, clutched his neck with one hand and whipped him with the other, urging him, but his legs would not obey. He groped to the wall and lowered her into an old chair of mesquite. She was shouting, gesturing.

—I can't, he said. I want to but I can't.

She struggled up from the chair and lifted her chin and went to the stone staircase. He watched, knowing, as she tried to raise her leg high enough for the first step. She pulled at her stocking and her foot lifted but not enough and she turned to the falluquero and struck him across the mouth. He stumbled back and the chair caught him and he sat shaking his head.

—Don't hit me, Dolores, he said.

She turned away and stepped into the early darkness of the nave, moving slowly down the aisle like a saint carried in procession. Her dragging foot echoed in the cavern, and doves flapped and resettled themselves in the high windows. He followed her out the western door and into the yard. A faint moon still hung in the sky and he heard the single peep of an early morning bird. She paused for a moment and pointed at the roof, and when he looked away, she came at him and he sidestepped and she dismissed him with a hand and kept on toward her room. One stocking was gathered at her ankle and she nearly fell but went doggedly on in the dim light. A youth was crossing the yard. She stopped and scrutinized him and shook her head and went into her room and closed the door.

The falluquero stood in the shadow of the mission, the moon fading into a white sliver against the ripening sky. A rooster sounded and another answered, and women appeared in their doorways, calling to one another. Men were about, and the smoke of cookfires curled upward from the homes. He went around the front of the church to a chair beside a single orange tree, against the half wall, and he sat fanning himself though the morning was chilled. His heart hammered. He had not thought his strength would fail before Dolores'. A man crossed the street on strong and purposeful legs, a hoe upon his shoulder, going to the olive grove. He paused to inquire of Dolores' health, and went on.

The falluquero must have dozed, and when he opened his eyes, the sun had risen over the canyon wall and he found himself sitting in the presence of a man atop a mule. For a moment he felt confused, as though he were looking at himself in his younger years. He wondered if he had died in his sleep and was now watching the whole of his life play out before him, season by season, the lonely years and the wanderings and the fruitless trying. But still he sat against the half wall by the orange tree, and he was still an old man, not having died. His jaw hurt, and he remembered Dolores, and he stood up and wiped his face.

—I didn't mean to wake you, the man said.

The falluquero shaded his eyes and inclined his good ear toward the man, who rode a fine mule. All about the man was new—the hand-tooled saddle and tack, a clean embroidered shirt, unsoiled hat and boots, the polainas and armas smelling of leather freshly cut and sewn.

—Apéese, the falluquero said, gesturing, and the man swung down and said he was looking for a man from San Xavier who had business with him—or perhaps the hope of a business—at Comondú. Had the falluquero been to Comondú? The Eden of Lower California, people said. They had films there, and prominent families . . . the man grew very animated, and as he went on describing the venture, the falluquero again had the curious sensation of watching some version of himself as he had once been. The man kept talking and gesturing, and when the falluquero looked closer, he saw the man was his son, Carlitos.

The falluquero sat down. Carlitos perched on the half wall and the falluquero heard nothing of what he said, but dared to look at Carlitos as he talked on. He recalled the boy of that time long ago, the same bright eyes and quick hands.

Carlitos asked again of the man he sought, and the falluquero pointed to the house at the end of the street. Carlitos rose and replaced his hat and was about to mount up, but the falluquero held his arm.

—Carlitos, he said.

Carlitos shook his head and smiled and said that no one had used that name for many years. He looked at the falluquero.

—Do we know one another?

The falluquero shuffled his feet.

—I suppose I knew your mother, he said.

Carlitos took off his hat and looked closer. He said a name that was not the falluquero's name, and the falluquero said no. Carlitos smiled and studied him. He said something the falluquero did not catch, and he raised his voice and repeated himself.

—You knew my mother?

—Yes, the falluquero said.

He looked off, afraid to inquire. Finally he said, without looking at Carlitos, Does your mother still live?

—Yes, yes, Carlitos said. She is older now, but she stays on the ranch as before.

Carlitos tried again another name, and the falluquero said no.

—I'm sorry I can't place you, Carlitos said.

—I was only a trader, passing through.

Carlitos snapped his fingers.

—Falluquero! he cried. He held out a hand. I haven't seen you since I was a boy. I remember you spent some time in the mines . . .

He talked on, of Comondú where he was going, and the business he would undertake. He turned to look at the homes along the street. The falluquero could not take his eyes from him. His hair grew in the very same way as the falluquero remembered, from a small whorl now sewn with threads of gray. He remembered holding Carlitos on his lap, looking down at the tender crown, and how Noni had called for Carlitos to come away.

—I wonder if your mother might remember me, the falluquero said.

—She might, she might. Her memory is still good. She gets around all right.

—I wonder, the falluquero said. I wonder if she ever speaks of me.

—No, no, she never mentioned you. But she is a quiet one. And I have not been home for some weeks. I will go, once I settle things in Comondú . . . did I mention I have a quarter share of an automobile there?

He spoke again of the films, and brushed his hands, and said, It is good to see you again. Which house did you say?

—I'll walk with you, the falluquero said.

—Do not trouble yourself, truly.

But the falluquero was already getting to his feet, and Carlitos thanked him and came along, leading the mule. The falluquero went as slowly as he dared. He wished the walk were not so brief. He went more slowly still, until the mule was nearly urging them from behind. He wanted to speak again of Noni, and the goats and the red sierras and the rain or lack of rain. He wanted Carlitos to tell him everything he had missed in the span of those years. He felt he was nearly choking as they came to the final dwelling, near the stone cross that marked the entrance to the town, and he stopped, pretending to examine the doorway of the house as if he were not sure it was the right one. A young woman came out, and asked if the man was Carlos, and he said he was.

—All my brother does is talk of you, she said to Carlitos, and he laughed and said he himself had done nothing but talk of their new business.

—My brother is coming tonight, she said. You are welcome to stay.

She called to her mother and turned back from the door. The falluquero held Carlitos by the wrist.

—In my home I have room for you, he said.

—I hate to trouble you, Carlitos said.

—Please, the falluquero said.

The young woman reappeared with her mother but the falluquero was already taking Carlitos by the arm. Carlitos laughed and said he had never been so popular and he hoped people would receive him so in Comondú. He told the mother he would come again in the morning and he winked at the young woman and she looked at the ground and smiled.

They left the mule there and the falluquero suddenly thought of Dolores, that he had never left her alone for such a long time.

—There's a woman I take care of, he said.

Carlitos put a hand to the falluquero's back.

—It makes me glad, Carlitos said, to know that a man might still love a woman even when he is . . .

—When he is old.

Carlitos fingered his hat brim and smiled.

—Perhaps you could come with me, the falluquero said. To meet her.

—I'm free as the wind, Carlitos said. Until tomorrow, when the business begins.

The falluquero said her name was Dolores, and she could not hear or speak, and she was aging and in some confusion. He said they had been together for a number of years. Together in a way.

Carlitos followed him to the storehouse and the falluquero opened the door a thumb-width and looked inside. Dolores was sitting at the little wooden table. Her fingers drummed and she looked at the window to assess the time of day, and when he opened the door wider, she looked up. She began to scold him, but when she saw Carlitos, her hands fell into her lap. She searched Carlitos' face and strained up from the chair, coming to him, fingering the embroidery on his shirt. Taking him in. She reached for his hand and turned it, tracing the lines. Shaking her head in disbelief.

Carlitos took off his hat and laughed.

—I am a celebrity in San Xavier, he said, though I cannot say why. A man could grow accustomed to this.

He kissed Dolores on the cheek and helped her into the chair. The falluquero sat on the edge of the bed. Dolores would not take her eyes from Carlitos. She sat whispering. She reached for his hand again and stroked it, shaking her head all the while. Her eyes pooling. She pressed his hand to her cheek and Carlitos just laughed and kissed her forehead and said, What will my wife say, doña Dolores?

The falluquero remembered Dolores' son as a thin youth, sauntering, sometimes singing. Cut down by federales among so many others. Even thinner in death, skeletal from the moment he fell, people said. Who could say what he would have looked like, had he lived. But Dolores kept speaking to Carlitos as if he were that boy, explaining in her own language as she had never spoken to the falluquero in all those years. Carlitos listened patiently, nodding as if comprehending all, permitting whatever was needful. The falluquero had the curious feeling again of watching himself, the hand Dolores held so like his own. Dolores loving his younger self. As she kissed Carlitos' hand again, he felt his own hand burning, and he closed his eyes and sat listening to the rhythm of her murmurings.

Carlitos slept in the falluquero's jacal. The falluquero had given him the bed, and he himself lay on the floor, listening to Carlitos breathing. He thought of telling him, in the morning, of his many visits to Rancho La Falda before Carlitos was born, and his own memories of Carlitos as an infant, as a little boy. But to speak of that was to speak of Noni, and how was he to explain why he did not stay. Would he tell Carlitos he had not loved her. Or would he say that something compelled him into the greater world, and even for his own son he could not resist it? He would tell Carlitos some part of it, when morning came. Only a portion, so he might guess, might look at the falluquero's face and see his own, perhaps, and know.

The jacal was very dark. The falluquero could scarcely see the bed on the opposing wall. He heard the cry of a peacock and dogs answering, a crescendo of howling that abated and died away in unison.

—Carlitos, he said.

He heard the small start and a rustling and the creak of rawhide on the bedframe.

—What is it? Carlitos said. Is all well?

—All is well, the falluquero said.

—Did you call to me?

The falluquero did not answer. He lay under the cover of darkness, upon the hard earth. He lay very still. He heard Carlitos turn again, the long sigh of a sleeper taking stock of the night.

—Carlitos, he said again, this time nearly a whisper.

But Carlitos did not turn, and the falluquero listened to the breath of his son until the darkness gave way and the roosters began to cry in earnest.

In the morning, the falluquero asked if Carlitos would come again to see Dolores, but he was anxious to retrieve his partner and start for Comondú.

—Thank you for your hospitality, Carlitos said. Send my greetings to Dolores, who no doubt is in love with me.

The falluquero shook his hand.

—Send word, the falluquero said. Of the venture.

—I will, I will. You'll no doubt hear of me.

The falluquero reached for his hand again. He heard Dolores shouting, and Carlitos blessed him for his good heart and turned to go. The falluquero watched him—the eager gait, the familiar hurry. Carlitos nearly lost his hat in the wind, and he caught it and smiled at the falluquero and waved.

The falluquero returned to his jacal and prepared the tray, but when he came to Dolores' room, she would not eat. She tottered out into the yard and looked toward the empty street, worrying her hands.

—He's gone, the falluquero said. He pulled at her sleeve and she looked at him. He is gone, he said again, gesturing. She did not curse or strike him. They stood together and finally she turned and went to her room and lay down on the bed.

He sat with her while she slept. He told the old stories of Calmallí and the gold mines, and all the places she had lived: Cantamar and San Vicente and Camalú, San Ignacio and Santa Rosalía and now San Xavier. He spoke of Mexicali and the days of the revolution, when young men were laid like firewood in the streets, and old men raised their fists and voices but were relieved they were too old to fight. He recalled her true son to her, speaking of what he remembered, and her daughter, a child quiet and grave. Dolores lay with her eyes half-open, sleeping in her shoes as though at the ready.

In the days that followed, she did not resist him when he handled her, perhaps did not know him. He braided her thick hair, taking care to cover her ears. He bathed her, carefully dabbing the sun-mottled hands and face, and washing the pale assemblage of bones that no longer seemed to belong to the body he had dreamed of in his youth. At times she wept when he was bathing her, from pain or consolation he did not know.

One afternoon the young woman from the house at the end of the street came to fetch him, finding him asleep beside Dolores. The falluquero was lying on his good ear, and the young woman resorted to touching his foot. He woke with a start.

—A woman is here, she said. With two children. Looking for doña Dolores.

He sat up blinking, wiping the sleep from his face. The young woman helped him find the sandals he had kicked away. Dolores was turned to the wall. He could see the thin shoulders rising and falling, and he pulled the cover up and she slept on.

—They are waiting in the church, the young woman said. I will stay with the doña.

He thanked her and went out, crossing the yard to the side door of the mission, pausing a moment on the single worn step before going inside. The woman waited in the crossing, her children beside her. The boy called to the ceiling to hear the echo, and the woman pulled his arm and he fell silent but looked at the girl smiling. A sparrow flushed from the high window and fluttered out. The woman turned to look at the falluquero. She was the image of Dolores as a younger woman, save for a deep scar cutting from eyebrow to opposite cheek like a puckered seam. He took off his hat and greeted each of the children.

—Salúdenlo, she said. The children stepped forward, first the boy and then the girl, identical in appearance and stature. Each offered him a hand and he took it. He told the woman his name and she offered her own.

—Does Dolores still live, the woman asked.

—She does.

Her expression did not vary. She stood examining him.

—You are the falluquero, she said.

—Yes.

—Then you know me.

—Yes, I knew you when you were small.

There had been no smile but her look grew colder and he was afraid to say anything more. From outside he heard a man calling to a neighbor. The rasp of a donkey, the stitch of a shovel into garden soil. A peafowl crying out. He waited, hat in hand, and the girl whispered something to the boy.

—Is she dying? the woman said.

—Yes. How did you know?

—I see it in your eyes.

The children fell quiet, standing like small statues with their arms at their sides.

—Are you her husband? the woman asked.

—No.

—Is there a husband?

—No.

The woman shook her head. I should not have come, she said. But I did. And so will you take me to her, or are we to stand here?

He wished she would keep speaking. Her words were the very words he had imagined Dolores to have, low and assured, flaying open everything before them. He turned and she followed, the children behind her. They crossed the yard and stopped at the door.

—She may not know you, he said.

—She never knew me.

She held the children's hands, and the falluquero opened the door. Dolores was propped up in the bed. The young woman said she had taken a little coffee. Dolores looked to where the others were standing, and her eyes took in the falluquero, the woman and the children. She leaned toward them, scrutinizing their faces. Her brow furrowed. She looked to the falluquero as if he might know.

The woman guided the boy and the girl to the edge of the bed and made a gesture to Dolores that the falluquero supposed was something devised between them long ago.

—Mother, she said.

Dolores shook her head.

—She has a hard time remembering, the falluquero said.

—She remembers, the woman said.

She began speaking in signs to Dolores, who looked away. The woman put a hand to her foot but Dolores twisted the bedclothes and let forth in a garbled tongue.

The boy and girl drew away toward the door.

—What is she saying? the boy asked.

—Nothing, the woman said. She says nothing.

She took the hands of the children and went out. The falluquero followed, and they could hear Dolores cursing as they stood in the yard. The little girl cried, and the boy patted her and led her to the step of the church door and they sat. The woman turned on the falluquero.

—I should not have come, she said. You yourself should not have come. Tell me you have a family somewhere, that you have someone to care for you. Because this woman has not cared for you. She will never care for you.

He looked toward the children. The boy had his arm about the girl's shoulders and she nodded as the boy whispered to her. The woman shook her head.

—She does not want you. She has never wanted you. Leave her to that young woman in there. And may God repay the one who cares for her, for she will not repay.

She called to the children and they came hand in hand. The girl stumbled and the boy bore her up and the woman smiled. She lifted the girl and kissed her cheek and turned to him.

—Goodbye, falluquero.

The boy raised a hand to him, and the girl copied the gesture, and the falluquero watched as the three passed in front of the church and out of sight.

At dawn, Dolores lay very still. He leaned down and listened to her breath. The young woman encouraged him to eat, but he would not. When the sun reached the mission bells, he asked her to go home and bring her father and another man to help.

The young woman returned with her mother. When the father arrived, the man with him was Carlitos. He entered gravely, hat in hand. He said that matters in Comondú were not as he supposed, but he was glad he could return to San Xavier to perform this service if he were welcome.

The falluquero tried to speak, but his voice caught. The mother spoke quietly to Carlitos and he went to Dolores and lifted her from the bed. She lay like a small child in his arms, her hand clasping the neck of his shirt. They all crossed the yard, and the mother carried a single blanket and a handkerchief of linen and they went into the mission.

The barrel of the nave was high and cool, blue in the morning light. Rays of sun streamed through the eastern windows. The group processed under a ceiling of plastered stars, the golden retablo shining on its own. San Xavier stood upon his pedestal, and the saints watched from their frames as the procession paused in the crossing and turned down the long aisle toward the sotacoro. The young woman opened the wooden gate that guarded the stairs, and Carlitos went up slowly and carefully. The father went ahead of the falluquero, helping as he raised one foot at a time, pausing and resting. They stopped at the choir rail, and the young woman and mother blessed themselves on behalf of everyone. They kept on toward the stairs that spiraled to the belltower.

The falluquero was winded. The father asked if he wished to be carried, but the falluquero said he wanted to go of his own accord. One step and another, trembling, trying again, spiraling up, the father buoying him, passing the porthole window with the early breeze cool upon his face. The young woman and the mother followed, encouraging, moving past the bells hanging silent in their ingresses.

They went out to the roof and the eastern wall. He saw the crowd below, women with covered heads among the stone mausoleums of the campo santo, men on their mounts in the street, the bells of their spurs sounding high and clear. Children who dared not run. All gathered before the dark fortress of the mission hewn from the black walls of the volcanic bowl in which it rested. Hats in hand and hands raised.

Carlitos carried Dolores to the edge, and held her to the early sun. Her face was buried in his shirt and her breaths came long and slow, as though calling forth from the depths. The falluquero stood beside her and took her hand, small and cold, and the women spoke their prayers. The group stayed there for some time, looking beyond the town to the mesas and the jagged mountains of the Giantess, and the wind carried the warming scent of the chaparral.

Chema

The Prison without Doors

HEROICA MULEGÉ

—1937—

In Mulegé—above the river that empties to the Vermilion Sea, above the adobe homes and streets and shops and the groves of date palms and orchards and vineyards—the Prison without Doors looms over the town, a fortress of whitewashed walls and battlements with a guard tower at each corner. There is one high gate of iron at the entrance, and at the hour of six o'clock each morning, the sergeant opens the gate, and the prisoners go into the town to work, to visit their women and children, to bathe and eat. At sundown the guard blows the conch shell and the prisoners file back up the hill and inside, passing the sergeant's office and the smaller gate to the women's cells, into their own block of four corridors that form a square, open to the sky. The inner walls are dinted with dark openings, one after the other, thirty-nine cells without doors. Each is a narrow room of stone with a high wooden ceiling. The prisoners walk freely around the four corridors, under a bright sky of blue, visiting one another and chatting with the guards, who are trapped in their towers for twelve hours of watching after the sergeant removes the ladder. Throughout the night the guards cry to one another in a soft, singsong voice—Alerta—a lullaby to the prisoners below.

The Cárcel sin Puertas, as the prison is known, has another gate of iron that leads to the inner courtyard, also open to the sky. In the innermost square there are more cells without doors, a stone pila at the center where men may bathe, and one cell with a pipe in the ceiling where in years past men were dripped with water as a punishment.

At the Prison without Doors, it is not the severity of the crime that determines who will be released to work each morning and who is never released. In the outer square reside men who committed crimes of the moment or of passion, and they may be forgiven, and the town welcomes them without judgment. But men of the inner square will do the same things again and again, and they cannot help themselves. Some are confused of mind, and they never stop pacing and talking to themselves.

In the evening when he could not sleep for thoughts of Rosalinda, Chema sat on his bunk with a small harp, built one year ago when he first arrived at the prison. Wang the shopkeeper had lent him the tools, and he carved the neck and pillar of ironwood, and when a goat fell down dead in front of the prison, the sergeant gave Chema the intestines to make the strings.

His cell was bare except for the bunk, his gray woolen blanket, and a single candle on the floor. Chema sat plucking the harp strings, playing songs of love. He picked up the letter Rosalinda had sent. She did not say she would see him, but she didn't say she wouldn't. She said her father did not want him at the ranch or anywhere near San Ignacio.

He leaned his head against the wall, and he must have drifted off because when he opened his eyes, the moon was up. He heard horses, and men shouting, and the guards in the two forward towers clacking their rifles. Other prisoners were already out of their cells, waiting for a new man to be brought. Chema could hear the thuds of blows and cursing, someone being dragged through the front gate.

—There's one for you, a man said to Chema.

Chema put a hand to the back of his neck.

The guards were bringing a man in leg irons, and the sergeant was with them. The new prisoner was a giant, towering over them all, and the corners of his mouth were white with froth. The sergeant walked ahead, directing the men with a slender truncheon, and the prisoner suddenly lurched and the youngest guard went down on a knee and jumped back up again.

The man was nearly bald, a round infant face atop a body like a circus bear Chema had once seen in La Paz. His great arms hung down, and he lumbered along as the guards prodded him forward. The young guard was rubbing his lip and it was already swelling and he walked sullenly behind. The prisoner was crying, or had been. His head swung from side to side on a thick neck, trying to see where the men were taking him.

—Watch out, the sergeant said, and the prisoners moved back.

—I'll come if you want me, Chema said to the sergeant.

—It's all right, the sergeant said.

The big man stopped and the guards kept pushing him but it was like prodding a wall. He looked at Chema. The guards gave a mighty shove and the man stumbled forward and nearly fell.

—Go easy, Chema said.

—Back to your cells, the sergeant said to the knot of men, but they hung in the doorways watching.

Now the prisoner began to move again, sobbing a little, shuffling with the half steps the leg irons would allow. The sergeant unlocked the gate to the inner square and they went through. Chema heard men jeering and the sergeant shouting them down, and when the sergeant and the guards came out, locking the gate behind them, the jeering started up again. The big man was howling and some others picked it up and their cries filled the air like a confabulation of coyotes.

The sergeant stood with Chema for a moment, studying the sky.

—What did he do? Chema asked.

The sergeant shook his head and gave Chema a cigarette.

—I'll call you if I need to.

He went to his office and Chema heard the squeak of his chair and his steady voice talking to Damiana, the sole woman prisoner at her gate across the hall. Chema waited a moment, listening, and walked back to the inner gate. He saw forms walking about the square in the moonlight, men who never seemed to sleep. Someone was at the pila splashing water on his face, but it was too small to be the new man. Chema heard the whining voice of Flores—the man who once ran off and nearly died in the desert, the one the sergeant sent Chema to retrieve. A few other voices he recognized. But he could not hear the big man.

Chema went to his cell. The candle had blown out and he relit the wick and picked up the letter from Rosalinda and read it again. He folded the letter and extinguished the candle with his fingers. The men of the inner square had settled down. Once he heard a sudden yap and that was all. He heard the main gate open and the sergeant preparing to go out, and the hooves of the sergeant's horse riding down the road into town.

He lay on his bunk, watching the shadow of the moon winking on the wall as clouds passed, and he fell asleep with the letter in his hand.

He woke to the trammeling of feet, bodies thudding against the walls and an angry blaspheming of voices: ¡Jesús, María, y José! He got up and went to the inner gate. Men were surging around the square, and Chema saw the big man go by in leg irons, dragging someone by the hair. A prisoner was beating him from behind but the blows had no effect; the big man kept going around the pila, swatting people out of the way.

The guards in their towers were shouting, and the young guard with the swollen lip came running. He stood with Chema and looked into the square and asked if Chema would go with him. Men from the outer court gathered around and they clapped Chema on the back and encouraged him: Take him, Chema! The guard opened the gate, and when Chema went through, the guard locked the gate behind him.

The prisoners had already gone to their corners. Flores went by with a hand in his hair and sat on the edge of the pila with his sandaled feet dangling in the water.

—He almost killed poor Flores, someone said.

—What'd you do, Flores? Chema asked.

—Nothing, I didn't do nothing, Flores said.

Chema found the big man in the lavatory cell, sitting alone on the toilet bench. The man looked at him and blinked, his pants around his ankles.

—What's your name? Chema asked.

—Mi mamá called me Leonardo.

—Come on out, Chema said.

The man looked past Chema to see who might be coming for him. Chema sat on the bench next to him.

—Are you a captain? Leonardo asked.

—No. I help out when there's trouble, Chema said.

—Is there trouble?

—People want to sleep.

—They do?

—Yes. And you're waking them up.

Leonardo looked down.

—Are you done making trouble? Chema asked.

—I thought I was. But then I wasn't.

He lumbered to his feet but he had forgotten his fallen pants and he stumbled. Chema caught his arm. Leonardo gripped the pants at the waist and came out. By now a small group had gathered around the pila, and they watched to see if another brawl was going to start. Flores looked darkly at Leonardo from under his heavy eyebrows. Leonardo glanced wildly around. He balled up his fists.

—How about we lie down, Chema said.

—I can't. I don't know which room is mine.

Chema led him to a corner cell.

—Here's a good one, Chema said. There's only one man in here.

—He can't have my bunk, Flores called out. It took me three years to get that bunk.

—Mi mamá always sang to me, Leonardo said.

—Where is your mamá?

The man lifted an anguished face and said he didn't know. He took Chema by the arm and gave him a little shake.

—I feel like something is going to happen, Leonardo said.

—Nothing is going to happen, Chema said. Lie down.

The young guard was already bringing the harp. Leonardo lay on the cot and Chema sat beside him. He held the instrument on his lap and softly pulled the strings. He sang a song his father had learned from his own papá, years ago:

Nana, nanita
El chiquito dormirá
en un ratito ya.

Nana, nanita
El niñito está
a punto de dormirse,
en un ratito ya.

Leonardo lay on his back, listening. His eyes rolled and drifted shut, and Chema kept singing, softer and softer, and Leonardo only opened his eyes once to ask, How come they got you in the prison?

Chema's grandfather had been a priest and his grandmother a mezcalera. Rosalinda had laughed about that, just a short year ago as they sat in the long breezeway in front of her father's ranch house at San Ignacio. Chema was thirty years her senior and had wanted to marry her even before she married the first time. Someone said she had a new hope chest her father built from palmwood, and she had already crocheted a tablecloth and two sobrecamas for the bed.

Her father was inside asleep. Chema and Rosalinda sat on cane chairs a little distance apart, under the roof of woven palm, eating date pie from wooden plates.

—We shouldn't be laughing, Rosalinda said. Let's just sit here.

—He wasn't a priest when he got married, Chema said.

—I said let's just sit. Do you want him to come out?

Chema wanted to work for her father, to show himself good, but her father would not see him. The whole region was in drought. Her father had held his cattle for too long, trying to keep them alive, and one by one the animals died. Her father was down, and he didn't want Chema or anyone coming around.

—Why won't you say yes, Chema said.

She lifted her chin and covered a smile with her hand.

—I'm going to say yes to someone, she said.

—I don't want you to say his name.

—I didn't. Keep your voice down.

There was going to be a dance in San Ignacio that night, at the house of the Torres, and Rosalinda told Chema not to come. She said the other man had asked her first.

—Is it because I'm an old man?

—You aren't an old man.

—Then why.

—Because he asked me first.

—You promised.

—No, I didn't.

—At the Torres. Before.

She laughed. But he remembered. He'd laid a handkerchief across his workworn palm when he danced with her, and on the third dance she had ticked it away, as if by accident. She had put her hand on his, small and warm, and he asked if she would marry him and she said she would.

—You already said yes to me, he said.

—I'm going to get Papá, she said.

—No, don't.

—You better go on.

When he got to the dance that evening, there were already horses and mules tethered outside. Light and music streamed from the windows, and a few men were gathered at the door. One of them turned and gave him an apologetic smile and stood aside. Chema looked in. The house was full of people, women on one side and men on the other. Some had cups in their hands. A small company of violins and guitars played from the corner, and couples were going around in a circle. The other man had his arm around Rosalinda, and her eyes were alight. The man held her waist and she had a flower in her hair.

Chema stood sweating in the doorway, though the evening was cool. He could not make himself go inside. A hand patted his shoulder, one of the neighbors succoring him. The song ended and everyone clapped except Chema. The couples drifted from the floor but the man held Rosalinda by the wrist. She suddenly had a serious look and the man was gesturing, entreating. Chema could not read her face but they were talking earnestly. Rosalinda caught sight of him in the doorway and she gave him a half smile and dropped the man's hand.

Chema turned and mounted up and rode off and he did not remember anything after that. Some said he took it from a house in town, and others said he got it from the old adobe behind the mission where the palms were blackened by fire. But whatever the case, he came back with a pistol and stood at the door of the dance for the second time and shot the other man's ear away.

Through the night, Chema did not hear anything more from Leonardo or the men of the inner square. At dawn he heard roosters and the keen notes of the little carboneros and the whine of Flores' voice. Chema took out the letter from Rosalinda and read it again. She said she would not stop Chema from coming but she would not wait for him either. She wondered what Chema had to offer but said she did not spend time thinking about it. Chema had sent his own letter, explaining that he was not a dangerous man. What he had done, he did for love. In a month or two he would go free, because he hadn't intended to kill anyone; he had only knocked the man's ear off. He told Rosalinda he did have something of great value to bring to the marriage. He would find it and show it to her.

He lay on his bunk in the half-light and thought of the other man, visiting Rosalinda and winning over her father, free to work and prove himself good. Sharing something sweet with Rosalinda under the eaves, free perhaps to taste of her sweetness himself. Chema had wanted to kill that man. Had tried.

He felt flushed and got up and flapped his shirt to bring a wind to his skin and then sat down again. Tucked into the letter he kept a leather-covered copper plate photograph of his grandfather, Magín Matías the priest. In the photo, the old man appeared as a bridegroom in an ill-fitting formal suit he must have borrowed. Chema's grandmother Inés stood beside him, more than twenty years his junior. In the picture her hand was blurred, and Chema imagined that at the moment of the photograph she had tucked her fingers into his arm. She was smiling, looking toward her husband slightly. He was thin, as though he had overcome some recent illness. He looked directly at the camera, and Chema believed that though the man did not smile, he wore an expression that might be called contentment. Inés stood very close to him. Magín Matías loved her, Chema's father had said, and Inés loved him in return, despite what he had done.

—He was a good papá, Chema's father said. He cherished me.

—Because he lost the Cochimí boy, Chema said.

—I believe he cherished me for myself.

—Was he ashamed of what he did?

—I don't know. He rarely spoke of it.

—And your mother?

—After he died, she told me some things. She was there at Mulegé. She was just a girl.

His father took Chema's hand. He was a good man, he said.

Now Chema could smell smoke from the cookfire in the women's court, and he heard Damiana with her skillets and spoons. He rubbed his eyes and slipped into his boots. Some men were already outside their cells, sitting on the short barrels they used for chairs and passing around the one mirror to shave. The sergeant came over when he saw Chema.

—You got him settled down, the sergeant said.

—It was nothing.

—Thank you for that.

A guard was coming with food Damiana had prepared. He held the tray and extended his hip toward Chema, who took the key from the belt and unlocked the inner gate. Chema followed the guard into the square. Men were straggling out of their cells. They took their breakfast and some went to the pila to wash and others walked the dusty yard, around and around, talking to themselves. Some were sullen on their bunks, eating and looking out of the caves of their rooms. Flores sat in the shade of the wall with a handful of coquina shells, tying them together with thread to make animals. He had some little burros in a basket at his feet.

Leonardo lumbered out of his cell in leg irons, his eyes on the platter of eggs and machaca rolled in tortillas. He took a tortilla and gave one to Flores and looked at Chema and grinned.

—I'm going out to work for a while, Chema said. I'll see you when I get back.

The big man stopped smiling. Chema put a hand on his arm.

—I'll bring you a coffee when I come. Will you wait quietly? Chema asked.

—I can work, Leonardo said. You can't know how I can work.

—Stay here with Flores.

—But how will I know when you're back?

—You'll hear the conch.

Leonardo looked uncertain. The whistle began to blow.

—Will you be tranquilo? Chema asked.

—Tranquilito, tranquilito, Leonardo said.

Chema patted Leonardo's arm again and went out with the guard. He lined up with the others. Damiana was at the women's gate, wiping a cup with a towel. She was a young woman with a sun-spotted face, flushed from the cookfire. She wore a long skirt sewn together from two other skirts. Her toes spread out in men's sandals and her braid was coming undone.

—Are you going to ask Wang today? Damiana said.

—I'm going to ask him this morning, Chema said. Before work, so he can think about it.

—He won't need to think about it.

—I don't know if I can find it.

—You will.

The sergeant stood at the door.

—He's all right now, Chema said. How about the leg irons?

—In another day we will see.

—Will you watch out for him?

—Go on.

The guard blew the whistle again, and Chema asked Damiana what he could bring her.

—The priest was already here, she said. He said the Lord bless me and keep me. I said the Lord could bless me if he wanted, but not keep me.

Chema laughed and she waved him on.

The prisoners filed out and started down the road to their work and families and breakfasts. Chema stood outside for a moment, looking over the little town. He smelled the salt air of the gulf and watched the palms rustling in the morning air. The breeze was still cool. He saw a tendril of smoke rising from Wang's store, and he saw the sergeant's house near the river, and Sombrerito Hill at the edge of the sea. Up the canyon, the old stone mission sat on the hill above the palms, the peeling whitewashed wall flashing through the swaying brush. He heard the bell tolling, echoing along the arroyo and drubbing out to sea.

Chema had the letter from Rosalinda in his pocket. He took it out and read it again before starting down the hill to Wang's.

The store was a long low adobe, dim inside, with fine dark cabinets of glass. Shelves were built to the ceiling, stacked with silk fabric, bottles of soda and perfume, porcelain dishes and cigarettes. Wang had barrels of figs and olives and quince and guayaba, and he sold wine to all except the inmates of the prison, who were forbidden to drink or go to dances at the government house, though they could stand outside to hear the music. At year's end, Wang provided a dinner to all the inmates of the prison, either on Christmas or New Year as they chose.

When Chema came into the store, Wang was at the register clicking the beads of his abacus. His littlest daughter sat on the counter in a frilled white dress, watching her father and swinging her feet. Wang smiled and said good morning and called to his wife Mimiberta to bring breakfast. Mimiberta brought coffee and two warm tortillas and some goat cheese and beans, and she greeted Chema and took her daughter's hand and they bustled out. Chema fingered his fork.

—What's the matter? Wang asked. Are you sick?

—No, Chema said. I had something to ask you.

Wang pulled out a chair and sat with folded hands.

—My grandfather did not die with anything of value except the love of my grandmother, Chema said.

—What more can a man ask? Wang said.

—They lived on the hill above the river. In a little adobe that is no longer there. The same house where my grandmother was born and grew up. They might have lived better. They had something they might have sold, but they buried it instead.

Wang waved his hand and smiled.

—Everyone has a grandfather or great-grandfather who buried gold coins or silver. I myself have such an ancestor.

—It was a pearl, Chema said. A perfect pearl of pink. My father never saw it, but he spoke of it. My grandparents buried it, for something my grandfather had done.

—What did he do?

—He killed a boy, Chema said. The boy was fishing for the pearl and he drowned.

Wang shook his head.

—I wanted to ask if you would buy the pearl, Chema said. If I can find it. They buried it at the foot of a tree, so my father said. That was how my grandfather made his peace.

Wang pushed his glasses to the bridge of his nose.

—Mulegé has many trees, he said. Trees in the orchards, trees along the river . . .

—I think it must be an old tree, an important tree.

—If he buried the pearl to find peace, Wang said, maybe it should stay in the ground.

Chema got up and ran a hand through his hair.

—What will you do with the money? Wang asked.

—There is a woman I want to marry, Chema said. Her father has fallen on a hard time. I'm going to buy him five cows and a bull, as soon as it rains.

Wang laughed. Does he like you? he asked.

—I'm going to fix his problem and then we'll see.

—If he won't have you without cattle, he said, he won't have you with. Take it from a father.

But Wang held out a hand and Chema shook it.

—I will buy your pearl, Wang said. If you find it.

Chema thanked him and shook his hand again. He chose some candies from the bowl and Wang wrote down the amount and Chema left one for the little girl and put the rest in his pocket for Damiana. He went out. He felt light and he greeted Wang's wife as she threw corn to the chickens and he walked around back where Wang kept his tools. From a wooden bin he took a machete and a rope and some cord and a tarp, and he put these into a wheelbarrow and went down to the river to the palm groves.

The other piscadores were already up in the trees, cutting dates. They were quiet men, quick of motion, descendants of the Cochimí. Mats of woven palm lay on the ground, piled with clusters, and women and children sorted the loose fruits. The men called down to Chema and he gave a wave and sat down and shucked off his shoes. He went to the edge of the grove and slung the rope around the trunk and tied it in a loose circle about his waist. He started up, gripping the rough bark with his feet. When he reached the top, he could see the mission where his grandfather had served as priest, and the river, and the little house on the opposite hill where his grandmother's adobe used to be. He hung on the trunk thinking, and then he began to cut the clusters, sliding them down the rope to the man below. He worked steadily in the trees until lunchtime, and said a prayer about the drowned boy, and came down.

He walked toward the old mission, following the path along the river that cut through the reeds, crossing to the other side when he came to the bridge. Pelicans floated on the water, paddling in a group. A girl and a boy had lines in the water and they greeted Chema and showed him two snook in a bucket. The girl offered one to Chema, who thanked him and said he would take it when he came back.

When he got to the top of the hill, he paused in the dirt yard in front of the small church of stone. He took off his hat and fanned himself. He had not been to the mission since he was a boy, passing through Mulegé with his father, and he did not remember if he had ever gone inside. The church was straight and square except for the arched entrance, semicircled by voussoirs of common quarry rock. A long wing jutted from one side. A gathering hall, he thought, or rooms where the priest slept and ate. Six white finials like flower vases sat atop the eastern wall, and one angled buttress hid a room behind—a side chapel perhaps. Two straight stone supports framed the main doorway, open and black in the glare.

He went in. The nave was cool and dim, and the outside noises fell to quietness inside the thick walls: the clop of a horse, the call of men, the trill of a flicker. Dove droppings covered the floor. The room smelled faintly of tallow. He held his hat in hand and stood just inside the door. The ceiling was vaulted. Arched windows and doors lined the walls, leading to rooms he did not know, all shuttered. There stood a few wooden benches, and a freshly painted statue of Santa Rosalía in a niche at the front. The church had no retablo of gold, as the grand churches of San Ignacio and San Xavier had, but only the single niche and the altar table. A solitary candle was burning, praying in someone's stead.

His grandfather had stood here more than a hundred years since, the man who became the aged father of Chema's own. Here he had lifted the bread and the cup, talked of body and blood, and then consumed the life of a little boy. A man with blood on his hands, the blood now buried somewhere in the ground. Chema sat down on a bench. He imagined his grandfather at the altar, holding the host aloft, turning his back to the people and partaking alone. Chema got up and looked around. Once there were no benches, he thought. The people sat on the ground. He imagined his grandmother as a young girl, watching the priest, unaware that she would later love him.

He did not know how to address his grandfather, had never addressed him. Abuelo or abuelito or tata. Padre perhaps. He did not know if a man remained a priest in heaven.

—I came to ask you, he said. I believe you already know I'd like to have it.

His words echoed in the stone expanse. Outside, a dog barked and another answered. The church was quiet. He moved down the aisle and stood before the altar. A penitent had placed a wooden lampion at the corner, the dry wick frayed at the end. The altar cloth was stained with waterdrops, sprinkled with the first fruits of someone's new well. A cat emerged and another followed, two dusty acolytes, eyeing each other. Chema licked his thumb and smoothed his eyebrows. He clasped his hands before him.

—You can say yes or no, but you don't have to be so silent. You got the woman you loved. I thought maybe you could help me do the same.

He scraped one boot atop the other. He thought of Rosalinda and knelt down and felt a little ashamed for the feeling of worship that lighted upon his breast. He wanted to savor it. But he could not help seeing the suitor standing beside her, and he saw again the pistol, recalling the cold metal in his hand, and his fingers itched to take it up. He stood and kneaded his palms and walked the aisle. He took some water from the shell of stone affixed to the wall, and he blessed himself and paused for a moment in the doorway. Hearing nothing, he shook his head and went out.

In front of the mission lay the small campo santo and he walked over and looked at the graves. There were only a few markers—some fine white monuments of marble that could not belong to the boy—and mounds of rock, crumbling and scattered, without cross or headstone. None of them identified. He walked among the stones and did not know if his grandfather had buried the boy or whether someone else had. He looked around. A few thin cardones were growing, knobby and unremarkable, and some spindly mesquites. There was only one tree of substance, the bright green trunk of a palo verde, in yellow flower, standing nearly at the road but not far from the graves. He imagined this whole hillside covered with the fresh mounds of the Cochimí. His skin prickled and he walked gingerly to the tree and knelt at the base and began to dig. The soil was hard and he wished he had brought a hand-trowel. He raked around the roots. When he had come full circle he went around again, probing deeper, until the soil became cold clay under his hands.

He sat back on his heels and looked up. The sergeant was riding up the road, and Chema dusted his palms and stood.

—I was just going back to work, he said.

—Never mind. I've already spoken to Wang. Get up here behind me, I need you.

When they got to the prison, Chema could hear Leonardo shouting, and the laughter of the men, and a communal cry of alarm and then laughter again. The sergeant's eye was going black. He unlocked the inner gate and Chema went in. Two guards were slouching against the pila, and when they saw the sergeant they straightened up.

Leonardo had gotten his leg irons off and he stood in the corner. Every so often he came out swinging the chains in a circle above his head. A group of inmates had clustered to watch. Flores darted in and out, the men cheering him on. Leonardo came out bellowing and barely missed Flores' head, and the leg irons left a divot in the flagstones.

—Get him, Chema! Flores cried.

Leonardo's bald head shone with sweat and he wasn't wearing pants. He gave the irons another swing in a wide circle that turned him fully around and sent the inmates stumbling back. A volley of profanity ushered from his mouth and the men cheered again. Chema went forward and flinched once when Leonardo swung toward him, but he kept going. The sergeant walked close behind, the slender truncheon raised. The guards had clustered at the wall and the sergeant turned and snapped his fingers and the men inched forward with brooding looks.

—Look here, Chema said to Leonardo. I brought you some candies.

Leonardo brushed the sweat from his face. He cursed again—¡Tu madre!—and swung the irons but not as widely.

Chema said his name and this time Leonardo looked at him. He blew through his lips as though displacing a fly.

—Did I hurt anybody? he asked.

—Look at the sergeant here, Chema said.

Leonardo came over, dragging the leg irons behind him. He reached for the sergeant's face and the sergeant blocked his hand with the club.

—You worked hard this morning, Chema said. Look at how you're sweating.

He took Leonardo by the wrist. Give your tools to the sergeant, he said.

Leonardo handed him the irons. The men groaned with disappointment and some of them exchanged cigarettes for their wagers and they went to their cells to get out of the sun.

—If he does that again I'll bring the ball and chain, the sergeant said.

—He won't.

—I won't, Leonardo said.

—And get him some pants.

The sergeant beckoned the guards and they followed him out. Chema could hear the sergeant berating them. He led Leonardo to his cell and found Flores already sitting on the cot. Leonardo plopped down on the bunk and the leather thongs stretched and creaked. Flores edged away. Chema handed Leonardo the candies.

—We have to be very quiet, Chema said. Very quiet until dinnertime.

—Is Damiana making something?

—I don't think much of that woman's cooking, Flores said. Every day frijoles de la olla. Not a bit of fat.

—The men said bad things about her, Leonardo said. I had to bash some of them.

Chema thought for a moment. Well, he said. That might have been right.

Leonardo got down and sat against the wall with Chema. Chema felt the cold of the stones coming into him. There was one bright line of sun just inside the door and he moved his legs away from it. Flores kicked off his sandals and lay down on the cot and turned to the wall.

Chema took out two cigarettes and gave one to Leonardo.

—Once there was a very fine pearl, Chema said. As precious as a child. And the pearl belonged to a couple and it recalled to them something sad, something they wished to forget. One night they took the pearl to a special tree and they buried it, and it lay under the ground hidden for many years until a small shoot began to grow from the place where the pearl was buried. The shoot sprouted leaves and buds and flowers, and one day a man came along and picked one of the flowers to give to his beloved.

—Damiana?

—No, not Damiana. Another woman. And the man unburied the pearl, and the woman accepted the pearl and she accepted the man.

Flores rolled over and looked at Chema with gleaming eyes.

—He shouldn't have dug up the pearl, he said.

—I thought you were sleeping, Chema said.

—You're not supposed to dig up people, Flores said.

—It wasn't a person, Chema said. It was just a pearl.

In the morning the sergeant called Chema to his office.

—The musicians from San Ignacio are asking for you, the sergeant said. To play a wedding. If you want to.

—I want to.

—I know you had some trouble there.

—I won't be trouble again.

—I didn't think you would.

Damiana had come to listen. She hung her arms out of the grate.

—Santo Dios, she said. I never get to go anywhere.

—What about Leonardo? Chema asked.

—We can handle him, the sergeant said. He'll teach those young guards what they need to know.

—How about me going to the wedding? Damiana said. You never heard me sing.

The sergeant smiled and shook his head.

—Don't be rough with him, Chema said.

—I won't if he won't.

Damiana whistled Chema over.

—What do you want to go there for?

—You know.

—You haven't even found it yet.

—I know.

—Bring me back something from San Ignacio, she said. Something good.

In the morning the sergeant brought a soft hide to wrap the harp, with two straps so Chema could carry it on his back. The sergeant loaded one of his own mules with a blanket and saddlebags packed with tortillas and dried beef and dates and a cantinflór of water.

—I need to tell Leonardo, Chema said.

—Hurry up.

The young guard unlocked the inner gate. Men were washing at the pila and others had begun their endless filing around the square. Chema found Leonardo sitting against the wall beside Flores, holding the basket of shell animals.

—Listen, Leonardo. I am going for a few days and I want you to behave yourself.

—I can come with you.

—No, you can't. But Flores is here.

—I don't want any of them. I don't.

Leonardo got up and his mouth was twitching. Flores edged away. Leonardo kicked the basket of animals and they skittered across the stones.

—Don't break the man's things, Chema said.

Leonardo paced back and forth, wringing his hands.

—I can't help it, I can't help it.

Flores scurried forward and tried to scoop up the animals.

—I'll only be gone a little while, Chema said to Leonardo. I'll bring you a date pie.

—Are you going to sing again?

—You bet. When I come back.

Chema walked to the gate and Leonardo followed. The young guard jerked Chema through, and Leonardo stood at the bars.

—Are you going, Chema?

—It's all right.

Chema asked the guard to bring breakfast. Leonardo reached a hand to Chema and he shook it and moved off. When he passed the sergeant's office, Leonardo was still standing at the inner gate watching him.

Outside, he lingered in front of the prison for a few moments, listening. He heard only the usual noises—a guard calling to Damiana in the women's court, trying to persuade her of something. A rooster sounding off. The whicker of the sergeant's mule answering another in a yard down the road. Someone chanting a song of a single note.

—Go if you're going, the guard in the tower called.

—I am.

He stood for another moment until the guard asked if he would like to stay locked inside for the day. Chema mounted up.

He rode down the hill and crossed at the lower bridge and followed the river to the sea. He thought he knew where the place was, for his father had shown him when he was a boy. But when Chema came out at the mouth of the river near Sombrerito Hill, he had not remembered how long and wide the beach was. Fishermen sat in chairs of mesquite beneath blankets on poles for shade, and they bantered to one another while hopeful dogs hung around. One little black-and-white snatched a fish head and the others followed half-heartedly. Chema shaded his eyes and looked out over the sea. A schooner was passing. The tide hissed on the sand and pulled away, and pebbles rolled down after the wave.

He got down from the mule and scanned the shoreline for trees. There were only skinny palms, one like another, and low mangroves that formed an island in the center of the river. Farther back on the beach sat one abandoned adobe with a gangly mesquite in front of the door, and that was all. He tried to imagine the place as it had been at the time of his grandfather. The jacales of the Cochimí and a few humble adobes. The monjerío of the women. The old mission fields. The reed canoes and the nets full of fish. The boy and the priest.

He walked the shore, leading the mule behind him, until he came to the tombolo his father had shown him: a sandy spit stretching into the sea, and the place where the Cochimí had dragged the boy's canoe ashore along with the boy himself. Standing in the brush, his grandmother had watched the priest running—so unseemly—and then the priest had fled.

If there had been a tree of stature in this place, it no longer remained. He looked once more to the hills, and mounted up and followed the road north along the coast. At Palo Verde he cut westward along the old camino, eating the goat meat and the tortillas Mimiberta had packed for him, and singing a song in which Rosalinda was every other word.

The journey took four days, and when he rode into San Ignacio he passed the parque with its young laurel trees and the tall mission of white stone with its single weathered bell tower. He saw people carrying flowers. Two little girls in low-waisted dresses with bows at their hips were jumping on the steps. One of the violin players saw him and waved. Chema rode up and handed the man the harp and said he would come back directly.

He took the road south, and when he came to Rosalinda's ranch he found her sitting in the breezeway in the shade of the palm roof. She had a bowl of mesquite beans, and a baby squirrel in a cage, and she was crooning to it. When she saw Chema she stood up.

He dismounted and secured the mule. He stood awkwardly, fingering his hat.

—I've lost my skill at courting, he said.

She only shrugged and sat down. The squirrel scrabbled at the cage, reaching its small hands through the bars. She handed a bean to it. Chema asked if he could sit.

—It's a free world, she said.

He drank a dipper of water from the olla on its forked stand and he took a chair.

—You better not stay, Rosalinda said. Papá doesn't want to see you here.

—Where is he?

—Down at the acequia, she said. He's coming up for lunch.

—I won't stay, Chema said.

Rosalinda pressed some more beans through the bars of the cage, and the squirrel accepted each offering with shivering hands.

—I thought you were in prison, Rosalinda said.

—I was. I am. I came for the wedding.

She did not reply. She tucked a strand of hair behind her ear and looked out to the road.

—Are you angry with me? he said.

—Yes.

—Do you want me to go?

—Yes.

But she kept sitting with him. The squirrel clambered about the cage, hanging from the bars and entreating her with black bulging eyes. She put her finger into the cage, and the squirrel latched on with its paws. When she unhooked the door, the squirrel darted out and Chema saw she had it on a string. She swung it up by the neck and put it back and fastened the door.

—How is your father? Chema asked.

—Unhappy.

—Because of me.

—Because of the cattle. Dios mío, not everything is about you.

—I plan to help him, Chema said.

—We'll see.

She put her fingers into the cage and scratched the squirrel's neck.

—So what have you got? In the letter you said you had something.

—I don't have it yet, he said. But I will.

She looked down toward the arroyo. He's going to come, she said.

—You're not saying no?

—I'm not saying what I'm saying.

—I wish I hadn't done it.

She got up and dusted her hands. I don't like rough men, she said.

—Just tell me if I should come back, he said. I need to know.

She began walking toward his mule as though seeing him out. He went with her and she stood by while he mounted up. He sat looking down at her. He thought again of the other man and he felt the back of his neck flush.

—I don't like that look, she said.

—What look?

—That murderous look.

He wiped his face with his hand. I guess I'll go, he said.

—Ándale pues.

—I heard there is a dance in another two weeks.

She said nothing. He turned the mule, going slowly toward the road. When he reached the gate, she called out to him.

—That wedding you came for, she said.

—Yes?

—It's the third daughter of the Torres, marrying some one-eared fool. Come back in two weeks if you want.

He returned to Mulegé by night, and did not go at once to the house of the sergeant. First he took the road along the hill overlooking the river, and he secured the mule to some trees in a vacant lot and told the mule he would come back.

He walked quietly up the road. At one house, a man came out to smoke, and Chema angled away from the lamplight of the open door and the man watched him pass.

Near the top of the hill sat the place where his grandmother Inés had lived with his great-grandfather the soldier. A house of cement block stood there now, with a roof of tin and a fence of cactus ribs and metal trellises at the windows. Flowering Mammillaria filled a small pot at the door. The house was dark, and he slipped around the side and into the yard behind.

One old olive tree grew in the corner, gnarled and ancient, with silver leaves rustling in the night wind and shining under the moon. The trunk was twisted and growing around itself, full of vents and splits and openings, the branches creeping over the wall. The night wind had come up, and a flock of cochines called to one another as they dipped and flitted away. He put his hand on the wizened trunk. The leaves rustled and the remnants of last year's harvest lay on the ground.

From here one could see out to the gulf. He thought he heard a sound in the house and stopped. For a moment he stood listening. Then he knelt down and started digging. By the time the moon had begun to wane, he had furrowed around the perimeter nearly to his elbows, and nothing lay underneath. He felt a rage rising.

He fished in his pocket for Rosalinda's letter and lifted out the picture of Magín Matías. One of the priest's hands rested on his knee, and the other hand lay upon his lap in a fist. Perhaps enclosing something. Chema tucked the letter under his arm against the breeze and looked at his grandfather.

—You greedy son of a butcher, he said. Why don't you want me to find it?

For another quarter of an hour he filled the trench and finally covered the place with leaves. He saw a candleflame appear in the house and he left the yard and took the mule and went down the hill. When he came to the sergeant's house, a lamp was burning. The sergeant came to the door in his nightshirt and stepped outside and closed the door behind him.

—I am very glad to see you, the sergeant said.

—The mule was tired, Chema said. The travel went slowly.

—Was there any trouble?

—Not on my side.

—Good, good.

—They are asking for me again.

—All right. Go on up, the guard will let you in.

Chema left the mule and walked the hill to the prison. He called to the guard in the tower, and after a moment another guard came to unlock the gate. Damiana was standing behind the women's gate as he came in.

—What did you bring me?

—A kiss if you are lucky.

She laughed and put her hand through the bars and gave him a push. He took from his pocket a cross of cow bone and handed it to her.

—From one of the old grannies, he said. She liked my music.

—Did you fight?

—No, I didn't fight.

Damiana put the cross around her neck and put her face to the bars.

—Did you find it?

—No.

—She never writes to you anyway, she said.

—I know it.

The young guard came and Chema took the harp into the inner court. Leonardo was sitting against the pila and he got up when he saw Chema. He had no pants and he scratched himself.

—Where's my date pie? he said.

—Did you make any trouble?

Leonardo screwed up his face in thought.

—Come on, sit down, Chema said.

He unwrapped the harp and played under the night sky and the ribbons of stars. The guards sang a little from their towers, and Chema could see men listening from the dark of their cells. A bat swooped down in a fitful arc and flew off. A light wind was blowing, and

Chema smelled the brine of the sea. When he stopped playing, Flores sat up on his cot and called out, Is that all?

Leonardo took Chema's arm. Flores came over and asked for a cigarette and Chema handed one to him and one to Leonardo. Flores leaned against the pila and smoked, a tiny red ember in the night. Leonardo's cigarette hung from his lower lip.

—Are you gonna live here with me? Leonardo asked.

—Just for a few days.

—Then where are you going?

—I have something to do.

Chema slept in the inner square with Leonardo for three nights, and in the morning the guard came for him.

—Come on, the guard said. The sergeant wants you.

Chema went with him, and Leonardo followed as far as the gate and hung his hands through the bars. He tried to put his face through.

—I'll be right back, Chema said.

The sergeant was at his desk, fanning himself. Some papers flitted to the floor, and Chema gathered them up. The sergeant put a stone on top of the papers and the edges flapped like small white wings in the breeze. Damiana watched from across the hall.

—We're going to have visitors, the sergeant said. Prominent families from El Boleo to see the prison. Administrators and their wives.

—Frenchies, Damiana called out.

The sergeant turned to Chema. I want you to take Leonardo out before they arrive, he said. Just take him to Wang's and let him work. And get him some pants.

Chema rubbed his chin. When? he asked.

—The day after tomorrow. Will you do it?

—For how long?

—Just the day and night.

Damiana stood across the way. She wiped a damp strand of hair from her eyes.

—I'll take him out if I can take Damiana too, Chema said.

Damiana put her face to the bars. Oh yes, she said.

The sergeant shook his head. Just Leonardo, he said. Just the two days.

—He likes Damiana. He'll stay with me if Damiana comes.

—He likes me, Damiana called. He truly does.

The sergeant got up and went to the women's gate. Damiana reached a hand toward him.

—We'll come back, she said. We will.

—Where will you take them? the sergeant said.

—To San Ignacio, Chema said. To play the dance.

The sergeant put a hand to the back of his neck.

—To San Ignacio?

Damiana took the sergeant by the sleeve. She looked down.

—Please, she said. I don't want those French women to see me.

The sergeant looked at her for a moment and freed himself from her grasp and turned to Chema.

—They don't go into the dance.

—Okay.

—Be ready at the whistle. I'll bring the gear.

Damiana jumped a little and kissed her hand and held it out to the sergeant. He smiled and went back to his office and she pressed her hand to Chema's cheek.

—I'll help you with him, she said.

The next day at dawn, the sergeant opened the inner square. Chema led Leonardo out. Men were lining up at the front gate for the whistle and Chema strapped on the harp.

—You mind Chema, the sergeant said to Leonardo. And wear your pants.

Leonardo looked down as though seeing the pants for the first time. Chema took his arm. Damiana sat on the bench outside the sergeant's office. She had a green flowered dress folded over her arm and she clutched a beaded purse. Her hair was braided around her head.

—You're so pretty, Leonardo said.

She stood up and smiled and scratched her skirt.

—Mimiberta sent me some things, she said.

—Go on, the sergeant said. Before the visitors come.

They went out front and three mules were ready. Chema opened the cojinillos hanging from the saddles, filled with dried beef and goat cheese and tortillas and dates. Two of the guards had come to see them off. Leonardo lifted Damiana on the mule and she sat astride. Chema took the green dress and her purse and packed them away and told Leonardo to get up, and when they were all seated, Chema thanked the sergeant and said they would come back directly. They started down the hill. Chema could see Wang and Mimiberta below, waving in front of the store.

—Go faster, Damiana said. Let's get out of here.

They rode toward the Sierra El Cuchillo and San Estanislao and they made a fire in the fallen walls of the old mission of Guadalupe. The mountains were high above them, the ridge drawn in a red line from the setting sun. Sparks popped in the fire and rose up and winked out like fireflies. They sat against the fitted stones, tumbled half walls in ruin. Chema took out the foodstuffs and handed them around. Leonardo found a small bag of guava candies and he already had a cheekful.

—Is this where the dance is? Leonardo said.

—We have a long way to go, honey, Damiana said.

—My grandfather hid in this church once, Chema said. He almost died.

—Ay, Dios, Damiana said.

—How come he almost died? Leonardo asked.

—He got sick. He was all alone. He wanted to go back to Mulegé for a woman he loved, but he was afraid to. Because of something he did.

—Did he bash somebody? Leonardo said.

—No, he was a priest. Or he had been.

—My Lord, Damiana said.

—And my grandmother made mezcal, Chema said.

—My grandmother drank it, Damiana said. And so did my mother. She was a revolucionaria. And so was her mother. Las dos pistoleras. What about you, Leonardo? Who was your grandmother?

The big man sat thinking and rubbing his bald head, sucking sugar from his lower lip. He tapped his forehead and kept tapping until Chema pulled his hand away.

—My great-grandmother was a santera, Leonardo said. A santera who made little santos.

He grinned and took another piece of candy and tucked it into his lower lip.

—Ándale, Damiana said. She held up her cantinflór and took a drink.

—To the santera! she said. To the mezcalera! To the pistolera! ¡Vivan las mujeres!

She put the canteen in her lap. Oh Lord, she said. I wish somebody had brought something real to drink.

Chema laughed. Damiana lifted the cantinflór again and took a drink and passed it to Leonardo. He drank until she took it from him and she handed it to Chema.

—So where are they buried? Damiana asked. The priest and the mezcalera.

Chema took a drink.

—In Mulegé, he said. In the panteón municipal.

—I don't like the panteón, Leonardo said. Once I saw a coyote going away with a bone.

He stood up and did a little side step. Wait till you see me dancing at the dance, he said. Just you wait.

—You can't go in, Damiana said.

—Why can't I?

—Because Chema doesn't want us there.

—That's not so, Chema said.

—Are we not going? Leonardo said. Are we not?

—We're all going, Chema said.

—He has a woman, Damiana said. He's going to forget all about us.

Leonardo looked at Chema, alarmed.

—No one is going to forget anyone, Chema said. Let's lie down. Let's go to sleep.

Leonardo turned to Damiana. You can lie next to me, he said.

She kept looking at Chema until he turned away. Finally he heard her brushing the floor, sweeping away the pebbles and thatch. She settled herself beside Leonardo. The wind gusted the fire like a bellows; adobe dust from the high gable wall swirled about them like spirits. Leonardo was snoring.

Chema watched the fire dwindle to coals. He kept thinking of Rosalinda, and felt a burning in his breast. He had told her he possessed something to bring to the marriage. Perhaps she would not ask him. But he knew that she would.

At some hour of the night, Damiana put a hand on him and he woke with a start.

—Why do you want her? Damiana asked.

He rubbed his eyes.

—What?

—You don't have any pearl or anything.

—She said to come anyway.

—She didn't mean it. She doesn't want you. That kind only wants to be wanted.

He lay down again. The night was cool and he stretched his feet to the coals. Damiana lay down on the other side.

—Hey, she whispered.

—What.

—Are you going to leave us behind? Once you convince her. Once you tell her.

—No, he said.

She turned over and Chema heard Leonardo speaking in his sleep. His legs were moving as though he were already at the dance. Damiana sighed.

—I said I wouldn't, Chema said to her.

The next day they followed the old camino into a narrow canyon. The walls were high and russet, and the ribbon of blue sky looked like a river itself. The dry watercourse channeled them along, and the animals ate chicura as they went until they came upon a twisted wild fig with a skirt of white roots growing over the rock. Chema stopped so the mules might eat the dried fallen leaves. A small spring bubbled from the rock and they all drank and mounted up and continued on. They went gingerly down the steep switchback to El Rincón and there they filled their canteens with water and kept going toward Santa Cruz and Cuevitas. On the fourth day they came to the outskirts of San Ignacio and they passed the panteón with its whitewashed tombs and markers and monuments and they rode to the parque in front of the mission.

They dismounted in the shade of the young laurel trees. Electric wires stretched across the lane for the lights of some future festival, and the high church loomed bright and weathered against the fading sky. Chema said Damiana could take Leonardo into the mission, that they could wait for him there.

—I want to go to the dance, Leonardo said.

—Come on, honey, Damiana said. We don't want to go to any old dance.

—I do, Leonardo said.

—So do I, she said.

—He'll tell the sergeant, Chema said.

Damiana dragged her sandal in the dirt.

—Are you ashamed of us? she said. In front of that woman?

—No, he said. I just don't want you to be in trouble.

She laughed a short bark of a laugh and put her arm in Leonardo's.

—We're not the ones in trouble, she said. When that woman finds out you don't have anything.

—Come on then, Chema said. You can stand outside. Listen to the music.

She clapped her hands. Let me put on my good dress, she said. Don't go without me.

She went into an empty room in the low side wing of the mission and they waited for her. Chema sat on the church steps. His stomach turned. He was afraid Rosalinda would not come to the dance, and he was afraid that she would. He was afraid another man would be with her and he was afraid of what he would do. She didn't like that murderous look, she had said, and he hadn't even known he was wearing it. He wanted to explain that he would not behave that way when they were together. But his hands were trembling again.

Damiana came out wearing the green dress and her hair was matted from sweat and travel but she was smiling. Leonardo brought tules from the arroyo to feed the animals, and Chema tethered them in the shade of some low pines beside the church. He said the house was close enough to walk. They started along the street toward the foot of the dark mesa and they could already hear the music, the violin and the guitar and the contrabajo.

At the house there were tables outside and someone had set up a little bar with warm Carte Blanche and wine from Comondú. He was going to tell Damiana to wait outside, but when he saw her face, he waved his hand and she took Leonardo's arm and they went in. Some of the men recognized Chema and called a greeting: ¡Quiúbole!

He looked around. The house was warm, though no one had started dancing. The gasoline lanterns were lit, and pots of young palms, bolstered by wire, lined the walls. Young women sat under the watchful gaze of their dueñas. One old abuelita with a half-closed eye was already sipping date brandy. Men laughed louder than was needful and they glanced with bright eyes at the women and took off their hats and put them on again. Someone was bringing more benches.

—So where is she? Damiana said.

—She'll come, he said.

He unpacked the harp and took his place with the musicians in the corner and they started up with El niño perdido. Damiana led Leonardo to the women's side. He sat on a three-legged stool and clapped and stamped his feet, and the crowd laughed and someone handed him a cup of mezcal with cinnamon and oranges and he downed it and asked for another.

—No more, honey, Damiana said.

Some of the men went outside to the bottles and glasses and others lingered and invited the women to dance. There were old men and bachelors and married men and young unmarried women. Chema kept playing, and Damiana got up to dance and Leonardo jigged his way around the circle with her as the people applauded. A man tapped Leonardo's arm and took Damiana's hand and Leonardo danced alone, following the two of them around. A little girl guided him by the pocket. Chema watched the door.

They played on past midnight, and at some hour Damiana went outside to sit at the tables in the night breeze and Chema heard her loud laughter. Leonardo slept in the corner, his head on his chest. Someone had covered him with a shawl. Then the guitarist gave a nod and the musicians began Las golondrinas and the people cried for them to keep playing; someone was taking up a collection for another hour. Chema kept watching the door and finally there she was.

Rosalinda looked around the room. When she saw him, she gave a half smile and waved and he stood up. She had on the same dress she always wore but she had a flower pinned to the front. Strands of hair were curling around her face and she wore a faint blush of something red on her lips. He left the harp and started to walk over when he saw a man coming in behind her, a skinny cowboy who smiled nervously and looked around. He had a gray hat of wool felt and it was newly soaped and starched with palo Adán and he wore a black string tie. Rosalinda turned and said something to him. His head bobbed like a gaunt turkey and he kept nodding even after she had turned away.

Chema stared at the man. He felt a hand on his arm but didn't know whose it was. He wasn't aware of the room or any of the people, or whether the musicians were playing or breaking up or whether there was anyone there at all. Rosalinda herself was drifting in a fog along with others but the skinny man stood there as clear as the moon, the only thing in Chema's eye. His hands burned hot and he shook them out and he was aware of himself starting across the room and someone was hanging on him. A mouth was at his ear and he heard Damiana's voice.

—Let's go, she said. Let's go.

In five steps he was at the man. Chema grasped him by the string tie and the skinny man surprised him by striking him full in the face. Chema staggered back without feeling any pain and went down on one knee and got up again. Some of the musicians were grabbing him but he plowed forward with them hanging on and went at the man again. The women backed to the wall and someone was covering Rosalinda's eyes. The skinny man was ready with both fists up. He said he didn't want to fight but Chema was already falling into him. They went down and suddenly Leonardo was in the frame and he threw Chema off. Chema saw him bringing his thick fists down on the cowboy, over and over, and four men were trying to pull him away but he was like a machine of iron, pounding and pumping and grinding. He was joyful and careless, half of the blows landing on the floor. The cowboy writhed and Damiana hung on Leonardo's arm, going up and down with the great fists, and she let go and took Chema by the ear and shouted into it.

—He's going to kill him!

Chema was in a fog, and the people were moving as languidly as old donkeys. He saw Leonardo's fist slowly coming down, saw Leonardo shake the sweat from his eyes, the droplets hanging in the air. He saw the cowboy raising bony hands to cover his face. He saw the man's hat roll to the wall and tip over. He saw Rosalinda crying at the door but could not hear any sound. He saw a man coming behind Leonardo with an iron spade in his hand.

All clicked into its proper speed. He heard the cries of women and the thundering boots of men, and he felt Damiana's rough hand grasping the sleeve of his shirt. He shook it off and leapt forward and caught the spade. He got Leonardo by the collar and put his face in front of Leonardo's.

—That's enough, Chema said.

Leonardo blinked and gave the skinny cowboy one more half-hearted slap and knelt there with his other fist in the air. Chema took hold of the fist and held it in his hands. His own knuckles were smarting. He opened his mouth and felt his jaw pop back into place. Damiana knelt beside Leonardo and she was crying.

—The dance is all over, honey, she said. It's time to go home.

Leonardo blew sweat from his lips and stood up.

—Okay, he said. I don't want to dance anymore.

Chema reached to touch Leonardo's face. The man's cheek was red with the imprint of a boot heel. Someone helped the skinny cowboy to his feet. Rosalinda wiped his face with a wet kerchief and he waved her off and someone else helped the cowboy to a chair. He shook his head. Someone handed the man a glass and he held it to his torn lip with shaking fingers.

—Híjole, he said.

A few of the men laughed and one handed Chema a drink. He pressed it to his cheek. The host of the house held up his hands and said everyone was welcome to stay and he himself would pay for three more songs. Chema shook his head.

—Take him outside, he said to Damiana. Walk him to the church.

—Are you coming? Damiana asked. The green dress was torn at the hem where she had knelt on it. She had Leonardo by the hand and the big man was looking around with interest as though he had just arrived.

—Just go on, he said. Just take him out of here.

She led Leonardo to the door, and the women of the house looked at Damiana's torn dress and unravelling hair and glanced sideways at one another. The skinny cowboy was sitting at the table with another glass in his hand, and men around him were already recounting the fight, mimicking the blows. Someone beckoned Chema over but he turned to the harp and began wrapping it. He hefted the harp to his back and thanked the host and said there was no need to pay him. The host winked and pressed some coins into his hand and said they'd gotten more than they'd paid for. An old woman was mopping the cowboy's forehead. The cowboy gave Chema a nod, and Chema nodded back. His jaw hurt and he moved it from side to side and felt it catch. He spat but did not see any blood.

Rosalinda was standing beside the skinny cowboy with her hand on the man's shoulder, but she was watching Chema. The red flower was half-hanging off the dress. From behind the man's back, she mouthed words at Chema.

—Hey, she said. Hey, listen.

She took a step toward him.

—Papá said you can visit, she said.

He laughed and waved a vague hand. She started to speak again, and he turned and went out while she was still talking.

Outside, the drinkers had extinguished the gas lanterns and gone. People were already walking down the street in the dark, and he heard the faint voices and their footfalls on the lane. He hurried unsteadily down the street toward the mission. He was afraid Damiana and Leonardo had left him, but in the parque he heard Leonardo's anxious voice and Damiana answering. They were standing with the mules. He heard Damiana say, Here he comes, here he comes.

They slept that night in one of the stone rooms in the long wing of the mission and Leonardo complained of the cold. Chema whispered to him that they would be warm again as soon as they left the town. In the morning, Chema readied the animals before first light. The streets were quiet. Whatever lanterns had been lit to stave away the night had been snuffed out. The air was calm and blue, and Chema breathed it in. He mounted up. Leonardo lifted Damiana and swung into his own saddle and they rode abreast in an easy silence. By the time the sun had risen above the mesa and touched the mission bells, the three were already long on the trail and not one of them looked back.

Epilogue

In the municipal cemetery of Mulegé there is a great tree, a bitter mesquite at the southern end. It stretches above the stone wall, rising higher than the Greek pediment that marks the entrance and the inscription wrought there: Aquí chocan y se estrellan a porfía todas las hipótesis de filosofía.

The mesquite has bloomed, its yellow flowers borne in catkin-like clusters that dangle from the branches. Bright green seed pods hang like strings of beads swaying in the hot wind. Beyond the wall, mules stretch their necks to the drooping limbs and pluck the young pods.

The glorious thorny canopy shelters the graves below, covered in the fallen pinnate leaves of the tree. Relics of men and women in their resting places, supine and prone and spread out like starfish, some curled like infants with artifacts and curios surrounding them: tatters of clothing, photographs, votives and letters, lockets and flasks. An old cleric in ecclesiastical dress, face to face with a woman shrouded in a handkerchief of lace. Sharing a grave. Brows together and fingers touching, arranged in the familiar manner of the marital bed. Mouths agape in reverence for what they have beheld, or now behold. Que en paz descansen.

Two women, dressed in white, are coming to the cemetery. One carries a hand broom, the other a trowel of palmwood. They pause inside the gate, taking in the scene: cracked urns and low mounds of red brick among the weeds, a hundred graves like domed ovens plastered with peeling white cal. Dried flowers blow between the headstones like bright tumbleweeds. The women pass short fences of rusted iron that encircle stone mausoleums like small houses, adorned with false columns and barred windows and fitted with proper doors as though someone might return home.

At the far edge of the cemetery, just inside the wall, stands the mesquite. The women approach quietly, tarrying in the half shade beneath the crown of feathery leaves, dots of brightness on their faces. In the dappled light they circle the trunk, the bark rough and fissured under their hands. They speak to each other in low murmurs. Now they stop and kneel. One takes the trowel, but the other stays her arm, inserting her fingers into the soil. Her companion whispers encouragement.

Now lies the pearl in hand. The women rise and move toward the gate, and beyond them the town: homes of adobe and wood and brush, horses circling their corrales, donkeys ambling along the road. The river of palms, emptying to the Vermilion Sea beneath a vast sky of blue where a solitary tern takes flight. Below, the white fortress of the penitentiary and the mission with its flat cruciform roof. The women two small figures among white tombs like scattered grains of rice, the cemetery wall a tiny ring upon an expanse of desert between two seas.

The women stand together, inclining their heads toward the pearl. With a breath, one launders away the dust from its shining surface, beholding it in the fold of her palm. Nothing to be interred; nothing to abandon to the loam. Neither to spend nor to hoard. She extends her hand, holding the pearl to the sun, bearing it into the light of light.

THE FLANNERY O'CONNOR AWARD FOR SHORT FICTION

David Walton, *Evening Out*
Leigh Allison Wilson, *From the Bottom Up*
Sandra Thompson, *Close-Ups*
Susan Neville, *The Invention of Flight*
Mary Hood, *How Far She Went*
François Camoin, *Why Men Are Afraid of Women*
Molly Giles, *Rough Translations*
Daniel Curley, *Living with Snakes*
Peter Meinke, *The Piano Tuner*
Tony Ardizzone, *The Evening News*
Salvatore La Puma, *The Boys of Bensonhurst*
Melissa Pritchard, *Spirit Seizures*
Philip F. Deaver, *Silent Retreats*
Gail Galloway Adams, *The Purchase of Order*
Carole L. Glickfeld, *Useful Gifts*
Antonya Nelson, *The Expendables*
Nancy Zafris, *The People I Know*
Robert Abel, *Ghost Traps*
T. M. McNally, *Low Flying Aircraft*
Alfred DePew, *The Melancholy of Departure*
Dennis Hathaway, *The Consequences of Desire*
Rita Ciresi, *Mother Rocket*
Dianne Nelson Oberhansly, *A Brief History of Male Nudes in America*
Christopher McIlroy, *All My Relations*
Carol Lee Lorenzo, *Nervous Dancer*
C. M. Mayo, *Sky over El Nido*
Wendy Brenner, *Large Animals in Everyday Life*
Paul Rawlins, *No Lie Like Love*
Harvey Grossinger, *The Quarry*
Ha Jin, *Under the Red Flag*
Andy Plattner, *Winter Money*

Frank Soos, *Unified Field Theory*
Mary Clyde, *Survival Rates*
Hester Kaplan, *The Edge of Marriage*
Darrell Spencer, *CAUTION Men in Trees*
Robert Anderson, *Ice Age*
Bill Roorbach, *Big Bend*
Dana Johnson, *Break Any Woman Down*
Gina Ochsner, *The Necessary Grace to Fall*
Kellie Wells, *Compression Scars*
Eric Shade, *Eyesores*
Catherine Brady, *Curled in the Bed of Love*
Ed Allen, *Ate It Anyway*
Gary Fincke, *Sorry I Worried You*
Barbara Sutton, *The Send-Away Girl*
David Crouse, *Copy Cats*
Randy F. Nelson, *The Imaginary Lives of Mechanical Men*
Greg Downs, *Spit Baths*
Peter LaSalle, *Tell Borges If You See Him: Tales of Contemporary Somnambulism*
Anne Panning, *Super America*
Margot Singer, *The Pale of Settlement*
Andrew Porter, *The Theory of Light and Matter*
Peter Selgin, *Drowning Lessons*
Geoffrey Becker, *Black Elvis*
Lori Ostlund, *The Bigness of the World*
Linda LeGarde Grover, *The Dance Boots*
Jessica Treadway, *Please Come Back to Me*
Amina Gautier, *At-Risk*
Melinda Moustakis, *Bear Down, Bear North*
E. J. Levy, *Love, in Theory*
Hugh Sheehy, *The Invisibles*
Jacquelin Gorman, *The Viewing Room*
Tom Kealey, *Thieves I've Known*

Karin Lin-Greenberg, *Faulty Predictions*
Monica McFawn, *Bright Shards of Someplace Else*
Toni Graham, *The Suicide Club*
Siamak Vossoughi, *Better Than War*
Lisa Graley, *The Current That Carries*
Anne Raeff, *The Jungle Around Us*
Becky Mandelbaum, *Bad Kansas*
Kirsten Sundberg Lunstrum, *What We Do with the Wreckage*
Colette Sartor, *Once Removed*
Patrick Earl Ryan, *If We Were Electric*
Kate McIntyre, *Mad Prairie*
Toni Ann Johnson, *Light Skin Gone to Waste*
Carol Roh Spaulding, *Waiting for Mr. Kim and Other Stories*
Iheoma Nwachukwu, *Japa and Other Stories*
A. Muia, *A Desert between Two Seas*

Anniversary Anthologies

TENTH ANNIVERSARY
The Flannery O'Connor Award: Selected Stories, edited by Charles East

FIFTEENTH ANNIVERSARY
Listening to the Voices: Stories from the Flannery O'Connor Award, edited by Charles East

THIRTIETH ANNIVERSARY
Stories from the Flannery O'Connor Award: A 30th Anniversary Anthology: The Early Years, edited by Charles East
Stories from the Flannery O'Connor Award: A 30th Anniversary Anthology: The Recent Years, edited by Nancy Zafris

THEMATIC ANTHOLOGIES
Hold That Knowledge: Stories about Love from the Flannery O'Connor Award for Short Fiction, edited by Ethan Laughman

The Slow Release: Stories about Death from the Flannery O'Connor Award for Short Fiction, edited by Ethan Laughman

Spinning Away from the Center: Stories about Homesickness and Homecoming from the Flannery O'Connor Award for Short Fiction, edited by Ethan Laughman

Rituals to Observe: Stories about Holidays from the Flannery O'Connor Award for Short Fiction, edited by Ethan Laughman

Good and Balanced: Stories about Sports from the Flannery O'Connor Award for Short Fiction, edited by Ethan Laughman

Down on the Sidewalk: Stories about Children and Childhood from the Flannery O'Connor Award for Short Fiction, edited by Ethan Laughman

A Perfect Souvenir: Stories about Travel from the Flannery O'Connor Award for Short Fiction, edited by Ethan Laughman

A Day's Pay: Stories about Work from the Flannery O'Connor Award for Short Fiction, edited by Ethan Laughman

Growing Up: Stories about Adolescence from the Flannery O'Connor Award for Short Fiction, edited by Ethan Laughman

Changes: Stories about Transformation from the Flannery O'Connor Award for Short Fiction, edited by Ethan Laughman